IMA-GIN-ATION

ON THE ROCKS, BOOK 2

SAM E. KRAEMER

This book is an original work of fiction. Names, characters, places, incidents, and events are either the product of the author's imagination or used fictitiously. Any resemblance to actual persons, living or dead, business establishments, events, or locales is entirely coincidental.

Copyright ©2022 Sam E. Kraemer
Cover Design and Formatting: Arden O'Keefe, KSL Designs
Editor: Beau LeFebvre, Alphabitz Editing
Proofreader: Mildred Jordan, I Love Proofreading
Published by Kaye Klub Publishing

These characters are the author's original creations, and the events herein are the author's sole property. All rights reserved. No part of this book may be reproduced, scanned, or distributed in any form, printed or electronic, without the express permission of the author. Please do not participate in or encourage piracy of copyrighted materials in violation of the author's rights. Purchase only authorized editions.

All products/brand names mentioned in this work of fiction are registered trademarks owned by their respective holders/corporations/owners. No trademark infringement intended.

New To On The Rocks Series?

Start at the beginning!

Whiskey Dreams (Book One)

Other books by Sam:

The Lonely Heroes Series

The Men of Memphis Blues Series

May/December Hearts Collection

Weighting... Complete Series

My Jingle Bell Heart

Georgie's Eggcellent Adventure

The Secrets We Whisper To The Bees

Unbreak Him

FREE Books by Sam:

Kim & Skip (The Men of Memphis Blues #0.5)

The Holiday Gamble

The World was Perfect

Seth – Mi Guapo Amor

STALK SAM E. KRAEMER'S EVERY MOVE

Join Kraemer's Klubhouse

Get Sam's New Release Alerts

Follow Sam on Bookbub

Follow Sam on Amazon

Follow Sam on Instagram

I'd like to take a moment to thank my team—Arden, Beau, and Mildred. Without you fine folks, I would never be able to tell my stories and put them out for everyone's entertainment. I appreciate all of the work that goes into these books by you three, and I'm sure I don't tell you enough, but thank you so much.

I'd like to thank my patrons on Patreon for their interest in what I publish and "how the sausage gets made!" I offer future book ideas, exclusive excerpts, and first-look cover reveals. If you'd like to become a patron, go to Sam's Patreon and choose your level!

Finally, I'd like to thank Special K and Sweet A for their support and listening ears. I can't tell you how much it means to me that I have both of you in my corner.

I truly hope you enjoy "Ima-GIN-ation, On the Rocks, Book 2!"

SUMMARY

Can an architect and a bar owner build a stable relationship? Not without a strong foundation and a shot of Ima-GIN-ation!

Leo Anderson is about as confused as a guy of twenty-eight can be. All his life he's been denying a part of himself, and now, with the appearance of a dashing architect in Leo's simple life as a bar and restaurant owner, that side of him—the side that is attracted to men—comes exploding from the closet like a battering ram.

Cameron March, a forty-something architect, discovers his attraction to men and women—after he's married with a family. Being a responsible father, he buries those feelings deep inside himself for the sake of his two sons until one-day, his wife decides she's done with the marriage… nearly fifteen years later.

When Leo contacts Cam about expanding On the Rocks, the beach bar Leo owns with his singer-brother and best friend, Cameron's immediately attracted to the barman—and the timing couldn't be worse. Cam's divorce is final, but he's still fighting his ex-wife to keep her from taking his younger son to live in the Pacific Northwest where she wants to begin her new life.

How can Cam and Leo explore the possibility of a relationship without Cam losing his son? It'll take a lot of Ima-GIN-ation…

PROLOGUE
LEO ANDERSON

"Hi, Leo. I thought I'd stop by for lunch."

I glanced in the mirror behind the bar where I was drying glasses to get ready for the evening crowd and froze.

It took everything in me to keep from throwing the pint glass in my hand—or, better yet, squeezing it like I wanted to squeeze the asshole's neck.

My adrenaline shot up from one to one hundred in a millisecond as I turned around to look him in the eyes. After what happened the last time I'd seen the man, I prayed I never saw him again. Clearly, I wasn't in favor with those higher powers everyone spoke so eloquently about.

"Big breath in... Release, one... two... three... four... five." I remembered the male voice of my meditation app reminding me to count as I exhaled. It was a new thing I'd started trying, and I hoped to hell it worked. The jury was still out on it.

I was going through some personal upheaval since my little brother had come to South Padre Island to visit me. I'd suddenly realized I wasn't the man I thought I'd been my entire life, and I was spinning.

I'd developed a lot of anxiety about my newfound realizations and had started looking for outlets to overcome my confusion at my new reality. I'd tried several ways to handle it—meditation had been one that seemed most beneficial when I'd attended a few classes at a yoga studio across town, so I downloaded an app for guided meditation, and I made time to do it every morning. Most days it helped, but I had a feeling today wasn't going to be one of them.

I plastered on a fake grin, my heart still nearly beating out of my chest. "I thought you didn't want to come to the island unless it was work related. You definitely didn't like it when I stopped by your office to drop off the deposit for the reno work," I reminded the new arrival, keeping my composure as cool as possible. *Maybe you should become a drama queen?*

Never in my life had I felt like such an idiot as I had two weeks earlier when I'd thought I was doing a good thing... I had to be the dumbest idiot on the planet.

"What are you doing here? I told you my son Grayson comes by the office from time to time, and he's here today. I can't have you just dropping by like this. Please leave before he sees you," Cameron had hissed at me.

I had been standing in the lobby of March & Stenson, having asked the receptionist to call Cam March to come meet me so I could give him the cashier's check in my hand. It had been the deposit so Cam could begin work on the blueprints for the renovation at On the Rocks, the beach bar I co-owned with my little brother Kelso, the country star and his boyfriend, Tanner Bledsoe —who also happened to be my best friend.

I'd stood there, stunned by what Cam March had said to me —as if I'd been the sort of guy who would show up at someone's job for a booty call at ten o'clock on a Thursday morning. He'd acted as if I'd been chasing him all over town, which I most certainly hadn't.

I couldn't lie and say I wasn't attracted to the man. My banker had given me his name to consult on the expansion to the bar, as suggested by Kelso. Cam had come into On the Rocks a few times to look around so he could prepare the plans, and we'd had nice conversations—nothing more. Meeting him, though, had put me into a tailspin.

I'd been so embarrassed by his chastisement that I'd left without even giving him the check, and I hadn't called or tried to contact him since. I had seriously considered finding another architect and forgetting Cam March even existed.

Never let it be said that Leo Anderson was clingy or believed that every man he met was interested in him as possible boyfriend material. I was a confused twenty-eight-year-old man who had only dated women up to that point in my life, and I suddenly found myself inexplicably attracted to an older man who, it seemed, was fresh off a divorce with teenage sons. Nope, that wasn't my style at all.

Without waiting for Cam to say anything else about why he'd dropped by, I walked from behind the bar and into my office, retrieving the envelope from my middle desk drawer. As I headed through the kitchen, I saw Tanner glance up from where he was changing out the fry oil, which seemed to be his weekly favor to Miss Yvonne.

"Everything okay, Leo?" Tanner asked. I nodded and continued on my way. If I tried to explain how I was feeling at that moment, I'd lose my shit. My best friend didn't deserve my suddenly sour mood.

When I walked back behind the bar, I saw Cameron March scrolling through his phone, reading glasses on the tip of his nose. I slapped the check down in front of him, getting a shiver of satisfaction when he jumped because he hadn't noticed my return.

"I *had* planned to find another architect, but we all liked your ideas for the bar, so we'll continue with the arrangement we made when we spoke on the phone last. From now on, you'll deal with Tanner." I stood a little taller and stomped off to the kitchen without another word.

"Tanner? Could you please go deal with Mr. March about the reno? I need to run an errand." I hurried upstairs and into the kitchen of the apartment, taking a seat at my old kitchen table—my thinking, worrying, and crying spot.

I put my head down on the table and practiced my breathing techniques again, trying to decide if I'd just made a huge mistake or had done the smartest thing possible in light of the current circumstances. The desire to scream was stronger than the need for control.

The clicking of dog toenails on the wooden floor caught my attention. I turned to see my brother's lazy mutt—who everyone loved at the bar—stroll into the kitchen and stretch downward-dog fashion before he *woofed* at me. I felt eyes on me and lifted my gaze to see Kelso dressed in a bar t-shirt and a pair of shorts, his hair wet from a shower.

"What's wrong?" my little brother asked as he took a seat—uninvited I might add. I didn't answer.

"What's wrong, Leo?" Kelso repeated—demanded.

I exhaled. "I need time away."

Kelso had just returned from a European tour, and now Tanner was back to his happy self. It was time for me to rely on my partners and get what *I* needed for once.

"Okay. Where would you like to go?" Kelso asked.

"I don't know. Somewhere that's not here," I responded without much thought, that familiar feeling of failing everyone in my orbit consuming me once again.

Kelso retrieved his phone from his pocket and glanced at me. "Beach or mountains?"

I chuckled. "Not the beach. I've got all kinds of beach here that I see every day. Maybe somewhere up north? It's almost Halloween, so the leaves are turning, right?"

I'd been to New York once in the fall for a class field trip in high school. The bus ride from my hometown of Tyler, Texas, had sucked, but I remembered the leaves were pretty. I wouldn't want to live up North, but it would probably be a nice place to visit for a week or two.

"I've got a better idea. You like gin, right?" Kelso questioned.

I was a bit taken aback by his question. "Not in excess, why?" I enjoyed a gin drink on occasion, but not to the point of having a problem with alcohol. I didn't think a successful bar owner could have a drinking problem. It seemed too easy to drink away the profits, and I'd worked too damn hard to establish the bar to let that happen.

"Okay, there are several gin distilleries in the mid-Atlantic. How about I set you up with tours? There are three in the DC area. You ever been?" Kelso suggested.

It sounded like it could be a bit lonely, but then again, when was the last time I'd ever taken a trip by myself? Maybe it was time to do some introspection of what I wanted from my life and my future, just as my therapist had suggested when I'd gone for an appointment to discuss why I was suddenly attracted to a man for the first time. I had some shit to sort out, and ninety-eight percent of it had to do with Cameron March.

"Okay, tell me what I need to do to book it," I acquiesced.

Kelso's face lit up. "Really? You'll do it? Oh, please let me handle everything!" His hand fluttered in dramatic fashion, and it made me grin.

The enthusiasm in his voice at his offer kind of scared the hell out of me, but maybe Kelso was right? Maybe it was time for me to get out of my comfort zone and use my Ima-GIN-ation …

1

CAMERON MARCH

THE STOMPING UPSTAIRS was giving me one hell of a headache. "Any idea what that's about?" I asked Naomi. She was a wonderful woman of sixty-two who had been with me since Jess and I split four years earlier. She came in once a week to clean our home and do laundry. With Grayson off to college, I was sure it was a chore when he came home with a bag full of his dirty stuff from school, but Naomi never complained about any of it.

"Most likely girl trouble, Mr. March. I had the same thing with my Davey before he finally settled down. They don't call it the *Terrible Teens* for no reason," Naomi stated. I'd never heard it called that, but she was definitely spot on. I wrote her a check for the week and escorted her to the door, thanking her for all her hard work. I then returned to the kitchen to attend to dinner for the three of us. The stomping from upstairs, however, was even worse.

"*Grayson!*" I yelled after my oldest son. He'd rushed upstairs to take a call as Naomi was finishing up, and I had no idea who he was talking to or what had apparently pissed him off. His tantrum needed to stop.

I'd had the worst fucking day in recent memory, and I just

wanted to sit down with some of my brother's gin and some tonic. I wanted to turn on some good music and try to figure out what the hell had caused Leo Anderson to get so angry at me, but I had two growing boys who ate me out of house and home on the weekends, and I was already late getting dinner started.

Last week when Leo had dropped by my office in Brownsville, I'd just hung up the phone with my ex-wife, and I was in a shitty mood. When I saw Leo standing by my assistant Nichele's desk, my heart beat a little faster, but then I remembered where I was and who was there with me—my son, Grayson, home for the weekend.

His roommate had dropped him off at the office after lunch, and he was in the conference room across from Nichele's desk doing homework—or so he claimed. The last thing I needed was for my son to see a hot young guy dropping by to talk to me… and me smiling about it like the cat that got the cream.

Grayson had interned at my office all summer before he'd started college at Texas A&M on a basketball scholarship, and I didn't want word getting back to my ex-wife, Jessica, that I was interested in a guy—especially someone as young as Leo.

I'd panicked that day, and I'd hurt Leo's feelings. I'd gone to On the Rocks on South Padre Island a few days later to talk to him, but he'd barely spoken to me before he'd stormed out of the restaurant, leaving me to discuss the expansion with Tanner, one of his partners.

Tanner Bledsoe was a truly nice guy, but I'd been looking forward to working with Leo and getting to know him better. Unfortunately, I'd totally fucked it up to the point I doubted he'd ever speak to me again.

"That's burning."

I looked down to see the taco meat I'd been browning was beyond blackened and heading into scorched territory, so I quickly moved it off the burner as I turned to see my thirteen-year-old son, Archie, wearing his ever-present smirk. Apparently, everything I did was a goddamn joke.

"What's wrong with Grayson?" I asked as I spooned the overcooked beef into a serving bowl and began to create a taco buffet on the breakfast bar in the kitchen. Grayson had come home from college for the weekend because he was expected to attend an event at his old high school, but I could tell he wasn't happy about something—as evidenced by the booming racket coming from upstairs. If I didn't know better, I'd have sworn we were herding buffalo up there.

I'd received the house in the divorce because Jess had never liked it, or so she told me when we were in mediation for our settlement because she'd wanted to move our youngest son to Seattle where she'd accepted a new job as corporate counsel for a major tech firm. I'd balked, and she was livid, now working the job from Texas but planning to move after the new year.

At the time the divorce was initiated by Jess, we'd agreed on joint custody so having my youngest in Seattle hadn't sat well with me. I'd fought her, which had put a kink in the divorce proceedings and pissed her off to high heaven. Up until that point, we'd been able to agree on everything, but with me now fighting her on relocating Archie since he lived with her most of the time—he'd changed schools to attend one in her neighborhood when we'd separated—the settlement couldn't be finalized even though the divorce had been, and Jess' *new life* with the fisherman, Dane, would have to wait.

If I'd allowed Jess to take Archie to Seattle, I'd have only been able to see him if I went there, because he'd have school nine months of the year. It had definitely moved things from amicable to volatile, and we were mostly still at a standoff. We were just unable to reach an agreement on the custody situation, and until we could, Jessica saw it as being *stuck* in Brownsville.

"Uh, I think he and Chelsea are breaking up. He was yelling at her about how they were expected to crown the new king and queen and go to the dance together. I'm guessin' she didn't agree," Archie, my budding journalist, informed me as he picked at the shredded cheese I'd put into a bowl.

"Get your hands out of that. Should I go up there?" I asked. Romance wasn't my strong suit, whether it was my own or someone else's—as had been proven by my divorce.

The crash of something echoed through the house, so I took off my apron, which had been a gift from Landon Stenson, my partner in the architecture and contracting business. He'd give me the apron when he took me out for a celebratory dinner after my divorce was final.

On the front of the black apron was a big white arrow that pointed up to the neckline, and printed in large white letters was the quip, "This guy rubs his own meat." Landon had a twisted sense of humor, the jackass, which had proven to be remarkably accurate in my case. He had been entertaining over the years, and I wouldn't have made it through the last four without him as my friend.

"I'd say if you like your stuff, you better go up there," Archie suggested as he reached for a corn taco shell that I'd just taken out of the oven.

"Don't burn yourself. I'm not gonna tell you to wait because we both know you won't, but please, leave enough for us," I instructed. Archie had hit a growth spurt, as evidenced by his jeans, and a shopping trip was set to take place that weekend—provided the house was still standing after Grayson's fit.

I took the stairs two at a time until I hit the landing and rushed to Grayson's door. I knocked, but there was no answer, so I tried the handle, surprised to find it wasn't locked. Archie had a bad habit of intruding, and more than once, he'd walked in on his brother doing something I'd later had to explain to my youngest, and I hadn't been the smoothest at it. Grayson had started locking his door after that.

We'd had a stripped-down version of the birds and the bees talk, and after I finished, Archie laughed and told me his mother had given him the talk when he turned ten. Jess had moved out and found a house to rent, and I'd been working on a big project for the City of Brownsville back then, and I wasn't around much during the week for my sons. My workaholic tendencies were at the core of my divorce, or so I thought back then, and I was trying to break the habit to be around more, even though I was completely unsure of the right thing to do as a parent most of the time.

"I'm coming in," I announced as I pushed open the door to find Grayson sitting on the floor with his knees up and his head in his hands as he leaned against the side of the bed. He didn't look good.

There was a shattered picture frame on the floor near the dresser where a picture of Grayson and his high school sweetheart, Chelsea, had once taken up residence. It was from their high school's Courtwarming ceremony—which was the basketball season's equivalent to Homecoming. Grayson, the captain of the team, and Chelsea, the head cheerleader, had been elected King and Queen of the Court.

The ceremony and dance had been the previous year before Halloween, and it was the last official event Jess and I had attended together when we were trying to remain civil. After the first of the year, all hell broke loose, and I found out why Jess was really done with me.

"You okay, son?" I asked. I sat down on the foot of the bed and put my left hand on his shoulder, feeling him shake and hearing him sniffle.

"She didn't come home this weekend. Chelsea's not going tonight. We broke up last week, but I thought I could talk to her, and we could work it out. She's already datin' somebody else," Grayson explained, his heart breaking with every word.

To be honest, I'd expected it. There were several hundred miles between them, and college had a way of changing a situation. I didn't even want to get started on what marriage did to a relationship. He didn't want to hear it, and I didn't want to discuss it, so I just sat with him for a few minutes to let him get it out of his system.

Heartbreak, in whatever form it manifested, was devastating, or so I'd heard. By the time Jess and I had called it quits, we'd pretty much beaten any love we had for each other to death. It had actually been a relief to close the book on it.

SATURDAY MORNING, I had an idea that may or may not have been inspired. Since Chelsea had determined she wasn't going to the Courtwarming festivities, Grayson had decided to only go to the game and attend the half-time ceremony, choosing to skip the dance.

I went for a run per usual, and when I got back home, I found Archie in the television room with cereal, watching cable news as I'd expected, and Grayson was in the kitchen dressed to go for a run himself.

"Good morning, son. How are you?" I asked as I went to a cabinet for a glass and then to the fridge for the orange juice.

"I caught Arch drinking out of the carton," Grayson reported. Instead of pouring it into the glass, I poured it down the drain.

"Son of a... *Archer James!*" I yelled. The loud laugh in return confirmed he knew why I was yelling.

I turned my attention to my eldest. "I'm sorry about Chelsea," I offered, hoping I was offering him any comfort at all.

"Yeah, well, it's my own damn fault. She's said she wanted to break-up before we went to college, and I'd told her we could have a long-distance thing. Everybody does it. I guess I knew it was over when she agreed so quick. Half the time when I'd call her, she was too busy to talk, and she never called me back. Basically, I was in a relationship by myself," Grayson explained.

I nodded as I handed him the water pitcher after he opened an insulated metal water bottle. I poured myself a glass of water as well. "You feel like going over to South Padre for lunch? Maybe to that beach place where we went to watch the surfing competition before you left for school?" I suggested as nonchalantly as possible.

Grayson looked up at the clock as he tied his shoes. "Okay. I've gotta be at school by six. The game starts at seven, but Coach asked me to come early and sorta give 'em a pep talk. I don't know what I'm gonna say," he stated.

"Is this something you want Archie and me to come to with you?" I asked, likely sounding like an asshole—or a dad. I believed in my sons' eyes the terms were synonymous.

Grayson grinned at me. "Thanks, Pop, but that's okay. The guys are picking me up here at 5:30, and after the game, we're all gonna go get somethin' to eat and hang out at Fart's house to play pool. I'll be home late, or I might spend the night at Fart's. That okay?" Grayson asked.

I chuckled. Alan Farthing—or *Fart* as he'd become known for passing gas during basketball practice in eighth grade—had been a nice young guy who Grayson had played ball with in middle and high school. There had been a group of those boys who used to spend a lot of time at our house during their high school years. Seeing them all grown up made me a little sad. It had seemed like just yesterday when they were playing horse on the driveway, but there I was now with a son in college. It made me feel my damn age.

"Yeah, that's fine. Go for your run, and when you get back, the three of us will go get some lunch. I'll have you home in time to meet the crew," I suggested as I went to my wallet in the kitchen desk and pulled out some cash for him.

"Thanks, Pop," he told me as he pocketed the money and kissed my cheek before he rushed out. I truly hoped he was okay about the breakup. I supposed it was my job to worry about him. At least I did *that* well.

We pulled into the parking lot of On the Rocks, where I finally found a spot at the back of the lot, reminding me the place was popular. I looked around for Leo's Chevy SUV, but, of course, it wasn't there. He'd been talking about moving out of the second-floor apartment he'd shared with his brother and best friend, the former two being a couple. Who the hell could blame him if he had moved? Nobody wanted to share a place with people in love.

Leo had mentioned he'd been looking at a nice place in South Padre to rent not far from the beach, so I wondered if he'd already moved. I felt the nerves balled up in my gut at the idea he might not be there. God, there was no fool like an old fool.

"I remember this place. That lady was pretty," Archie decided.

"What lady?" I asked.

Grayson rolled his eyes and opened the door to get out while Archie leaned forward and patted my shoulder. "It's okay, Dad." I had no idea what the hell he meant, but I'd learned not to ask unless I wanted an honest answer. The kid was nothing if not frank.

We went inside, and the hostess, Dewanna, was at the desk and offered a friendly smile. "Hi, Mr. March. Inside or outside?" she asked. I glanced at Archie to see the kid had his mother's eyebrow, and it was cocked and ready.

"Outside, if possible," I responded.

"Come here often, *Mr. March*?" Archie asked, his voice dripping with sarcasm even though it was yet to drop. I glanced at Grayson to see his head was down, staring at his phone as usual.

"Knock it off. I've come here for business. I'm doing the plans for their remodel and expansion. Uncle Lan will be doing the construction," I informed him.

The place was crowded with college football fans, but we were able to secure a table on the patio. I glanced around the place, the blueprints I'd been drawing up for the back patio running through my head again. Tanner had liked my ideas, and

I was due to meet with him the next week to finalize the renovation schedule before we began preparing for the demo.

The patio was closing the first weekend in November so work could begin, and Landon had already lined up a crew to begin ripping the place apart. My business partner was a damn good contractor, and I had complete faith in his decisions when it came to the jobs we signed on to do.

Landon Stenson had become my best friend since he'd taken me on as a partner when we were both much younger. When Jessica and I fell apart, he became my rock, as had my twin, Cordon, but he lived the life of a nomad, finally settling down in Maryland about a year ago.

Cordon was more of a gypsy soul than me. He had a small scar on his chin and his hair was a little darker than mine—because he didn't have teenagers—but we were barely discernible as we'd grown older, and as kids, we were completely identical. Even our father couldn't tell us apart. I think we had our right big toes painted purple and blue until we were old enough to learn our own names. It was the only way Dad could tell us apart. Of course, Mom knew easily enough because she was a mom. I truly missed them both.

"Hi, and welcome to On the Rocks. Can I get you something to drink? We have game day specials on this sheet, and of course, we have the lunch specials," the young server, Gina, listed off.

"I'll have a Hefeweizen draft. He'll have a lemonade, and Grayson?" I prodded, seeing my oldest was still busy scrolling his phone.

Grayson glanced up and smiled. The girl was pretty, and she was about five years too old for him, but if she got his mind off Chelsea, then I was grateful. "I'll have an Arnold Palmer, please," Grayson asked, just as polite as anything, which was definitely a new thing for him. Usually, all anyone got was a grunt.

After the young lady left us, we started watching football.

Grayson went back to his phone, and Archie was busy playing his Switch because he didn't have a phone yet—one thing Jess and I agreed on. No phone until he was fifteen.

"Mom said you guys are going to court again in December," Archie brought up.

I felt myself cringe internally. It was another meeting where Jessica was going to try to get me to let her take Archie, and I was going to fight her tooth and nail. That kid... I couldn't imagine my life without him around with his smartass comments and big goofy grin. My sons were my world, and it was hard enough only seeing them every few days as it was, so yes, I'd fight her every fucking day. I had a hard enough time adjusting to Grayson going away to college.

"Yeah, we are, but that's nothing you need to worry about," I said, trying to put Archie at ease about the whole thing.

"I told her I don't wanna move to Seattle. I wanna stay here. I wanna learn to surf, Dad," Archie protested. I wanted to tell him to tell Jessica the same, but I wouldn't use my kids. I absolutely refused to put them in the middle of our quarrels.

"Hey, Cam," Tanner greeted, changing the subject for me.

"Wow! What happened to your..." Archie's mouth started running before I could put my hand over it to stop it, but thankfully, Tanner just chuckled.

"I didn't eat my vegetables, and the darn thing just popped out one day," Tanner teased, referring to his eye patch. I'd never asked about it—I was raised by a good mother and father to keep my mouth shut unless someone wanted to share something with me. Apparently, I had been remiss with my youngest.

I glanced at Archie to see him swallow hard. "Just popped *out*... Really?"

I saw it as a great opportunity. "Yeah, isn't that something? I'd eat the sweet potato fries if I were you," I suggested, pointing to the menu.

I glanced at Tanner and winked, seeing him holding a laugh. "Grab a chair. You want to join us for lunch? Oh, these are my sons. That's Grayson, and the smartass is Archie. Boys, this is Mr. Bledsoe. He owns this place," I introduced.

"Grayson. Archie. Nice to meet you both." Tanner then looked at me with his kind smile. "Is everything on target to start construction as planned in December? Leo's gone until just before Thanksgiving, but Kelso will be back from Nashville, so we'll be around," Tanner explained.

My beer was delivered along with the boys' drinks. The server looked at Tanner. "Anything, boss?"

"I'll have a sweet tea. You guys ready to order? Lunch is on me," Tanner suggested. I started to protest, but he waved me off. We ordered, and after Gina left us, Grayson started playing the game with Archie, paying no mind to us.

"So, where's Leo?" I asked after I sipped my beer. I'd noticed Tanner didn't seem to drink alcohol, which wasn't really any of my business. Everybody had a story.

Tanner smirked. "He's on vacation. He, uh, I understand there was an issue between the two of you. Leo's a great guy, and I hope the fact the two of you didn't hit it off won't be a problem, right? We'd discussed getting a new firm to do the work before he left, but in the end, Leo suggested we stay with Stenson & March."

I nodded, glancing at the television to see Clemson was leading ten to three. I had no idea who they were playing but hearing that Leo had been the one to stick up for me had caught me by surprise.

"Okay, uh, where did he go? Leo, I mean," I questioned, not that I was owed any explanations.

Tanner looked at me with an odd look on his face. "I didn't think you'd care." With that, we didn't discuss Leo anymore. We talked about the bar, Kelso's career, and the renovation. Anything but Leo, which bugged the hell out of me.

Tanner ate with us, and I had a couple of beers as Tanner and I discussed random shit. When it was time to go so Grayson could get home in time to meet his friends, I gave him the keys to my twin cab Silverado and got into the back seat, allowing the boys to sit up front.

The fact Leo was gone had me confused and concerned. I'd wanted to apologize for being such a dick, but he hadn't given me the chance. I didn't have the slightest idea how to feel, but something unsettled took root in my chest.

Finally, I asked Archie a question that had bugged me a little. I leaned forward between the seats and touched him on the shoulder, startling him as he played his Switch. "What did you mean when you said it was okay that I didn't notice the hostess?"

"You never notice girls, Dad," Archie replied.

That comment floored me. Was that right?

2
LEO

THE PLANE LANDED IN BALTIMORE... Baltimore/Washington International Thurgood Marshall Airport. It was like they couldn't decide on a name for the joint, but as I looked around, I decided maybe it had such a big name because it was such a big place. I collected my luggage and got my rental car to drive to the quaint little town of Frederick, Maryland, excited for a new adventure—and relieved to be away from all thoughts of Cameron March.

Kelso had gone out of his way to get me a nice Hilton hotel, and I knew I owed him something great for all of his efforts. I settled into my room early that night after having a burger at a small burger joint near the center of town. It was a unique place with a lot of history, as I was finding out while driving around.

My brother had given me a list of activities I could enjoy, but all I really wanted to do was sleep. I leafed through all of the pamphlets I'd collected from the hotel lobby, considering the various tours that were available—everything from ghost tours to electric bicycle tours, but none of it really appealed to me.

I walked over to the window in my room to take in the view. "One, two, three... Damn, five church steeples?" I observed. I was talking to myself, of course, as I took in my reflection off the glass. I was nearly thirty, and I guessed I wasn't ugly, but I wasn't sure if anyone would call me good looking. Though, as I thought about it, I'd been checked out by plenty of women in my time. I wondered if I'd been checked out by any guys, as well.

With so many churches in such a small town, I was curious what people in Frederick, Maryland, thought about people in the LGBTQ+ community. Hell, I was coming to believe it was *my* community, and I wasn't sure how I felt about it. Would they ostracize folks under the rainbow, or would they treat them like any other neighbor—wave from the porch… bring in the mail when you're on vacation… talk over the fence? Could I see myself in a community like Frederick? Was it too much like my hometown of Tyler, Texas, that I wouldn't fit in like Kelso hadn't when he was younger? Why the hell had I ignored that part of me that was attracted to men—one Cameron March, in particular—that was suddenly rushing to the forefront of my mind after all these years? *Yeah, why?*

Being away from the beach was a bit unsettling as I stood there taking in the little town through the glass. I was used to having my windows open in the apartment, and the new duplex I'd leased had a beach view from the crow's nest built on the roof. I'd just moved in before I'd taken off for my trip, and I was still wondering if I'd done the right thing by moving away from the beach.

Living with a couple in love—Tanner and Kelso—was hell, especially considering my conflicted feelings circling around the thoughts I'd been trying to avoid because a certain man was driving me batshit crazy.

I'd been fighting with myself about Cam March, trying not to think about him. He'd offered me no explanation as to why my showing up at Stenson & March was such a horrible thing. His reaction to seeing me there had made me embarrassed, as well, and I definitely hadn't wanted to be anywhere near him until I got over it. It was definitely a great time to get away.

I settled myself into bed, looking at the itinerary Kelso had emailed me. I saw he'd scheduled me for tours of a few small vodka and gin distilleries, the first at eleven in the morning, so I set my alarm for seven so I could get up and go for a run around Frederick to see some sites before my tour.

I arrived at the first distillery at ten-thirty the next morning, invigorated by my self-guided jogging tour around Frederick. It was larger than I'd thought, and I was impressed by the old homes and town squares. I could imagine how the place looked pre-Civil War because a lot of it hadn't changed. They'd kept the old-world vibe alive and well.

I was met by a nice young woman with a friendly smile. "Welcome to McClintock Distillery. I'm Betsy McClintock, and my husband is looking forward to meeting you. Your brother called us yesterday to ensure we were ready for you, so I'll be taking you around for a private tour myself."

I was a little uncomfortable that Kelso had done such a thing, especially when I saw a group of seven people with a young guide who was talking them through a display designed to teach about the fermentation process that I would have liked to study.

Betsy took me through the whole distillery, explaining things to me in passing before finally introducing me to her husband, Mark. "Mark, this is Leo Anderson, Kelso Ray's brother," Betsy introduced, a lilt in her voice at mentioning my brother's name. It still surprised me that so many people knew the guy I used to aggravate mercilessly when we were younger. He certainly didn't act like he was famous.

Mark McClintock was tall—nearly seven foot if I were guessing. He looked like a doctor with his long white lab coat, safety glasses, and white hair covering. He was wearing neoprene gloves, and he was standing next to a table with numbered test tubes on it, perusing some sort of report on his computer.

"Well, hello! It's a pleasure to meet you, Mr. Anderson. We're so pleased you included us in your tour of mid-Atlantic distilleries," Mark welcomed. He removed his gloves and shook my hand, which was nice. Of course, who knew how much Kelso had told the couple. My little brother had a big mouth.

"Thank you, and I really don't want to take up your time. I'm just beginning to look into what distilling entails. I own a bar on South Padre Island, and I'm in the process of making renovations. I'm thinking about adding a small batch distillery, and wanted to explore my options, so any guidance you can offer is welcome," I explained to the couple.

Betsy giggled. "Don't do it!"

I was a bit taken aback until Mark started laughing with her. "Yeah, I'm obsessed with making botanical infused gin. I work too many hours according to my wife." He then turned to look at her and smirked. "But we spent enough time together to have three kids, so I think we have a pretty good balance, right?"

They were cute together, and it was nice to see their interaction. Sadly, it reminded me of what I was missing in my own life.

Mark and Betsy took me around the distillery again, Mark explaining in meticulous detail about the botanicals McClintock infused into their gin—juniper berries being the primary flavor profile and rye being the base of their mash. After he walked me through the whole process, I completely understood Mark's obsession, and I was quite interested in delving further into it. The idea of distilling small batch gin in Texas had me completely psyched more than anything I'd been doing recently.

"And now, how about we have a sample or two?" Betsy suggested, leading me out into the tasting room so Mark could get back to work. Hell, how could I refuse?

As I was tasting a citrus flavored gin, Betsy went to wait on a customer who was ordering some of their specialty blends. Mark came out of the back, having shed himself of his previous garb and stepped over to me, lifting the other glass of gin to his nose and taking a sniff as he swirled the liquor in the glass. "Orange blossom. This is one of the first I created," he commented before he put the glass down in front of me.

I picked it up and smelled the contents as Mark had done,

feeling the rush of orange blossoms flood my nose. "Wow, that's incredible. How'd you learn to do this, to create something as great as this?" I asked, eager to learn how one could develop such a skill.

Mark grinned. "I actually apprenticed with a guy who now works in Sykesville after I graduated with a degree in chemistry and took a job at a research lab. I absolutely hated the job and started looking into distilling alcohol—my grandfather was a moonshiner in southern Virginia for most of his life, and my great uncle was a bootlegger, so it sort of runs in the family. I'm just doing it the legal way," Mark joked, bringing a great laugh from me.

"Cordonmarch is the guy's name," Mark said very quickly. The guy spoke at breakneck speed, so I had to pay close attention. He then continued, "He used to teach at IBD, uh, Institute of Brewing and Distilling in London, before he came back to the US and went to work for the Maryland Distiller's Guild as a judge in competitions on the eastern seaboard. He's a master at his craft, and he's the head distiller at Oriole's Nest Distillery. It's a newer place, and I've heard he's doing great things, but I also heard the place is owned by the mob, so who knows, really."

"I'd love to hear more about your grandfather," I replied as I took another sip of the sample.

Mark checked his watch. "You wanna get some lunch? It's kinda early, but my wife has an appointment at the hairdresser's this afternoon, so I'll be working the tasting room by myself, but if you're willing to go now, I'd love for you to join me," he invited.

I decided I had absolutely nothing to lose, so I accepted. "I have a tour scheduled at two o'clock at Chesapeake Distilling, but I have no plans until then," I admitted.

"I'll be right back. I need to get my cell phone from the lab," Mark advised. He left me, and I took a sip of the delicious orange blossom gin. I could imagine it in all sorts of cocktails that would work well at the beach. My excitement was growing with all of the ideas going through my head. I couldn't remember being so enthusiastic about something since I'd moved down to the beach years ago.

Betsy stepped over to me. "It was truly nice to meet you, Leo. I can tell you've been bitten by the bug, so if you have a wife or girlfriend, you'd better warn her she'll be spending a lot of time by herself," Betsy suggested.

Nerves raced up my spine and sweat popped out over my top lip. It was just an off-handed statement anyone would make in her position. Why did it feel like a life-changing moment?

I grinned cautiously, taking in her demeanor. I didn't notice anything that would give me any indication how she would react if I answered honestly. "I, uh, I'm single, but I'll let any future boyfriends know ahead of time." I attempted to laugh it off.

Her facial expression didn't change at all. "Ah, shortsighted of me. I apologize but warn him that you'll have a new love in your life," she replied with such grace, I was impressed.

"Say, how much do you think it would cost for me to start up a small distillery? Something like this, but on a much smaller scale?" I asked, thinking of the renovations that were set to take place at On the Rocks and how much more it would take to start up an operation like Mark and Betsy's.

"Double check with Mark, but I'd guess you can probably start it up for around thirty thousand," Betsy answered. The price didn't scare me. It all sounded like a fun new plan.

3

LEO

FOR THE NEXT WEEK, I made the rounds to about five distilleries in Eastern Maryland before I stopped at Maryland Distillers Guild in Baltimore. I spent an hour talking to an older gentleman, Lucas Lawson, who'd once owned his own distillery. He'd proven to be quite knowledgeable on the subject of spirits.

Mr. Lawson, the docent at the Distillers' Guild, told me about selling his distillery ten years prior. "My wife got the cancer, and I just didn't have time to devote to it like I wanted. It was right around the time when flavored liquors were trendy, and I couldn't give the business the time I'd been devoting to it before. Rather than run it into the ground, I sold it to three sisters who grew up on a vineyard in France and wanted to try their hand at distilled liquors," he explained.

"I see. Is it still around?" I asked.

"Yeah, yeah. It's Black-eyed Susan's Distilling Company. They kept the name, which made me happy. My wife's name was Susan," Mr. Lawson told me. I didn't ask any more about his wife, getting the impression she'd passed away.

"Oh, Ava, Marie, and Lena Dubois? Yeah, I went there. It was really nice. I did a tour day before yesterday. Did they keep your recipes?" I asked him.

He smirked. "I gave them my basic batch recipes, but I kept some of the good ones for myself. Would you like to sign the visitors' book? They send a quarterly newsletter to distillers and connoisseurs to alert them to new innovations in the industry." I nodded and signed the book he'd spun around. It looked pretty full, which was a good indication I might be onto something that wouldn't be a flash in the plan.

Luke picked up a map, marking a route on it before he walked with me to the door of the guild, handing it to me. "You might wanna check out a fella in Sykesville. He's got a following because of his ability to mix some intriguing spices and botanicals. Each batch is only twenty liters, and he holds an auction for some of the special batches that fetch a pretty good price. You should check the place out before you leave the area," Luke suggested as we stepped out onto the front porch of the building.

"Thank you, Mr. Lawson," I replied as I held up the map he'd given me to Sykesville. He'd marked the best route, and I was looking forward to getting on the road the next morning.

When I got back to my hotel, I settled into my room and called the bar. "On the Rocks. How can I help you?" It was Dewanna.

"Hello, Dewanna. It's me, Leo. Is Tanner or Kelso around?" I asked.

"Hi, Leo. Kelso's out walking Whiskey, but Tanner's behind the bar. You wanna talk to him?" she asked. I glanced at the clock on the nightstand to see it was just five in the evening. It was supposed to snow, and I was a little worried because I wasn't good with driving in snow, but I'd wanted a change of pace, and I was getting it.

"Yeah, please," I requested.

I heard the shuffling as the phone was passed. "This is Tanner."

"Hey, man, how's it going?" I asked one of my partners. I was never so happy as I was when we signed the paperwork that made Tanner and Kelso my partners. There were no better guys than the two of them to be in business with, and the fact they were in love was just a plus. Tanner had been through hell, and he deserved every good thing coming his way, and my little brother—it seemed as if he was Tanner's every good thing.

"We've been dead, Leo. I think people mistook that when we put up the sign that the patio was closing on November 1, we were closing the whole thing. When you get back, we need to plan some events so they know we're still open," Tanner suggested, before he asked, "How about you, man? How's Maryland?"

"It's actually really cool. The days are nice—about sixty-five, and the nights are a little chilly, but it's a nice reminder that there are four seasons. I highly recommend you and Kelso go somewhere when I get back and he's not in the recording studio," I told him.

Tanner chuckled. "And leave you here alone with Cam March? What would we come back to? You in jail and him buried on the beach with Whiskey's help?" Tanner joked, and I laughed.

"Probably. Is he being a pain in the ass?" I asked him.

"Actually, he came in with his boys on Saturday. I had lunch with 'em. They're damn nice, Leo. I mean, I don't know what Cam's issue is, but they were all cool when they were here. Kelso sang some songs, and they hung out for a while. Archie, the youngest, is funny as hell, and he took Whiskey for a walk for us. I'm not pushing you to give Cam a break, but..." Tanner trailed off.

What Tanner didn't exactly know was how stupid I'd felt when Cam had basically chastised me for showing up at his office to drop off a fucking check. No, I didn't give a shit how nice he was because that fucker wanted the money we were set to spend on the reno. Nothing more, nothing less. Of course, I wouldn't say it to Tanner to sour him on the man, but nobody would ever make me believe anything else.

"Let's just keep it professional, Tanner. Can one of you go by my place to check on my plants?" I asked. After I'd moved out of the apartment I'd been sharing with them, I'd bought a few hard to kill plants to have another living thing in my space. I'd never been a fan of living alone, but I was determined to give it a try.

"Sure, Leo. Where are you off to next?" Tanner asked.

I chuckled. "I'm going to some distillery in Western Maryland. It comes highly recommended. A lot more goes into the process than I ever imagined, and I've got some thoughts on the matter I want to share with you guys when I get back. We might be able to bring something new to the beach," I dropped before we said goodbye. Every successful bar needed a niche, and maybe I was finding ours? It was damn well worth a shot.

I PULLED the rental into the parking lot, taking in the large stone building. The town was quite lovely, and it was an incredibly sunny day, so I was looking forward to the visit. Mr. Lawson had suggested the place as a must see, and as I took in The Oriole's Nest, I could understand why.

I got out of the car, tossing my jacket inside before I closed the door since it was warmer than I'd anticipated.

I traversed the gravel to the concrete sidewalk, taking in the architecture of the building. There were three windows across the front, two on one side of the door, and one on the other. The window frames were painted a bright white, and there were window boxes with colorful flowers spilling out of them. It was different from my beach shack but equally inviting.

The front door, which was a federal blue, was propped open by a boot jack that looked to be a hundred years old. I stepped into the large room, taking in river rock walls and the split oak bar tops, complemented by open oak beams. The ceiling was high, but there was another floor above it where a bar and restaurant were advertised.

The specials had been posted on the chalkboard outside, and I was actually looking forward to the crab cake sandwich with some fries. The smells coming through the doorway of the building were mouthwatering.

I walked inside, taking a minute for my eyes to adjust from the bright sunlight to the darker room. When I was finally able to focus, I was met with a cute little store showcasing various local delicacies—jams, jellies, pickled vegetables, salsas. It was really cool, much like some of the little shops in South Padre.

I stepped up to one of the counters, noticing a wooden top that showed wear and tear just enough to make it interesting. There were bottles behind the bar and small tasting glasses lined up beneath them. Some of the bottles appeared to have flowers or herbs of some kind marinating inside, which was quite interesting.

"Welcome to The Oriole's Nest. I'm Lynn. What can I pour for you?" an older woman asked with a welcoming smile. She handed me a list of the day's offerings, and I was impressed.

"I'd like to meet the distiller if they're available. I met a man in Baltimore at the Maryland Distiller's Guild who told me about this place. I'm interested in starting my own distillery in South Texas," I admitted.

The woman smiled. "Let me check if Cord is in the back. You're exactly the kind of person he loves to meet. I'll be right back," Lynn confirmed before she went through a back door, leaving me alone for a few minutes.

There was a picture hanging behind the bar from a nail that looked as large as a railroad spike. The black framed photo was of five men in black suits, the woman I'd just met, and a man wearing a white button shirt and jeans with black boots. He appeared to be nonplussed by the formality of the picture, which was intriguing.

The man in the middle looked oddly familiar to me. His hair

was slicked back and he had a full beard, but it didn't hide his big grin. I couldn't make out his face because the picture was from a distance to catch the entire building in the frame, so I pulled out my phone, focusing it on the man in the middle. I enlarged my phone screen with my index finger and my thumb, and my breath caught. "It can't be…"

A familiar laugh sounded behind me, and when I turned, there he stood… Cameron March.

4

CAM

I stood at Nichele's desk looking at the courier deliveries that were on the rack to the right. I saw "Beach Reno" on the side of one tube, and I grabbed it and took it to my office, spreading it out on my drafting table.

"Knock, knock." I turned to see Nichele and Landon standing in the doorway, Nichele with a cocked eyebrow and Landon with a smirk.

"What's the rule, Cam?" Nichele prompted. No wonder Landon was smirking—he was usually the one to get in trouble.

"I… Uh, sorry." I rolled them back up and put them in the tube, closing it and handing it back to her. She had to check the order so she could authorize payment for the copies, and I'd taken the blueprints before she had the chance. I was definitely the one in the wrong.

There'd been a mix-up with plans another time that cost us money. Lan took the wrong set to the jobsite, and we were delayed by a week while we waited for the right plans to be sent again because the other set had been misdirected to another client.

It had been a clusterfuck, so we'd made a rule—nobody was to touch the plans until Nichele logged them in. She would deliver them to us when they were accounted for, and we were able to keep the mix-ups to a minimum as long as we all followed the rule—the one I'd just broken.

Nichele took the tube, offering a friendly wink before she left us. Landon came into the office and closed the door. "What's wrong with you?"

So many thoughts rushed into my head, but none that I was willing to share. "How do you mean?"

Lan flopped into the guest chair and put his feet up on my desk, crossing them at the ankles. "Well, my friend, aside from the fact you've been a real prick to deal with lately, you haven't said a word about your date with your neighbor last weekend."

I cocked an eyebrow at him. "What date with what neighbor? Old Mrs. Preston?" I asked. Mrs. Preston was an eighty-year-old widow with a fat Cocker spaniel that shit in my yard every morning.

The old woman refused to clean up after the damn thing— Mitzi—and Archie had threatened to feed it rat poison on more than one occasion when he had to trash his sneakers because he stepped in dog shit when he got off the bus on Wednesday afternoons.

"Archie told me you were going on a date with… What's his name? Donovan Gullett? The neighbor guy who lives in Mrs. Preston's basement," Landon explained. I was surprised my head didn't spin off my shoulders!

"What? Donovan… Donovan is twenty-six, Lan. He's way too young… Archie was bullshitting you, Lan." My heart was pounding in my chest, and I felt my palms begin to sweat, the heat rising up my neck as my stomach flipped. In my protest, nowhere had I mentioned the fact he was a guy.

WTF? Can he… Does he know about me? Does my son know I'm attracted to…? No! This can't be happening…

Suddenly, Landon cracked up. "You're too fuckin' easy, Cam. Arch told me you guys went out to the beach without me, and I was just gettin' back at ya. What the hell is going on with you?

And, for the record, Donovan Gullett is over eighteen, so I'd say he's perfect dating material if one were so inclined. He's got a great ass," Landon offered with a grin, having met Don at a barbecue I'd had over the summer and invited my neighbors to. Don had joined us. Thankfully, Mrs. Preston and Mitzi had stayed home.

I swallowed my panic attack and sat back in my chair, putting my feet up on the desk, as well. "Oh, please tell me when you started looking at my neighbor's ass?" I asked.

Lan was a single guy of about fifty, and he'd dated some over the years, but nothing ever seemed to stick. Now, I had to wonder why.

My friend looked at me for a moment before he chuckled. "I'm bisexual, Cam. I didn't realize I had to spell it out for ya."

I stared at him, waiting for the punchline, but when none came, I sat up. "You're bi? Why didn't you ever…?"

"Because you and Jessica are so damn tight-assed about everything, I wasn't about to lose my best friend over who I fucked. She's judgmental, and you were always easily swayed by her opinions. What the hell else was I supposed to think but that you'd stop being my friend?" Landon asked.

I sighed. He really wasn't wrong. I went along with Jess because it was easier than fighting with her, which she'd honed to a fine art. For the sake of my sons, I did what she told me like any henpecked husband would do. The woman wielded fear and dominance like a Samurai with a katana.

To be honest, I was simply too fucking lazy to do anything about my miserable existence with Jess. She finally did it for me when she told me we were getting a divorce. At the time, she hadn't told me why, but she got pissed enough during our mediation process to tell me she'd found a *real* man and had been seeing him for years.

He was a former Naval commander who owned a commercial fishing business in Seattle. His name was Dane. Jess told me she met him at a coffee shop at Pike Place Market when she was on a business trip. She'd been getting coffee, and he was throwing fish—whatever the fuck that meant.

They'd secretly been having a relationship for two years while she waited for Grayson to graduate from high school. I wished to fuck she'd have just told me and gotten it over with much sooner. Maybe I could have gotten my nuts back a lot quicker.

"I'm sorry, Lan. She wanted people to think we were Texas royalty, and that stupid church we went to was where she showed how pious she was... we were. Queers, people of color, the poor... They were to be pitied but not extended any kindness. She wanted to sit on high and cast a withering glare at anyone who wasn't white, straight, and wealthy," I confessed.

Landon, my best friend, laughed. "Yeah, well, when she was shtuping the guy in Seattle, I'm sure she believed it was god's will. My grandmother was part Jewish, by the way. I'm sure Jessica would have had a field day with that knowledge."

I felt about two feet tall, learning that my best friend couldn't be himself around me. "I'm really sorry, Landon. You never talk... I figured you didn't speak to your family," I admitted to him.

My folks were dead, and they'd never learned about my attraction to guys because I hadn't been willing to admit it to anyone. They were nothing like Jessica and her snobby family, but I was too afraid to take the risk of telling them and having them reject me or just look at me in a different light. In my gut, I knew my folks weren't like that, but I was too chickenshit to take the risk.

Lan chuckled. "I see my parents twice a year when I make the trip to Costa Rica. I don't have a timeshare down there like I've claimed over the years. That's where Mom and Dad live now that they've retired. They have an adventure business. Zip lining; jungle hiking; shit like that. It's their passion, and they're living out their dreams. I think they want to forget they have a son who's almost fifty because it reminds them they're in their seventies, and neither wants to admit that. I just thought that information would be too hippy-dippy for you and Jessica, so I didn't share it," Lan related.

"God, I feel like a total bastard right now. Why did you put up with me?" I asked, really hoping he answered me honestly. I couldn't say I'd do the same. "I have a twin brother," I blurted out.

Landon's face showed his surprise. "Where is he? You mean to fucking tell me that we've been business partners for nearly ten years, and we've been keeping all this shit from each other? This stops now. Let's go get a beer and have a *real* talk for once? What do you say?"

I glanced at the clock on my desk to see it was just after ten. "It's a little early, don't you think?"

Landon laughed boldly. "Brother, if you gotta put your beer on a schedule, you might wanna consider if it's a problem for ya. I, on the other hand, have a beer when the urge hits me. You might wanna live a little, Cam. You're a free man, and pretty soon, you won't have to answer to that bi... woman for any fucking reason."

Well, he did have a point.

"HELLO?" I answered on Friday afternoon. I'd been ruminating on everything Lan and I had shared on Monday morning/afternoon when we'd gone out together. We'd taken a rideshare back to work and had both slept it off in our offices before we'd gone home at five o'clock that evening, as usual. It had been cathartic to tell Landon a lot of shit I'd held back for years—but I couldn't bring myself to tell him I, too, was bisexual. I still had no idea why.

"Cameron, it's me." The voice still grated on my ears like nails on a chalkboard, as it had the whole time we were married.

I wanted to kick my own ass for not doing something about it sooner.

"Yes, Jessica. What can I do for you?" I asked, bracing myself for whatever fresh hell she was about to unleash on me.

"I'd like to talk to you without the lawyers, Cameron. Can we meet for a drink? I'd prefer you not say anything to Archer about this," she requested.

My gut said *no fucking way*, but I still held out hope that maybe—just maybe—she'd find a tiny morsel of humanity in her stone-cold heart and not use our sons as bargaining chips. Sadly, I couldn't hold out a lot of hope.

"Okay, when and where?" I responded, already second guessing my judgment.

"Meet me at a place called Bar-B. It's on East Tenth. I doubt we'll run into anyone we know there. Seven tomorrow night," she demanded and then hung up without waiting for my answer. Unfortunately, I was far too used to taking orders from her to be surprised or complain.

Friday night, I pulled into the parking lot of Bar-B. From the outside, it just looked like a hole-in-the-wall joint, and there were a million of them in Brownsville.

I parked my Silverado and stepped out, heading toward the red wooden door when I saw two men walk out hand in hand, the two of them laughing together. They were obviously a couple—a happy couple at that.

The bar was new if memory served me correctly. After the couple left, I stepped onto the sidewalk, looking through the window beside the door to survey a mixed crowd.

I didn't miss Jess sitting at a high top, phone in hand, ignoring the crowd as she scrolled. She glanced up, looked around, and then took a sip of her red wine before she went back to whatever she was reading.

My stomach roiled a little at the thought of having to carry on a conversation with her, but I'd already taken about ten antacids, so I was as ready as I was ever going to be. I was determined to get through whatever she wanted to discuss because she clearly had a reason for setting up the meeting. I just had to figure out what it was.

Just as I was about to open the door, a heavy hand clamped down on my left shoulder. I spun around, and much to my surprise, there stood Tanner Bledsoe and Kelso Ray.

"Hey, Cam. What are ya doin' here?" Tanner asked, his big grin in place.

My heart slowed to a normal rate at friendly faces. "I'm supposed to meet my ex here to discuss our settlement, I think," I replied.

"This is a gay bar, Cam. Why would your ex-wife want to meet you at a gay bar?" Kelso asked, not letting go of Tanner's much larger hand.

I answered honestly. "I seriously have no idea. I just want things settled so my boys and I can live our lives happily."

Tanner pulled me around to the side of the building. "You got your phone with ya?" I nodded, holding it up.

"Make a voice recording so she can't misstate anything. It's legal to do it in Texas as long as one person gives consent—which would be you," Tanner advised.

I chuckled—doing my best to keep the nerves at bay. "How do you know that?"

Tanner grinned. "I studied law while I was in prison. Lots of time on my hands, and I had a curious disposition. You'd be surprised at the random shit I know," he stated with a chuckle. I laughed with him and Kelso.

Tanner looked up at me, his hand resting on my shoulder in comfort. "Care for a little advice?" I nodded. "Go in like you don't know us. We'll sit as close as we can to your table to act as witnesses if you need us to testify later. Think long and hard before you volunteer any information."

I nodded and went inside, stopping to look around as if I didn't know precisely where Jessica was sitting. When I caught her eye, the impatience on her face took me back to the end of our relationship where she believed I was nothing more than a buffoon.

Jess glanced at her phone, and then she scowled. I was ten-minutes early. She couldn't bitch about me being late, and it clearly pissed her off. I was a little smug at my unintended coup.

I did glance around the place, seeing a few smiles before I took a seat and finally relaxed. "Jessica, you look upset. I'll remind you that you chose the place to meet."

She pasted on her *business* smile. "Yes. I thought it might be more comfortable for *you*."

I turned on the recording app on my phone and placed it on the table, upside down, just as Tanner had suggested. Just then, he and Kelso came in and sat down at the bar, making friendly conversation with the handsome bartender, who they seemed to know pretty well.

I turned my attention back to Jess. "I'm not sure why you'd think I'd be more comfortable here as opposed to anywhere else," I commented, keeping the panic at bay by the skin of my teeth.

"You and Landon have been fucking for years, Cameron, haven't you? I just don't know why I didn't see it. Who do you think the court is going to believe? Me, a neglected housewife with two sons who has tried to hold my family together with no support from you, or you, a fag who has been cheating on me with his boyfriend/business partner?

"I have pictures of the two of you together, Cameron. I also have names and contact information for everyone at that bar who will testify on my behalf that you two are regulars. Drinking during the day and then fucking in the bathroom after," Jess threatened.

I couldn't believe what I was hearing until she tossed a manila file folder on the table and photos spilled out. There were the two of us, Landon and me, having beers at Alberta's up the street from the office. It was the previous Monday, and when we finished our conversation, Landon gave me a hug, and we walked out the door and back to the office.

"These are from Monday. Why do you think this makes Lan and me a couple?" I pressed, deciding that if he and I were so inclined, we'd make a damn good-looking pair.

Jess leaned forward, hovering over the phone. "I've got more pictures of the two of you I've had taken over the last year. No judge with any morals will let two queers raise a fourteen-year-old boy," she stated.

I chuckled. "I don't know how the hell you think you got incriminating pictures, but go ahead," I goaded.

"You forget, I have resources you can't even begin to imagine, Cameron. I'll build the case against you, and by the time I'm finished, the judge wouldn't let you have a fucking hamster. I don't need it to be true. I just need it to *look* true," Jess hissed at me.

Movement caught my attention. The waiter appeared with a smile for me until he glanced at Jess. His welcoming grin turned to a frown in record time. "Welcome to Bar-B. What can I bring you to drink?" he asked me.

I thought of Cordon. "You have any craft gins?" I asked.

The young man gave me an odd look. "Craft gins, sir?"

"You know—gin that's been enhanced with botanicals?" I explained.

"Uh, no sir. We don't," the young man answered, looking a bit embarrassed.

I chuckled. "If you lived in Maryland, you'd know what craft gin was, young man. I'll have a gin and tonic, please. Jess?"

"I'm done. He's got the check. You drink up, Cameron. I'll be sure this is your last celebration, you cock sucker," she snapped at me as she gathered her pictures to leave.

Suddenly, you could have heard a pin drop. A stocky guy walked over to the table and looked at me. "Is she giving you trouble?"

My heart grew wings at the juxtaposition of the situation. I watched as Kelso Ray pulled out his phone and began recording the altercation. "As a matter of fact, she is. I think she might have been overserved. Maybe she needs to be escorted out?" I suggested.

The bouncer looked at me and grinned. "That's probably a good idea." He then led Jess over to the door and walked outside with her, which brought a rousing round of applause from the crowd. The bartender even rang the bell hanging over the bar.

Tanner and Kelso came over and sat down with me as my drink was delivered, which was a relief. I flipped over my phone and stopped the recording, placing the device back on the table. I looked at Tanner and smiled. "Well, counselor?"

Tanner turned to Kelso Ray, whose star was definitely on the rise in country music and motioned his head towards me. Kelso retrieved his phone and showed me the video he had of Jess being escorted out of the bar. "Send me those. I think I want them for my personal photo album," I joked.

Both men laughed, and the three of us had a drink. I resisted the urge to ask about Leo. I still had some thinking to do, and now with Jess's new strategy, I was completely terrified to even think about him, much less voice any desire to know his whereabouts.

5

LEO

"Wait, how..." I couldn't think, and apparently I couldn't speak a full sentence. Who was this doppelganger for Cameron March? The hair was longer and had more pepper than salt. His eyes seemed to twinkle, which was weird, but his demeanor came across much lighter than the Mr. March that I knew. I was stunned.

"I'm Cordon March. I'm the distiller here. *You are...?*" the man introduced himself.

"I'm... March? Are you related to Cameron March?" I asked. It was a stupid question, because obviously they were related in some fashion, or it was the biggest fucking coincidence in the whole world! The man grinned and held out his hand to shake.

Suddenly, my common sense took center stage, and I lifted mine in return. "I'm so sorry. I'm Leo Anderson. I live in South Padre Island, Texas. I know a Cameron March, who you must be related to. The likeness is uncanny," I observed.

The man in front of me laughed heartily. "That's my little brother, Cam. I'm sixteen minutes older than him. It's a pleasure to meet you, Leo Anderson. Lynn said you wanted to speak to me... or rather, the distiller," he answered.

It was then I remembered what Mark McClintock had said—

very quickly. *"Cordonmarch is the guy's name. He used to teach at IDB, uh, Institute of Brewing and Distilling. He's a master at his craft, and he's the head distiller at Oriole's Nest Distillers…"* Clearly, I hadn't paid too much attention when he'd said the name because it had sounded like one name, not two.

"Ah. Do you remember Mark McClintock? He mentioned you when I visited his distillery. He speaks very fast," I informed him.

Cordon smiled. "Yeah, Mark's a good kid and he's always talked that fast. His place is doing well from what I've heard, but unfortunately, I don't get over that way often. This place keeps me busy. So, you know Cam?"

I swallowed. "Yes, sir."

Cordon tossed his hands in the air. *"Oh, God No!* Don't call me *sir* unless you're getting on your knees for me," he stated, which surprised me. Suddenly, he pointed to me and laughed.

"Sorry, but the look on your face is priceless. I seriously didn't mean to startle you, but I'm nobody special, so don't call me sir. How do you know my brother?" Cordon asked. He stepped forward and placed a hand on my back, steering me to a seating area in front of an old stone fireplace.

We took a seat, and I gathered my thoughts. "He's actually designing a reno for my bar on South Padre Island, Texas. It's a beach bar…" I started to explain to him.

Cord, as he insisted I call him, was a really personable man and an active listener as I explained about the remodel at On the Rocks. "I recently acquired two partners, my brother, Kelso, and my best friend—who happens to be dating Kelso—Tanner. We're hoping to expand the business from the little beach shack we currently have. I've been thinking about adding a small distillery, but aside from what I've read about it, I have no knowledge on the subject. That's why I took this trip."

Cord nodded. "So, Cam is designing your place? I'm surprised I haven't heard from him about the distilling rooms you'll need."

"Oh! I haven't actually told him that part yet. I'll need to have Tanner call him soon, I suppose. The plans will need to be modified to include the distillery," I thought out loud.

Cordon sat forward. "Is there a reason you don't talk to Cam yourself?"

I had to give the man props—he was astute. "We, uh... This is a little embarrassing. We had a disagreement a couple of weeks ago, and I turned over all of the planning to Tanner. He's going to work with Cameron now. Your brother seems to dislike me. I went to take a check to him at his office, and he was quite upset that I showed up there. His son was at the office, and for some reason, Cameron didn't want the kid to see me," I related.

Cord stood and walked over to the bar, hopping over the top of it. He began working behind it, but I couldn't see what he was doing. The lady who had greeted me when I arrived, Lynn, came out from the back and the two spoke quietly for a moment. "Get out from behind here, Cordon. You're no bartender," Lynn seemed to chastise.

The man laughed and hopped back across the bar, standing there to wait for her to do something. I couldn't help but notice he was quite fit, just like Cam. Cordon was definitely a mystery to me, but I had seen a twine braided bracelet in the PRIDE colors on his wrist, so maybe he was an ally? I felt a little more comfortable with those thoughts in my head.

Lynn, who I was curious to ask if she was his wife or partner, walked over to the table with a tray holding two rows of shot glasses. She put it down and winked at me before she walked away through a swinging door. Cord walked over to the table with a basket of oyster crackers like we used to put on chili when I was a kid.

"Palate cleansers," Cord responded to my unasked question as he placed them on the coffee table in front of us, taking a seat on the tan leather couch next to me at a respectful distance.

He rested his elbows on his jean-clad knees, his ponytail falling over his right shoulder. "So, if you met Mark, you might recognize some of these botanicals. I shared my basic recipes with him, and we each tweaked them to our personal tastes, but they're ostensibly the same," Cord explained.

He picked up a shot glass and pointed to the same on my end of the tray. I could see flower petals floating in the white liquor. "Do you leave the petals in for any particular reason?" I asked.

Cord took a sniff of the glass, so I did the same. "Looks pretty. Women love it," he remarked before he took a tiny sip. I mirrored his actions.

I watched as he rolled the taste around his mouth, so I did the same, tasting the natural juniper infusion, but then there was a subtle taste I couldn't exactly identify. "I get the juniper notes, but the other one... I just can't name it," I admitted.

Cord grinned. "It's honeysuckle. You're new to it. It takes a little time to get in the groove of discerning the ingredients. I've judged some moonshine competitions in the past, and it takes years to learn how to taste each ingredient. Just remember, your palate is your best asset in this business."

"I don't think I'm stupid, but can you explain to me why?" I asked, suddenly worried I might not be intelligent enough to even consider studying to become a distiller.

Cord placed a hand on my shoulder. "We experience taste with more than just our tastebuds. Sight and smell play a big part in it. No one I've ever met is too stupid to learn these things. If you ever research prohibition-era moonshiners, you'll see most were completely uneducated, but they figured it out. I have full faith you'll be a quick study." Cord followed it up with a wink, and for a moment, I wished he were Cam. I had the feeling Cord wasn't shy about letting people know where they stood with him. Cam... not so much.

"So, have you met my nephews?" Cord asked as we ate lunch at a diner near the Orioles Nest. I'd invited Cord to lunch because he'd been so kind as to take me around the distillery for about two hours, and I owed him something.

"I, uh, I haven't actually. Cam mentioned he has two sons, and I've heard from my business partners that they've been into the restaurant since I've been gone, but I've never met them. As I said, I seem to rub Cam the wrong way, so I'm not surprised," I responded.

Cord chuckled. "I have a feeling it's not what you think."

Before he could expound on his response—or I could ask any more questions—a young guy sashayed over and stood at the end of the table, staring at Cord. "You didn't call me," the small redhead lashed out.

Cord glanced up from the menu and cocked an eyebrow. "No, and I won't, just as I told you. I'd urge you to check your tone, young man," the ponytailed man chastised. Somehow, I got the feeling I was in the middle of a power struggle, and it was interesting to watch.

"You didn't seem to have an issue when I sucked your..."

"*Stop!* I didn't know who you were. It was a one-time thing. Now, are you going to take our order, or do I need to tell your father where I ran into *you* and all about that fake ID?" Cord threatened.

Hmm... Interesting...

"I'm twenty. I'll be twenty-one next May. I have my own car, and I pay my own way..." the young man protested.

"I'll remind you that you live in your parents' home and work in their place of business. You're not on your own until you are self-sufficient, and I'm not looking to raise a child. Now, I'll have the special. Leo?" Cord insisted before he looked at me.

The young man turned my way, snarling at me a little before he pasted on a fake grin. "I'm Brian. What can I get you to eat?"

"I'll have the hamburger deluxe, please. No mustard and a

side of potato salad," I ordered. The kid wrote it down, and I prayed to hell he didn't spit in my food.

Just as he was about to walk away, Cord grabbed his forearm. "Grow up a little and come find me, pet. Don't do anything to our food or I'll make you eat it," Cord warned, offering a wink to seemingly soften the blow. The young guy's eyes actually seemed to twinkle as he looked at Cord before he scurried off toward the kitchen.

Cord looked at me and smirked. "That sounded bad, but a few tequila shots at a club and a hot young guy coming onto me? Let's just say my better judgment was in the shitter that night."

We both laughed, and I had one question answered. The woman at Oriole's Nest was definitely not his wife.

We ate, making small talk about the Sykesville area and how he ended up there. "Is Oriole's Nest owned by the Mafia?" I asked, remembering that I'd heard it from Mark McClintock, though he'd said it in a half-joking manner.

Cord full-on laughed. "Lynn's mean enough to be a Mafioso, but no. She used to work for a big marketing firm in New York, but after her wife died from ovarian cancer, Lynn decided she needed a change of pace. I was judging an absinthe competition in West Virginia a few years back when I met her. She was interested in opening a distillery as an act two for her life, and the two of us hit it off," Cord detailed.

"I thought maybe she was your partner," I offered.

Cord's face scrunched up before he leaned forward. "Not on your life. I love her like a sister, but no."

"I meant no offense…"

"No need to apologize, Leo," he replied as he rolled up the sleeve of his denim shirt, revealing not only his PRIDE bracelet, but a PRIDE flag tattoo woven through two purple male symbols. It couldn't get much clearer than that.

"Does this bother you?" Cord asked as he pointed to his tattoo.

"No, not at all. Did you think it would?" I asked.

Cord lifted his hand, and Brian the server strolled over. "Your lunch should be right up."

"Thanks. Can we get two of the bourbon smashes?" he asked.

I looked at him with questioning eyes. "You make bourbon?"

Cord laughed. "I have in the past when I was learning the science behind various mashes used in distilling. I worked with a few moonshiners in Tennessee once upon a time, and I've found most bourbons are pretty great how they are, so I don't try to improve on perfection. Besides, Brian's dad used to be a moonshiner in Kentucky. He makes some of the best bourbon this side of the Mason-Dixon line. I wasn't about to compete with him."

Brian came back with our drinks as another young guy came out of the kitchen with a tray carrying our meals. Mine was the burger, and Cord's was chicken-fried steak. I almost wished I'd ordered that meal.

I thanked the two of them and waited for Cord to eat or drink before I ventured into those waters. If he trusted Brian, then I'd give it a try.

Cord held up his drink to Brian. "Take a sip, sweetheart." Just then, a man walked over to the table with two drinks. "Cord, how the hell are ya? Brian, son, go wait in my office."

I glanced up to see a bear of a man with a quick smile. He placed a drink in front of me and placed the two we'd been served onto the tray the other guy was carrying. "Thanks, Will." The other guy nodded and walked away.

"What did he do to 'em—spit or piss?" Cord asked.

The man laughed. "Actually, I saw him with the hot sauce. I was curious who he was makin' 'em for."

Cord chuckled and pointed to me. "Leo Anderson, this is Arlo Teague. Arlo, this is a new friend of mine, Leo," he introduced.

The man extended his hand, so I stood and shook it. "You'll have to forgive Brian. He's young and has an attitude about everything. Nice to meet ya, Leo. Where you from?" the man asked. He had flaming red hair, just like his son, but the man had tats on his face, which was a bit unusual, though I could remember men with them when I'd gone to visit Tanner in prison. I swallowed. "Tyler, Texas, sir."

The man, Arlo, laughed. "Welcome to Maryland. I spent about six lifetimes in a Texas jail once. I have no desire to go back there anytime soon," he offered.

I nodded and sat back down while Cord and Mr. Teague chatted for a minute. Finally, the redhaired man looked at my plate and grinned. "Damn. Sorry, guys. If it's cold, I'll send out new meals," the man offered.

I bit into my burger, which was stacked with onion rings, tomatoes, pickles, and shredded lettuce. I tasted the charbroil of it, and I had no complaints. "It's great, Mr. Teague." No way was I going to cross the man.

"We're fine, Arlo. It's still hot, man," Cord thanked. Arlo nodded and left us alone.

"You said Brian's father was a moonshiner in Kentucky and you worked with him. When was he in prison? Seems risky that he'd make moonshine, or did he do it before prison?" I asked.

Cord cut into his steak and chewed it as he studied me for a moment, making me nervous. Finally, he wiped his mouth with his napkin. "Arlo is Brian's uncle. Arlo's sister took off from their home in eastern Kentucky when she found out she was pregnant with Brian. Arlo went looking for her and found her working the stroll in Dallas, and he put her pimp in the hospital for turning his little sister out when she was pregnant," Cord explained.

"Oh, wow," I commented, thinking of Kelsey Lee and her baby by that son of a bitch, Gil McGovern. She should be due any day, so I could imagine how Arlo felt about his sister having a child on her own.

"Stacy was Arlo's sister's name. She had Brian on a Wednesday, and she overdosed on Friday. Silas, an emergency foster father who worked with social services in Dallas at the time, took Brian in. The baby was in withdrawals from Stacy's heroin addiction, and he took care of the boy until Arlo got out of jail and could take him," Cord explained.

I couldn't hold my tongue. "How did you not know it was Brian when you hooked up with him? You know the family, right?" I had no real business questioning his actions. I was only in town for a few days, but it felt as if I needed to know what happened to be able to see if the boy was really in any danger. I had no problem telling his father what had happened if I felt Brian needed to be protected. I owed Cordon March nothing.

Cordon chuckled. "Cool your jets, Leo. I only met this family a few years ago. The night I ran into Brian, we were both at a play party, and he was wearing a puppy hood until after our encounter. I've felt dirty ever since, okay?"

As I stared at him, I saw he was definitely serious. *Puppy hood? WTF?*

6

CAM

Bzzz. Bzzz.

I glanced over to my desk from my drafting table to see the intercom light flashing. I slid off my stool and hit the button. "Nichele, why didn't you buzz my cell?" I asked with a bit of a bite in my tone.

"You wanna check the battery power and apologize to me?" she responded.

I looked at my cell to see it was dead. "I apologize."

Nichele chuckled. "Accepted. It's Cordon March."

I inwardly groaned because I owed my brother a call, and I knew he was going to give me hell about it. "That's my brother. How's he sound?" I asked.

"Sexy A-F, boss. That man has quite a lovely voice," Nichele taunted. Cord had a deeper voice than mine, which was probably due to the lifestyle he led. I was the stupid geek to his cool bad boy. Life wasn't fucking fair when it came to me and my twin brother.

"Thanks, Nichele," I replied before I went to the desk and hit the speaker button on my phone. "Cord?"

"Little brother, how the fuck are ya?"

I walked over to close the door in the event Lan was having a client in. We were trying to project ourselves as a professional organization after all. Nothing about my moonshining brother was professional.

"I'm well—as well as I can be with the shit hitting *my* fan. What's up with you?" I replied.

"How are my nephews? Grayson doing okay at college?" Cord asked. It was the way he procrastinated telling me why he'd actually called, and I had the feeling it was because he had bad news, though I couldn't imagine what it could be.

"Doing great in light of the circumstances. His girlfriend broke up with him so he was in the dumps for a few weeks, but he's back at school, and I think he's better now—unless he contacted you to say he's in trouble," I pressed.

I knew Grayson and Cord were friends on social media—which pissed me off because my son wasn't friends with me, barely speaking to me when he was at my place for weekends, much less contacting me on the few social media outlets I was on.

Cord laughed. "Nope. He hasn't called in a month or so. How about you? Are you surviving the divorce wars?"

One good thing—I could bitch to my brother about my stupid mistake. "Oh, Jess has a new tact. She's pressing that Lan and I are dating—have been dating for years, and she swears she has the pictures to prove it. She says no judge will allow me to raise Archie when she finishes stacking the deck against me," I answered, feeling the anger flare inside me at the memory of the meeting at Bar-B when she came up with that bullshit about Lan and me being a couple.

"Seriously? She's gonna try to push that you're having a relationship with your business partner? The man you've been friends with for years? What the hell is she smoking?" Cord asked.

I had to laugh because I'd thought the same thing. "I guess the money her boyfriend makes isn't enough to support her extravagant lifestyle. I honestly have no fucking idea. How about you? What are you up to?" I inquired.

"I'm curious to know what you can tell me about one of your clients. He turned up at Oriole's Nest a day or two ago. His name is Leo Anderson," Cord informed.

"Wh-who?" I asked, unsure how in the hell Leo had ever ended up in Maryland and come across my brother. Had he gone looking for Cord? Was he stalking me?

"Leo Anderson. Gorgeous blond about six-foot tall. Big smile, and sexy as fuck. He's doing a distillery tour in the mid-Atlantic, and he showed up here. He met a student of mine over in Frederick, and Mark sent him here. He says he knows you," Cord explained.

My common sense told me to just make light of our acquaintance, and with the shit I was facing with Jessica, it was the smartest thing to do. At least I hadn't let my paranoia take over with that stalking bullshit. "He's a client—that's all. He's a nice guy."

Cord laughed. "That's the best fucking news I've heard in a long time. I'm taking him to a club tonight. The guy has a gorgeous ass, and I'm intrigued. I plan to suggest he stick around for a few weeks. He wants to learn distilling, and damn if I don't want to teach him that and more," my twin seemed to taunt.

Cordon and I were polar opposites when it came to relationships—I was more of a caretaker, which was why Jess walked all over me. Cord was a more dominant personality. I knew he'd dabbled in BDSM over the years because he never made any secret of anything he did. Cord was an out and proud gay man, and I was… well, I wasn't sure what I was.

"Don't… Uh, I don't know him that well. I'm doing work for him and his partners. They're expanding their business in South Padre Island, and Stenson & March are doing the reno work. Is he thinking about adding a distilling business?" I asked, moving away from his comments about Leo's ass. Hell, I'd already noticed it.

Cordon snickered. "I think I better let the two of you discuss that. So, what else is new?"

"Archer is giving me a run for my money. He doesn't want to move to Seattle with Jessica, but I'm worried about how everything will flush out," I admitted.

We spoke of nothing for a few minutes until I couldn't take it any longer. "So, did Mr. Anderson say when he's returning to South Padre?"

"I'm trying to convince him to stay for a month or so. I think the two of us have a lot in common, plus, like I said, I'd be happy to teach him the science of distilling and then some. I suppose we'll see what happens," Cord told me.

My anger simmered, though I had no right to be mad about anything. Yes, I was attracted to Leo Anderson, but I'd been a horrible jackass to him out of fear, and I couldn't say my worry was going anywhere anytime soon.

EARLY ON THE Wednesday before Thanksgiving, I drove out to South Padre Island to check on the demolition of the patio behind On the Rocks. Jess had Archie for the long weekend, and Grayson was going to spend the holiday with her, needing to return to school on Friday for a basketball tournament to support his team.

Grayson had been redshirted for his freshman year, being relegated to the practice squad and the bench during games, which had pissed him off. I'd explained to him that not many freshmen played in games that first year and being redshirted would afford him the opportunity to extend his playing time to a fifth year, giving him an extra year of his scholarship to get his masters if he so desired. He'd finally seen my logic and was taking it in stride—not happily at all.

With the boys gone, I saw no reason to be home alone for the holiday, so I rented a beach place for the weekend. I picked up the key for the duplex, finding the address included in the envelope through the GPS. I was happy to see it wasn't too far from the beach, so after I unloaded my things, I decided to drive out to the bar. Tanner and Kelso were great guys, and the staff were friendly. Hell, I was lonely, and I needed some familiar company.

I turned into the lot and saw it was full, so I drove around to the back, finding a spot near an industrial-sized dumpster. Apparently, the demo was going well. I walked around the back of the building to see the patio covering and the tiki bar were both gone, which was sort of sad. They'd had a lot of character.

I could see footings had been set. There was a vacant lot next to the space, and a sold sign in front of the property made me wonder if my brother was right. Was Leo Anderson planning a distillery next door?

I was standing in the sand when I felt paws on my leg. I looked down to see Whiskey, Kelso's dog, panting next to me. "Hey, bud," I greeted, ruffling his ears. He seemed happy to see me, too.

A shrill whistle caught my attention, and when I looked up, expecting to see Tanner, I saw Leo standing on the beach. My breath caught in my chest. I was completely awestruck at how much I'd missed him.

Whiskey stayed with me, frolicking around as I trudged through the sand to the two steps leading from the beach to the deck where Leo stood, handsome as ever. "Hey, stranger," I greeted, my heart ticking up at the sight of him.

He looked at me, not smiling. "Hello, Cameron. Whiskey, get up here."

The dog looked at me, his tail going a million miles an hour as it scraped the sand back and forth in snow angel fashion, before he finally succumbed to Leo's order and walked up the two stairs to Leo, sitting on the deck and leaning against Leo's leg in hopes of getting a little affection. I envied the dog, wishing I could do the same damn thing.

"You, uh, you went on vacation," I remarked, trying not to sound too eager for details. Cordial but detached seemed like the best approach.

Leo chuckled. "Yeah, and I was lucky enough to meet your brother. That was a mind-fuck because I didn't know there was another *you* out there. Thankfully, *he* didn't throw me out of his place."

His comment was like an arrow through my heart, but he wasn't lying. I'd been a stupid prick that day when he'd shown up at the office in Brownsville, and there was really no excuse for my overreaction. He was there to put down the deposit for the project, which really wasn't a big deal. I'd completely panicked because I was attracted to him and Grayson was hanging out at the office to wait for me to take him home that Friday. I was afraid my son would see my attraction for another man and judge me for it—he was half his mother's son.

"Yeah, uh, I'm sorry for that. I freaked out for a ridiculous reason, and I took my panic out on you," I offered as a weak excuse for bad behavior.

Leo sighed. "Let's just forget it. Come on inside. We had to make a temporary bar in here to get us through the renovation. Lan's pretty creative," he replied.

I followed him through the messy outside and inside the former bar/restaurant area, seeing a temporary bar top had been created in the dining room where people used to sit to look out the window.

The entire bar had been ripped out, the space taken down to the studs and temporary framing put in place with heavy-duty plastic tarps to keep the wind out. Lan had set up a makeshift bar with some Formica remnants he had in the warehouse and built a temporary frame for it. He'd created some shelves in the window after covering the panes with blackout film so the liquor wouldn't be ruined by the sunlight, and he'd even put up the cute sign that was originally over the tiki bar. My friend had outdone himself, and I planned to quiz him about it the next time I saw him.

I sat down on a stool and rested my elbows on the bar. "I liked your other bar better," I offered.

Leo walked behind it and grabbed a shot glass and a beautiful, hand-painted bottle that I recognized. He poured the liquor into the small glass and slid it in front of me. "Cord said this one is on him. I'll be heading back to Maryland after Christmas for more training. Your brother is incredible," Leo opined.

At that moment, I was suspecting Cord was a son of a bitch and showing off to me that he'd charmed the handsome bar owner. Cord knew I had played around with guys before, the bastard. I had the feeling he could tell I was interested in Leo, and I had no doubt he was up to something devious. Oh, he'd hear from me, all right.

I picked up the glass and moved it under my nose to smell the aromatics. I could definitely smell some lavender and a little bit of sage, I thought. "Lavender and sage?" I asked.

Leo grinned. "Yep. Your asset works really well."

I wasn't sure what the hell Leo meant by it, but I took a sip of the gin, tasting the herby goodness of it. It was one of Cord's favorite blends to make, and it was delicious with a little white soda and a squeeze of lime.

Cord had brought me a bottle of it when he made the one trip to Brownsville to see Archie when he was born and Jessica was in the hospital. When Grayson had been born, my twin was in Europe plying his trade.

Unfortunately, Jessica had been horribly rude to him that time, and he'd never returned to Brownsville after that, though he'd send me a bottle of his craft gin from wherever he was at the time, and I did love the surprise when it arrived.

Shame on me for not making the goddamn effort to go visit him, either, though he'd moved around a lot once he'd returned to the States. He'd lived in Maryland the longest since we'd left home the year we graduated high school—me to college and Cord to see the world.

"So, how *is* my brother?" I asked Leo as he made me a gin and tonic, adding a splash of sweetened lime juice as I liked it.

Leo handed me a menu. "Well, considering I just met the man a few weeks ago, I'd say he's fine. He was kind to me. I worked with him for a week at Oriole's Nest, and I fell in love with distilling. I bought that lot next door to build a distillery someday. I need to look into all the rules and regulations of it to be sure it's all legal, but I could see it being my new passion. Thankfully, I have a built-in outlet for the liquor right here," Leo described with a smile, seemingly talking to himself and ignoring me. I definitely understood why.

"Is it your *only* passion?" I asked out of the clear blue. I hadn't even really thought about it. It just came out.

The blond turned his eyes to me, their green and gold irises seeming to dance in the overhead lights. "I... I honestly think it could be. Your brother said it's his, and I completely understand it after being there. That's why I'm going back to train some more," Leo informed. I certainly didn't like the sound of that, but I had no say in the matter, did I?

"So, today's special is chicken-fried steak, mashed potatoes, and green beans. Miss Yvonne was quite jealous of some of the food I had when I was in Maryland, so she's trying to show me she can outcook anybody in the mid-Atlantic. It's damn good," Leo praised before he walked down to the end of the bar counter and left me alone, heading toward the kitchen.

I saw Tanner carrying a dish bin filled with beer over to the bar with Whiskey on his heels. The slow smile on his face made me feel welcome—a lot more than Leo had, but that was my own fault.

Tanner placed the bin on the floor behind the bar and stood, offering his hand to shake. "How're you doin'? As you can see, Lan's been hard at it," Tanner greeted with a big grin.

"Yeah, he's certainly gotten a hell of a jump on the demo. How's Kelso? Is he coming home for Thanksgiving?" I asked.

Tanner's happy chuckle answered my question immediately. "Yeah. He's coming home tonight. We're all having dinner at Leo's place tomorrow afternoon. How about you? Where are Archie and Grayson?" Tanner asked as he began loading the beer coolers that had been relocated into the space near the windows.

"They're with their mother for the holiday. I actually rented a place not far from here for the weekend. I was going to see if it was too late to pick up a premade meal at the grocery because I was sure you guys would be closed, and I bought a lot of crap I wouldn't let my kids eat. I'm looking forward to stuffing myself with junk food and watching football," I admitted.

"You should come over to Leo's place for dinner," Tanner invited.

I smirked at him. "I don't think your partner would like to have me there after my bad behavior the last time I actually saw him, but thanks, Tanner." I appreciated his kindness, but he didn't need to waste it on me. I'd already made my bed. It was time to relax in it.

7

LEO

I paced the width of the kitchen as Miss Yvonne worked around me. We knew we'd be busy on the Wednesday night before Thanksgiving, so I'd scheduled everyone to work. Tabitha had worked a split shift, god bless her, and I was planning to give her a bonus for Christmas, plus the week off.

Tabitha worked quite hard to help Miss Yvonne in the kitchen, and she had even brought a few of her own recipes into the restaurant, which Miss Yvonne and I had tasted. The woman was an incredible cook, and I could see that even Miss Yvonne was impressed.

"Leo, honey, what's goin' on? You tryin' to wear out the tile? I happen to like it, myself," Miss Yvonne joked.

I didn't know how to really answer her because what Cameron March had done to me a month ago was physically painful when I dwelled on it. I'd pushed it aside while I was back east but seeing Cam in person brought it all rushing back. I had to get over it because I'd quasi-accepted the man's apology, and he was working for us at the bar. Besides, being around the handsome architect did things to me that I didn't know how to handle.

I stopped pacing and looked at Miss Yvonne. "What the hell do you do when you want to be important to someone, but they don't see you as... How does someone get over a person who wants nothing to do with them?"

Miss Yvonne grabbed my arm and dragged me over to the office, pushing me inside and closing the door. "Goodness, you're like a chicken on a hot plate, darlin'. Now, tell me exactly what the heck has you so on edge?"

I helped Miss Yvonne sit in the only chair other than the desk chair, and then I sat down on the desk, preparing myself to confide in her instead of Kelso or Tanner. "*IthinkI'mattractedtoaman!*" I said really fast. I expected her to be horrified, but all she offered was a kind smile.

"I can see this is upsetting to you," Miss Yvonne announced, her smile not fading.

I couldn't hold back. "I played football in high school. I dated a lot of girls. I had sex with some, and I'm... I'm a *man*," I defended.

I watched Miss Yvonne closely, expecting her to scowl at me and walk out of the kitchen, never wanting to return. She stood all right, and she walked to where I sat on the desk, wrapping thin arms around my neck as she quietly cried, rocking me back and forth as my mom, Loretta, used to do when I was a kid and got hurt while doing one fool thing or another.

"I know from Kelso that you boys grew up with parents who didn't cherish the fact they had two wonderful sons. I lost my boy... Well, honey, I can tell you that there are pains at losing a child that are hard to get over. My RJ, he was one who was attracted to men and women." Miss Yvonne offered, her words shocking me.

Her quick acceptance of my words caught me by surprise. "So, you don't think I'm going to hell like my parents thought about Kelso when he was younger and came out?"

Miss Yvonne laughed. "Leo, son, why do you give a good

goddamn what anyone thinks about who you choose to love? My word, life is way too short for that business," she said, the sincerity on her face offering a comfort I hadn't expected.

"Yeah, okay, but he's straight. He has kids and a wife, though she might be an ex-wife. I'm afraid I'm into a guy who will never be into me," I grumbled.

Miss Yvonne's blue eyes became as wide as saucers, and then she laughed. "Leo, I never took you for one to throw in the towel without a fight, honey."

I was a bit stunned by her comment. "Yvonne, the man's not gay."

She stood and took my hand. "Leo, what about you?"

I sucked in a breath. "I'm attracted to Cameron March, and I don't know what to do about it."

Miss Yvonne chuckled. "Now, Leo, you're gettin' somewhere."

I CARRIED out Cameron's dinner plate—the chicken-fried steak special—and I placed it in front of him. "Here ya go. Miss Yvonne gave you an extra-large portion. I hope you like it," I offered as I placed a flatware roll on the counter next to him and went about loading a glass crate with dirties and carrying it back to the kitchen. We'd had to sacrifice water at the bar because we didn't want to run a water line. I missed it a lot.

I shoved the tray in the dishwasher and went back out to find Tanner and Kelso giving each other the breath of life in the middle of the dining room. It made me smile. Whiskey was right there next to them, tail going back and forth like a windshield wiper. I was happy to see Kelso, too.

I waited until their lips unlocked, and then I walked over to hug my little brother. "Glad you're home," I told him.

Kelso pulled back and looked at me. "What's wrong? Did you not enjoy your vacation?"

"Yes, and I owe you for it. I coulda paid for it," I whined, not sounding very gracious. "Sorry. Thank you so much. It was so fun. We can catch up tomorrow. You guys take off," I suggested.

Tanner chuckled. "Nope. Wouldn't do that to ya. If anything, you take off. You're the one hosting all of us tomorrow," he reminded me, not that I could forget it. I'd ordered a turkey and sides to keep Miss Yvonne from killing herself to cook for us. There would be Tanner, Kelso, Miss Yvonne, Tabitha and her daughter Celia, and me.

I did need to get home and make sure everything was in order, but it was only seven in the evening, and I felt better being there since I knew how much money was coming into the place. They didn't call it "Drunksgiving" for nothing.

I went to the back to grab a flat of glasses and headed back to the bar, seeing Cameron was still sitting there. He had another drink, which I was guessing Gina had made for him, and his plate was cleared.

I placed the plastic flat on the beer coolers behind me and began wiping pint glasses. "Big plans for Thanksgiving?" I asked.

Cam didn't answer, so I glanced up to see him staring at me. "Leo, I can't apologize enough for how I treated you that day. I won't bore you with my sad story, but I was panicked, and I didn't expect you to come into my office. I was rude, and there's no reason for it. Please forgive me."

I studied his face to see he was completely sincere, and I decided I should just let it go. Besides, I was planning to see Cord after Christmas, so there was that. Carrying a grudge just wasn't my style.

"Cam, chalk it up to a bad day, and let's forget it. We'll run into each other professionally, so let's call a truce," I suggested.

"Thanks, Leo. I'll take my check if you don't mind," he requested.

I decided to offer him an olive branch—a friendly gesture since we'd need to work together on the expansion. "This one's on me, Cam. Happy Thanksgiving," I said as I extended my hand to shake his.

"Thank you. Happy Thanksgiving to you as well," he responded before he downed his drink and left the bar.

I felt a lot better for taking the high road. My karma could use the boost.

I LET myself into my place, seeing a strange pickup parked next door and the lights on in the other side of the duplex. I'd found out the owner of the two places had decided to rent out the other half as an Airbnb when he wasn't living there, so I was guessing people were staying there for the holiday.

I went back to take a shower and change into sweats and a t-shirt so I could do a little housekeeping. I heard music through the wall in the kitchen, so I walked over and closed my eyes, trying to figure out what the guest was listening to. The baseline was familiar, so I got a glass and put it up to the wall like I'd seen in old movies. All that did was muffle the sound even more, which wasn't a help at all.

Suddenly, the volume was a little louder as the water was running in the kitchen. When the water was turned off, I heard my brother's tenor voice, clear as a bell. It was The Tex-Sons, my brother's band, number one song, "Whiskey Dreams," which made me smile. At least my new neighbor had good taste in music.

Ding.

The sound came from my pocket as I ran some hot water in the sink to wipe down the counters and eventually mop the floor. I wanted the place to pass Miss Yvonne's strict standards of cleanliness. The woman used to give me shit about the apartment when she'd stop by, and I wanted her to see I was now able to keep a house clean. Her approval meant a hell of a lot to me.

I was scheduled to pick up the turkey and all the fixings at noon the next day. We were eating at two o'clock in the afternoon, and I needed to ask Miss Yvonne how to keep it all warm, but I decided I'd call her in the morning; she deserved a quiet night at home after such a busy day and evening.

I reached into my pocket and retrieved my phone, glancing at the screen to see it was a text from Cord.

Happy Thanksgiving Eve, Leo. How'd you find everything back home?

I grinned at his thoughtfulness. I wanted to let myself fall for Cordon March. I could move to Maryland and make a life there, but as crazy as it was, I hadn't been attracted to him. He was a really nice guy, but that was as far as it went for me. I smirked as I responded.

Warmer here than where you are! The reno is underway at the bar, so that's good. I was wondering if you'd mind if I came back to Maryland after Christmas and worked with you some more? I'll get a place to stay, and I won't be a pain in the ass, I swear. Will you think about it?

I thought about deleting my message to him, thinking it sounded too forward, but I decided to do something out of my comfort zone again. I'd done it when I'd taken the gin tour Kelso had planned and paid for, and the world hadn't ended when I left Tanner in charge of the bar, so I hit send.

My phone rang a second later. I checked the screen to see it was Cord. "Hey," I greeted.

"Leo, how the hell are ya? Trip home okay?" Cord asked, his ever-present smile evident in his deep voice.

"Yeah. Turned the car in at BWI-Marshall and got home by six. How's everything at Oriole's Nest?" I asked.

"Things are kinda in flux, as a matter of fact. Lynn's sister got into a car accident in Pennsylvania, so Lynn's gonna close the place for a few weeks. That's what I called to tell you. I'm storing the liquor I've already distilled in the root cellar of the Oriole's Nest, and then I guess I'm looking at a whole lot of down time," Cord explained.

I had a fantastic idea hit me just as his sentence ended. "Why don't you come down here to the island? I mean, your brother is here, and I'm sure he'd like to see you. He said you guys haven't seen each other much over the years, so now's your chance to catch up. You're welcome to stay with me. I've got a two-bedroom duplex not far from the beach," I volunteered before my brain finally engaged.

"Duplex? Are there a lot of those down there?" Cord asked, which seemed quite odd to me. I thought there were duplexes everywhere.

"I wouldn't say an overabundance of them, but there are some, why?" I asked.

"What are the odds? I'll fly in on Friday. I don't want to disrupt your Thanksgiving," Cord offered.

"Can you get here tomorrow? I'm having a few people over, and I'd like you to join us," I suggested. Apparently, I had diarrhea of the mouth all of a fucking sudden.

"Oh, yeah? Let me see if I can get an early flight. I'll text ya when I know," Cord assured.

"Okay. I hope you can work it out," I replied. We hung up, and I hurried to the spare room, looking around at all the fucking boxes that still needed to be unpacked. I started to move them into my bedroom when my phone chimed at the same time as the doorbell.

I hurried to the kitchen where I'd left my phone on the charger to see a text from Cord.

I was lucky enough to get an early flight. I'll be in about noon. Don't worry about a place for me. I've got a friend in the area. What time's lunch?

I chuckled and responded.

Two o'clock. I'll keep a plate warm for you! Safe travels.

I went to the door and pulled it open, surprised at who was standing on my little porch.

What were the chances???

8

CAM

I WAS SITTING on the couch of my rental after I'd made some popcorn and grabbed a beer from the fridge. I turned on the television, grateful for satellite, and I started channel surfing.

I wasn't really a boob-tube kinda guy—and I was dating myself with the boob-tube reference. Of course, I watched the news to try to keep abreast of what the hell was going on in the world, and occasionally, I'd watch an old detective show, but I worked a lot and didn't waste time on gossip and speculation, which was all there seemed to be on television. Archie, however, was a child of the television era to be sure.

When I was working on a project, I didn't stop until the muse took a break, and even then, I went back and refined what I'd already gotten down. TV seemed like something bored people and little kids enjoyed. I was neither.

My work habits had been the scapegoat for the end of my marriage with Jessica. When Stenson & March really took off, Grayson was just starting kindergarten. I'd worked for the city of Brownsville as an inspector before that, which was where I met Landon. The more involved I got in our fledgling business, the less time I had at home, and I thought it suited Jess just fine back then because she never said a word. Hell, if I was being honest, it suited me just fine, too.

Archie had been a surprise—Jess called him an accident—but if he was an accident, he was the best one I'd ever had. Jessica had suffered from post-partum depression after Arch was born, and I ended up taking off work for three months to care for the boys so she could concentrate on her health, which sort of turned into me becoming the primary caregiver to them while Jessica pursued her legal career with fervor.

My phone buzzed on the couch next to me, so I picked it up, happy to see it was my brother.

You got room for me to spend a week or two with ya? It's your twin brother, by the way—the better looking one.

I chuckled at his asshole behavior while inviting himself to stay with me.

I'm at the beach for the weekend. You're welcome to join me anytime.

The phone rang, so I answered. "What's up, cocksucker, and I mean that with all the love in my heart," I joked.

"Yeah, you oughta try suckin' a cock. It'll give you a whole different perspective on the world," Cord punted back. It was funny how we slid into old behaviors so quickly.

I laughed. "Yeah, maybe. It probably would have kept me from umpteen years of bullshit," I assessed, remembering the day I came home from work to find the house nearly empty. My loving wife—*haha!*—had hired a moving company to come into our home and remove everything *she* wanted. She left me the furniture in my den and the spare bed.

My clothes had been dumped onto the floor where the dresser and chest had been, and she had left my pillow without the pillowcase because it had matched the bedding set she'd picked out. Even as empty as the house was, it felt a hell of a lot warmer without her there. I'd really missed the boys, though, because for the first time since Archie had been born, she'd taken responsibility for them.

Cord chuckled. "Maybe, maybe not, but it's a lot more fun. Anyway, where are ya?"

"I'm at the beach... Well, at a duplex not too far from the beach on South Padre Island," I answered. I saw lights shine through the window of the kitchen, but I was too comfortable to get up and check. The place I was staying was an Airbnb, and the owner told me the next-door neighbor had recently moved in, so I was determined not to be a pain in the ass as long as they didn't start shit with me.

"You got room for me to crash on your couch?" Cord asked.

I laughed. "You long-legged bastard. There isn't a couch long enough for you to sleep on in all of Texas. No, I can do you one better. I've got a second bedroom with a king-sized bed you're welcome to use if you get here before Monday. Otherwise, we'll be at the house in Brownsville," I replied.

"Duplex? You know who else lives in a duplex?" Cord asked.

I sighed. I hated his goddamn guessing games. "No fucking idea."

"Leo Anderson. He told me about moving to a duplex near the beach so his brother and partner could have the apartment over the bar. Isn't fate interesting? I'll see ya tomorrow," Cord tossed out before he hung up, the dick.

I turned off the television and walked into the kitchen, turning on the radio because the place was too quiet. I dumped the swill of my beer down the drain and rinsed the bottle before turning up the radio. Kelso Ray and his band were playing that song they had charting at the moment, so I turned it up and went to look out the kitchen window, not too surprised when I saw Leo's small SUV parked next to my pickup truck. I wondered if he recognized it was mine? I stood there for a few minutes wondering what to do as I stared at the night sky filled with stars.

I finally grabbed an empty coffee cup, turned down the radio, and went out the front door, pushing the doorbell on the attached unit.

The door popped open to reveal Leo's handsome face, and I held up the cup. "Hi. I'm the jackass next door, and I wondered if I could borrow a cup of sugar for my morning coffee," I lied.

Leo chuckled. "Come on in. You want a beer?" he asked as he stepped aside to invite me inside his half of the duplex.

I looked around, seeing boxes on the floor of his living room. "You need help moving those?" I asked.

"I don't, but thanks. I thought Cord was going to stay here with me, but I guess he's staying with you, huh?" Leo surmised.

I smirked. "Yeah. I still don't know how he figured out we were neighbors this weekend. He'll stay with me here for the holiday, and then probably go back to Maryland," I speculated.

"Oh, actually, Lynn closed the distillery for a few weeks. Her sister was in an accident, and she's going to Pennsylvania to help out. You settled in next door?" Leo asked as he headed to the kitchen, me following behind.

Suddenly, something popped into my head that I hadn't considered until that very second. "So, uh, you and my brother hung out a lot?" I asked, taking the beer he offered as we each leaned against the opposite counter in the galley-style kitchen, studying one another carefully.

Leo had one arm over his chest and his hand under his pit while the other arm was bent holding his beer. His body language seemed a little closed off, and I wondered if it was because there was something going on between him and my brother or because I really had no business asking him anything about his personal life. That being said, I still stared at him, waiting for an answer.

"He's, uh… He was kind enough to sort of show me the ropes… Wait!" He held up his hand, a kind grin tipping up the edges of his sumptuous lips. "Let me back up. I went on a distillery tour after…" Leo looked away for a second before turning back to meet my eyes.

An anguished look overtook his features, and I immediately felt the guilt churn in my stomach. Leo then continued. "Well, you humiliated me, Cam. I thought maybe we were becoming friends, and I didn't think it would be a big deal to drop by while I was in the neighborhood to give you the deposit check for the work at On the Rocks. I'm not sure what you thought I was going to do to you. I was so embarrassed that I left town," Leo explained, his face covered in shadows that my actions had put there.

Man, I felt like I was about two-feet tall, so I swallowed my pride. "I'm really, really…"

"No, you already apologized, Cam. I accepted it, but that's why I went back east. I toured five distilleries, and then I went to Sykesville where Cord works. I nearly had a heart attack when I saw him. His hair is long and a little darker than yours, but you two are otherwise identical," Leo said.

I laughed, feeling the nervous tension between us finally snap. "Our father couldn't tell us apart when we were born, either. Mom painted blue and purple polish on our toes to help Dad out, but until Cord fell off his tricycle at three and busted open his chin, we were literally identical," I clarified.

Leo chuckled. "Well, he has a beard now, so there's no scar to see. If he cut his hair and shaved, I don't know if I'd be able to tell the two of you apart," Leo affirmed, his smile nearly hypnotizing.

"*You* might be able to since you know Cordon, but yeah, that's probably true," I replied.

"How would *I* be able to?" Leo asked, looking confused.

I smirked at him. "I'd be the one with the devil horns coming out of my scalp," I joked, bringing a raucous laugh from the attractive man.

Leo took a sip of his beer, a smile forming around the bottle as he looked at me. "I don't know about that. I'm guessing if somebody looked, they'd find the same ones on Cord's scalp, not that I did any exploring." We both tittered at his comment, which was probably true.

"So, you bought the lot next to the bar to build a distillery?

You liked the process that much? Cord's tried to explain it to me over the phone, but I don't get it," I admitted.

"Yeah, I did. It's harder to understand what goes into making gin and vodka if it's explained without seeing the distilling process in person, I'm certain. I'm more of a hands-on learner, myself. I did well in school with chemistry, so I understand the mechanics of it, but there's a lot that comes from trial and error. I'd like to build a small still to experiment, but I have no idea where I'd put it," Leo explained.

I gave it a minute's thought and smirked. "I'll get Lan to put a couple guys on building a shed on the new property that could be moved when you're ready to build out. It won't take but a day or so. It should be about fifteen by fifteen so you have space to store grain and stuff. They can insulate it to be able to maintain the temperature and keep out the vermin. It'll work while you're learning and experimenting," I suggested to him.

"Yeah? That'd be cool. That means I can get your brother to help me build a still while he's here. Think we could run a hose to the building so I can have water inside?" he asked, his mind seeming to go a million miles an hour.

I considered his idea, but thought another option was better —we should go ahead and put in a water line to the newly purchased property. "Let me talk to Landon about the water. He's out of town right now, but when he gets back, I'll ask him about the best way to suit your needs temporarily. So, you don't go home for Thanksgiving?" I asked, changing the subject to more personal matters.

I wanted to know more about the guy in the worst fucking way, especially since I got the feeling he and my brother were only friends. I could see Leo was a little shy, and with my regularly guarded demeanor, we'd never get anywhere if we went about things as we had previously.

"Let's sit down. Want another beer?" he asked, seeing mine was empty. *Why the fuck not?*

"Yep. I'll be right back," I told him, hurrying over to my side of the two-family dwelling. I grabbed my popcorn and the rest of the six-pack I had in the fridge and went back to Leo's, happy to see he hadn't locked me out.

I placed the popcorn bowl on the table in front of the couch, and I took the beer in the kitchen where Leo was running water and adding some lemon-pine scented disinfectant.

"Something wrong?" I asked, looking around for a spill.

Leo chuckled. "Miss Yvonne is coming over tomorrow, and she gives me shit about my housekeeping skills, so I was just gonna mop the floors and wipe the cabinets to prove I'm actually an adult. You'd think my driver's license would be enough proof."

I scrutinized the guy, which caused my dick to plump up and take up the space in the front of my jeans. *Yep, he's definitely an adult.* "One thing I know is housework. How's the bathroom?" I asked, beginning to roll up the sleeves on my flannel shirt I'd worn in lieu of a jacket.

I watched Leo's attractive ass as he moved around the kitchen, the easy motion of his body making me so bumfuzzled, I finally decided to take off the damn shirt, draping it over the back of a chair and pulling my t-shirt from my jeans to be more comfortable. I slipped off my socks because in my haste to see if my neighbor was indeed Leo Anderson, I'd neglected to put on shoes.

"Oh, uh, I can't ask you to clean my bathroom, Cam," Leo started protesting.

I laughed. "I have two sons, Leo. I won't tell you some of the sh… stuff I've cleaned up in a bathroom. Where're the tools?"

Ten minutes later, I was on my hands and knees on the bathroom floor scrubbing the shower pan with a brush Leo had in the utility closet. I heard a gasp behind me and turned to see Leo looking at *my* ass. *Now, what did I want to do about that?*

Once Leo's house was sanitized from top to bottom, I washed my hands and wiped them on my jeans so as not to mess up the fresh towels Leo had put out in the bathrooms. We'd moved all of the boxes back to the spare room from where Leo had started moving them into his bedroom, and we'd been chatting about his life growing up in Tyler, Texas, with parents who were less than supportive of their sons.

"I guess my sister's had her baby by now. They're very short sighted, my parents, and I feel for that poor baby if Kelsey lives with Mom and Dad and that kid has to grow up with the shit we did," Leo commented offhandedly.

I sighed, remembering how lucky Cord and I were when we were kids. Our parents supported us through everything, which made me even more ashamed that I hadn't been honest with them when I was in high school and college. Maybe if I'd have trusted them more, my life would have been different—though, I'd have never been blessed with my boys.

"Cord was a cliché when he was younger—he decided it was a good idea to come out on Thanksgiving of the year we turned fifteen. Dad had just said the blessing—we weren't religious, really, but on special occasions, we thanked the universe for our blessings. So, after that, Cord says, *'Pass the potatoes, please. I'm gay.'* I swear, I nearly fell outta my damn chair," I related, laughing at the memory.

Leo laughed hard, falling forward on the couch as we sat facing each other, eating the cold popcorn I'd brought over. "Oh, my god!! What did they say?"

I laughed louder. "My mom was very laid back. She hands him the potatoes and says, *'That's nice, dear. Pass your father the rolls.'* I couldn't eat, I was laughing so hard. I think Cord was trying to frazzle them, but they both just kept eating. When dinner was over, Dad asked him, *'Does the fact your gay keep you from doing dishes? Your mom worked all day to make this meal, so let's cleanup for her.'* My half-sister Meg was home from college at the time—she's from our father's first marriage—and she actually spit cranberry sauce all over Mom's white tablecloth. It was definitely a Thanksgiving not to be forgotten," I finished telling him.

We both chuckled some more, drank more beer, and killed my popcorn. Leo got out potato chips, and the two of us talked about shit from our childhoods. Finally, I got up my courage and told him something only Cordon knew for fact.

"I finally figured myself out when I was twenty-five. I'm bi. Of course, by then I was married to Jess. She'd gotten pregnant our senior year of college, so we got married when I was twenty-one, but she lost the baby about two weeks later. She was pregnant with Grayson when I admitted my sexuality to myself, but by then, it was too late to consider any options, so I just stuck it out," I admitted.

I glanced up to see Leo smiling sweetly at me. "I'm not much better. I'm twenty-eight, and I've just finally admitted to myself I'm not straight. I don't really know where I fall on the rainbow because I've never been with a guy. If I'm gonna be honest, I've only been with a handful of girls, but I wasn't really happy with the results, ya know? I'm pretty sure they weren't happy either," Leo confessed to me.

I slid closer to him on his couch and took his hand in mine. "This okay?"

Leo nodded, his face flushing and my mind blowing at the same time. "I'm relieved to know you're not straight, Cam. I'm really attracted to you, and I'd like to take you out on a date... Oh, unless you're already seeing someone."

I chuckled, unable to believe my own fucking luck. "No, I'm not seeing anyone. I haven't even thought..." I didn't get to finish the sentence because Leo leaned forward and touched his soft lips to mine. It was more of a brush than a full-on kiss, but I still felt electricity skitter over my skin.

His hand came up to my neck, grasping gently as he turned his head and continued the firm kiss. There was no tongue—dammit—but his lips were soft and pliant. When he pulled away, we were both breathless.

"Wow!" Leo whispered as he touched his fingers to his lips.

I grinned at him. "Yeah, *wow* is right."

Suddenly, he scrambled backwards to the other end of the couch. "I-I... I'm sorry," he sputtered, looking so cute that I wanted to hug him tight and kiss him all over his gorgeous face.

I almost couldn't believe how panicked he appeared to be. Hell, I wondered why I wasn't equally panicked, but then again, it wasn't my first time kissing a guy. That was something I needed to explain to him.

"Don't freak out, okay? It's not my first time kissing a guy. I messed around a little in high school and college, so I'm not entirely new at this, but I'm afraid my experience ends with kissing and mutual hand jobs," I informed him.

"It's mine," Leo whispered.

"Your what?" I asked, needing clarification.

"My first time kissing a guy. I've jacked off with other guys while we watched porn, but not... not like *together*. I was too afraid to be interested in other guys in high school, so this is my first time kissing a guy," Leo confessed.

"You okay with it?" I questioned, wanting so badly to touch him, but not daring to do it.

Leo took my hand and pulled me down the couch and into his lap, which was quite a feat. We were the same height, but he was more muscular than me. When I looked into his hazel eyes, I saw fear, which put me on edge.

"Look, don't let our attraction for each other make you do anything you're not comfortable doing," I tried to emphasize.

"I'm actually pretty relaxed right now. I just don't want you to jeopardize... Do the boys know? I mean, do your boys know you like guys, too?" he asked me. It was a good question I'd been afraid to ask myself, especially in light of my recent meeting with Jessica.

"Honest answer—I don't know. Did Tanner and Kelso tell you about the three of us running into each other at Bar-B a few weeks ago? I was there to meet Jessica—her choice of location, not mine. We're divorced, but we're still fighting over custody of Archie, and she accused me of having a relationship with Landon. It's not true, but she had pictures of the two of us having drinks and hanging out at a place near the office. She's planning to use them as a reason to keep Arch from seeing me," I laid out for him.

Leo was silent for a moment as his hand brushed up and down my spine in a comforting gesture. "I'm really sorry about that, Cam. Can she get away with it?"

I actually leaned forward and kissed his lips again, pulling away after a moment. "I don't know. I need to call my Niles about it, but I've been living like an ostrich—head in the sand and all. Archie is old enough to decide where he wants to live, I think, but this is Texas… With the wrong judge…" I didn't finish the sentence. The look on Leo's face told me he understood what I meant.

"So, a date would probably be a bad idea," Leo mentioned quietly.

My heart kicked up a little which was ridiculous in a man of forty-five, but it was sort of exciting to think of dating Leo Anderson. "I'd like to think we're friends, and friends can go out for drinks or dinner, can't they?"

We both smiled, and I kissed him again—this time accepting his tongue into my mouth when it brushed over my lips. He tasted salty and sweet, which I found to be my favorite flavor. The brush of his blond stubble against my cheeks had quite an effect on my downstairs, but I wasn't going to stop kissing the man for anything. Thankfully, he seemed as aroused as me.

Suddenly, Leo tossed me onto the couch from his lap and climbed up on top of me. I felt his hardness brush against mine through our clothes, and I wished we could remedy that, but we were sharing our first kisses—smoldering, mind-melting kisses —and it was the most amazing sensation to hold him in my arms.

I pulled back an inch, looking into his fiery eyes as he rested on top of me. "It's very tempting to take this further than either of us might be ready for," I whispered into the small space between us before I kissed along his prickly jaw, enjoying the soft sounds coming from him as my hands cupped his sumptuous ass.

Leo offered a soft smile that lit me up inside before he spoke. "Yeah, well, right now, I think I could get ready really quick, but I'd kinda like to take my time with this, if that's okay with you."

I pecked him on the lips as he started to get up. Suddenly, he relaxed on top of me again, and I relived my teen years, making out with Brady Hicks in his parents' basement. It was poor form to kiss one guy while thinking about another from at least thirty years prior, so I blocked Brady out and sunk back into Leo. It was extraordinary to be in that space with such a fantastic man in that perfect moment. I hoped to hell it wasn't the last one.

My face was raw when we finally got off the couch, but I could see Leo's looked red as well. I chuckled as I pointed to him. "Put some ice on that, maybe. You don't want your guests to wonder what you were doing tonight."

Leo smirked and pointed to my face in return. "Yeah, you better do the same, and it's no longer night. Please come over to eat with us later today. There'll be more than enough food. I ordered a twelve-pound turkey and all the sides. Plus, Cord is coming, so I don't know how you'll get away without being here."

I glanced out of the windows in his living room, seeing the sky was beginning to lighten to a pale purple, the stars quickly fading with the rising of the yellow sun. "Damn! What time is it?" I asked.

It had been one of those nights I'd only heard about in movies. We'd kissed; we'd laughed; we'd talked; but most of all, we became comfortable with each other, both confessing that we shared an attraction I didn't want to let get away from me. It was like a new day… literally and figuratively.

I left Leo's place at four-forty-nine that morning, leaning

against his front door until I heard him engage the locks on the other side. I couldn't wipe the huge grin off my face for anything in the world, and as I strolled across the shared front porch, I heard sappy love songs in my head.

Suddenly, there was a rustling in the bushes at the side of the porch by Leo's place. I looked around, but finally decided it was just a cat or a squirrel, so I let myself into my place and locked the door, heading straight to the bedroom.

I had dreams awaiting me, and I was gearing up to spend the day with a man I was extremely attracted to—unashamed of that attraction for the first time in my fucking life! I was nearly too excited to sleep, but sleep did take me, and Leo was right there with me, holding me in my dreams.

9

LEO

I TOSSED and turned in bed for a couple of hours until I decided I couldn't sleep. I looked up how to deal with beard burn because my face was on fire, and then followed the directions, applying some hydrocortisone cream I had in my medicine chest for a mild case of poison ivy I'd contracted while cleaning up weeds at the new lot I'd purchased next to the bar.

I thought about texting Cam to share the tip, but it was just after seven in the morning, and considering he'd only left two hours earlier, I jotted down a note for him and decided to tape it to the back door of our shared deck.

The buzzing of my phone at eight that morning while I made coffee brought me from the memory of the wonderful kisses and the reason my face was crimson red and prickled. I checked the screen to see it was Tanner. "Hey, man. Happy Thanksgiving," I greeted, happier than I'd been in a long time.

"Well, hello, Sally Sunshine. How are you this lovely morning?" Tanner asked, his voice sounding as happy as I felt.

"I'm fantastic. What's up?" I asked in return.

"Well, uh, since you are Kelso's only relative that he speaks with, I wanted to ask for your blessing to ask him to be my husband. With his schedule for next year, I'd like us to get married before he goes out on tour. What do you think? Will you give your blessing for your little brother to marry a jailbird?" Tanner asked.

I chuckled. "A jailbird? *No!* My best friend who has been like a brother to me all of my life and had an unfortunate piece of luck that he paid for? Happily."

Tanner's deep laugh over the line made me smile. Tanner and Kelso deserved all of the happiness that could come their way. "You ask him yet? Anything I can do to help out if not?" I questioned.

There was a knock on the back door, so I stepped around the counter to see Cam standing there with my note in his hand and a smile on his face. He had a pink bottle in his other hand, and I happily motioned for him to come inside.

"Actually, if you wouldn't mind, could we have this weekend off? I'd like to take him to one of those bed and breakfast places at the north end of the beach for a little staycation," Tanner requested.

Cam walked inside and set the pink bottle on the table next to where I was standing. I pointed to the coffee maker and raised my eyebrows. He nodded, so I set about getting cups, sugar, and creamer out for us.

"Yeah, sure, Tanner. I know we were going to be doing inventory tomorrow, but I can handle it alone. Saturday Miss Yvonne will be there, and I'll call in Gina or maybe ask Tabitha tonight while she's here for dinner if she wants to work your shift. She's always looking for overtime.

"You guys will have a great time, no doubt. Make sure and set up your phone to capture the moment so I can see it. Those idiots Kelso plays music with will probably want to see it, as well. I'll see you guys in a little while," I offered in support of the happy couple. I knew Kelso would be over the moon about Tanner's plans, and I loved the idea of my little brother being happy.

I plugged my phone into the charger and turned to face my guest. "Did you sleep?"

Cam grinned. "Just an hour or so. You?"

I shook my head. "Tossed and turned for a while but gave up. Great minds think alike, huh?" I asked, gesturing toward the pink bottle I recognized as calamine lotion.

Cam chuckled. "I looked it up and didn't have any of the stuff they suggested, so I went to the drug store on Bahama Street and picked up a bottle of this stuff. It works for rashes—Archie was my explorer when he was little, and the kid always had one kind of rash or another, so I can attest to its effectiveness. When I was coming over to leave it by your door, I saw your note," he explained, his face turning a little pinker than it had been before a big grin blossomed on his face.

I smiled in return. "Thanks a lot for thinking of it. You take your coffee with creamer and a teaspoon of sugar, right?" I asked him.

The coffee cup he'd brought over the previous night was still on the coffee table in my living room, which made me feel a little gooey inside—which was crazy. The first night he'd come into the bar, Cam had ordered coffee during our business meeting, and I hadn't forgotten how he liked it.

"Yeah, please," he confirmed. I made the two of us coffee and placed the cups on the kitchen table.

We both sat down, each staring at our cups as an awkward silence seemed to surround us. Finally, I looked up. "Any regrets?" Of course, I prayed he said he had none about how we'd spent the previous night, but with everything he'd told me, maybe it was too much for him to handle right now. I'd hate to settle for the friend zone with Cam, but he was a really nice guy. I could do a lot worse for friends.

As he was about to answer, there was a loud banging outside, so we both hurried to the front door. I opened it and chuckled at the sight before me. There stood Cordon March with a turkey hat on his head and the stump of a pipe sticking from between his teeth. Cam stepped out around me and started laughing like a madman.

"Of course, you'd show up with your head shoved up a turkey's ass! What's with the pipe? Tell me you don't smoke now," Cam seemed to chastise.

Cord laughed and stepped over to my door. "Leo, it's good to see you, my friend." He hugged me before he knocked the pipe on the handrail of my porch, proving it was empty.

Cord then turned to his brother. "I'm a smoked turkey, dumbass. Back in the day, I used it for weed, but I'm a little long in the tooth for it now. Come here, you bastard, and give your big brother a hug," Cord ordered, giving a smacking kiss to Cam's cheek.

Of course, Cam pushed him away, and the three of us stepped back into my place, closing the door. I led the twins through the duplex to the kitchen and reached for another coffee cup, pouring some for Cord to join us. I'd learned the man preferred his coffee black from my time with him in Sykesville.

"So, is this a regular coffee klatch I'm interrupting?" Cord asked, a hint of mischief in his eyes as he gave us both the up and down. I wasn't saying anything because the man was Cam's brother, and it was up to Cameron to tell him as much or as little as he wanted him to know.

"No, but we only just learned we were neighbors last night, as you damn well know. How the hell did you get here so fast?" Cam asked.

"Well, to be honest, I'd already book a flight to come down to see Leo today. Lynn had to go take care of her sister in Pennsylvania, and she's closed the distillery for the time being. After I talked to you, brother o' mine, I decided there was more going on than met the eye, and I was able to move my flight up and come investigate. This looks quite cozy, by the way," Cord assessed before he sipped his coffee.

I saw Cam wince at his brother's words, but he sat up and glanced my way, nodding his head before he turned to Cordon.

"It is, actually. Of course, with Jess looking for anything she can to keep Archie from me, it would look incriminating if it came out, but I'll deal with that later," Cam said, offering me a smile.

He was likely right. The two of us, both red-faced at eight-thirty on Thanksgiving morning could look bad for Cam. I held up my hand in protest. "We're friends who..." I began to lodge my objection.

Cam grabbed my hand. "No, Leo. I'm not ashamed of anything." I could see he meant it, but I could also see what he had to lose—his younger son. His older one would make up his mind about things in time, but the younger boy was still a minor. That was a complication.

"But, Cam, we didn't do anything wrong. We half-ass watched a movie, ate some popcorn, drank a couple of beers, and talked most of the night," I described.

Cord cleared his throat. "By the look of those faces, there was a little somethin' somethin' that went on, but I'm not here to judge. We'll figure this shit out with Jessica, Cameron. I won't let her pull any bullshit that would make you lose Archer."

I felt a sense of relief at Cord's appearance. Maybe he could help Cam keep from having his whole world torn apart? God knew, the man didn't deserve it.

"Leo, this meal could only be better if I'd made it myself," Miss Yvonne joked as we ate her delicious pies and had coffee. Everyone had come over to the duplex for the holiday. We'd closed On the Rocks for Thanksgiving, not planning to open up until Friday night at five to give everyone at the bar time off to be with family.

"Thanks, Miss Yvonne. I knew I damn well couldn't make a turkey," I joked, feeling Cam's hand slide over my thigh under the kitchen table. I'd put the leaf in so everyone could fit around it, and Cam and Cord had brought over chairs from the other apartment, so while it was a tight fit, the eight of us made it work, and it felt perfect to me. It was the most wonderful day since I was a kid and didn't know how awful our family really was, and by the look on Kelso's face, he felt the same way.

"I hate to cut this short, because it's been wonderful to spend time with all of you, but I need to take Celia home and get her in bed," Tabitha spoke up. I absolutely adored her daughter, Celia. That little girl was full of personality, just like her mother, who I was thankful I'd hired. That sweet little girl had wandered into the living room and sacked out on the couch with a cartoon to keep her company. She was absolutely lovable.

"Oh, let me carry her out for you," I offered. I rose from the table, missing the heat from Cam's hand on my thigh.

"I got it. I think she likes me better, anyway," Kelso taunted as he stuck out his tongue at me and rushed off into the living room.

Tanner, of course, followed after him to help Tabitha carry out the toys she'd brought along. I was excited for Tanner and Kelso to get engaged. They were like a hand in a glove.

After hugs all around, Tabitha left us, and it was just the four of us at the table. Miss Yvonne, who was never one to mince words, poured more coffee for everyone and turned to look at Cam. "So, this…" she moved her index finger between the two of us with a frown on her face. "This is for real? I absolutely refuse to work with Leo when he's on a tirade like he was before he took time off. If you're in, Mr. March—the one without the beard—then you're in."

Cord laughed at her bossy tone. "I'm with her. She's a wise woman," he agreed.

I glanced at Cam, the heat rising up my neck and onto my already red face. I'd showered and shaved earlier when Cam and Cord went next door to get Cord settled. I'd applied the—thankfully—clear calamine lotion to my face, but it was still a little red. Cam's was, too, which had made me laugh.

"My heart's in it for sure, but…" Cam answered, squeezing my thigh. I knew exactly what he meant—but it can't be at the cost of his son. I completely understood.

"So, what's the problem?" Miss Yvonne asked.

Without hesitation, Cord spoke up. "His ex-wife is a sadistic bitch. She's lost her control over Cameron here, and she's going to make him pay for not indulging her every whim any longer by allowing her to take their son, Archie, to live in Seattle. She had an affair before her and Cam were officially separated, and she wants to smear him in any possible way so her betrayal of her marriage vows isn't the focus of the custody battle," Cord summarized pretty well for those at the table.

Tanner and Kelso came back inside, Tanner's arm around Kelso's waist. "We're taking off, too. I've got a rehearsal tomorrow morning with the guys—we're doing a spot at a holiday thing in Nashville for a charity in two weeks, and we don't know any Christmas songs, so we're going to work on some on Zoom," Kelso explained.

Tanner winked at me. "And then, we're going on a surprise weekend getaway. I'll see you guys on Sunday after I drop Kelso off at the airport to go back to Nashville. Have a great weekend."

Hugs all around once again, and then they were gone. Miss Yvonne began loading the dishwasher, but I stopped her. "I've got plenty of time to do this. Do you need to leave, too?" I asked.

She flapped her hand at me. "Sit down. I think better when I'm busy," she replied, going back to work.

I sat down at the table and looked at Cam and Cord. They were remarkably identical—well, aside from Cord's beard and long hair. "You know, if you cut your hair," I suggested as I looked at Cord before looking at Cam, "and if you grew a beard, nobody would be able to tell you apart at all."

Cord laughed and pointed to Cam. "Oh, that has a lot of possibilities, doesn't it? But, instead of you growing a beard, I'll shave off mine," Cord offered.

"That's it! That's it! *Fuck* her!" Miss Yvonne shouted, causing the three of us to turn to look at her. It was quite uncharacteristic to hear her drop the "F" bomb.

"Uh, Miss Yvonne? You okay?" I asked, checking her over for any outward sign of distress.

"Leo, son, quit lookin' at me like I lost my damn mind." She then looked at Cord and Cam. "Does she know you're in town?" she asked, her gaze directed at Cordon.

"Not that I know of, why?" he asked her in return.

Miss Yvonne then looked at Cam. "When do you get to see your son next?"

"He'll come over to my place next Friday night for the weekend. I'm actually going to Archie's art exhibit on Wednesday evening at his school. We usually go for dinner that night, but he has to stay at school until nine to help clean up after the midyear art fair, why?" Cam answered her with Cord nodding along unprompted. I laughed. The two of them were very similar in mannerisms for certain.

"Okay, Cordon, go get a haircut and shave off your beard. Cameron, go with him so your hair is cut exactly the same," Miss Yvonne suggested.

Cam looked at Cord with concern. "I can't ask you to do that."

Cord glanced at me and then smiled at his brother. "I think Miss Yvonne is onto something. I need to cut it anyway. I look like a damn over-the-hill hippy. Time for me to become respectable like my little brother."

"Good. When you go to the art fair on Wednesday, take your brother with you. Make sure your ex-wife sees the two of you together, and then you and Leo can freely date as much as you'd like. You can claim Leo was with Cord, not you, if she starts any bull," Miss Yvonne predicted.

I couldn't say I was a huge fan of deceit, but Miss Yvonne might be a goddamn genius.

10

CAM

CORD DECIDED to turn in after Miss Yvonne left, so he went over to my side of the duplex while I stayed at Leo's place to help return the kitchen to normal. Even though all we did was heat up the pre-made meal, there were a lot of dirty dishes to unload from the dishwasher and pots and pans to scrub.

Leo turned on some music and poured each of us another glass of the rosé that Tanner and Kelso brought with them from the bar. It was pretty damn good, but I knew it wasn't an expensive brand. I was sure Jessica would have turned up her surgically enhanced nose at it without ever tasting it.

"So, this was really nice, Leo. Do you like to entertain?" I asked as I dried the pots and pans he was washing.

Leo looked at me and offered a mischievous smile, removing his soapy hands from the water and dotting suds on my face. He stepped back and smirked at his handiwork. "Yeah, let Cord cut his beard off. I like your handsome face without whiskers," he teased as he took a dry towel and wiped away the bubbles.

I pulled the handsome man closer to me and kissed his soft lips, being careful to keep our respective stubble in check so as not to harm each other again. When we pulled away, we both had goofy grins, I was certain.

"Thank you for letting Cord and I crash your party. It's one of the best Thanksgiving's I've had in years," I admitted.

"What did you do last year?" Leo asked as we resumed our tasks.

I glanced at the ceiling, remembering the hellish dinner I sat through with Jessica, the boys, and her parents. God knew, I'd wanted to choke on the fucking wishbone from the turkey rather than sit there with all of them.

"Uh… Last year, I went to Jessica's house for dinner with the boys and her parents. It was like hell on earth, but I was there for my sons, so I swallowed my pride, even with all the shit they said about me as I sat there. I stuck it out," I confessed. It was a funny thing I was learning about Leo Anderson—I could tell him shit I couldn't even tell my twin. With Leo, there was no judgment. He reminded me of my parents before they passed, and it was a wonderful, comforting reprieve from my day-to-day anxiety.

Leo rinsed his hands and dried them on a clean towel before he picked up a saucepan, drying it and putting it on the table to finish air drying. He didn't say anything for a moment, and then he stepped forward and wrapped his muscular arms around my neck, gently kissing my forehead, cheeks, jaw, and finally my neck, stopping by my ear.

"Never let anyone make you feel like you don't measure up to everyone else, Cam. I can see all of the good inside you. All of the love you have for your sons is palpable when you talk about them, and if *I* have to walk away in order for you to continue to have Archie and Grayson in your life, I'll do it without question. I care about you very much, and I want nothing but for you to be able to see and spend time with your boys as often as possible. That will make me happy," Leo whispered.

His pretty words tickled my ear, and the skeptic in me wanted to ask if he was bullshitting me to get into my pants. Fortunately, deep in my gut, I knew it wasn't Leo's style at all.

"You hated me when I came into the bar a couple of months

ago. What changed your mind?" I asked, dying to know how I'd been able to win him over and prove I wasn't really the asshole I'd been that day when he'd dropped by Stenson & March.

"Well, you did... Or my vision of you did. I thought you were a hotshot architect, and I didn't think I was anybody who would catch your eye. You mentioned bringing your sons in for the surfing competition, but that was my day off. I believed you were married, but I also thought you were a huge flirt. I couldn't help but flirt back," Leo professed, which made me smile.

"Yeah, and when Jess filed for sole custody the week before you dropped by the office, my balls crawled up into my gut. I've been the one to take care of them since Archie was born. Jessica had postpartum depression after Archie came along, so I took time off from my job to care for him and Grayson. I became the primary caregiver for those boys," I explained, reliving every goddamn moment of feeling my way through truths I'd never shared with anyone.

Leo held my face in his hands and rested his forehead against mine, not saying a word. It was a comfort I never imagined I'd need, let alone ever get. His kind demeanor spurred me to continue.

"Hell, I was lucky enough to get the job offer from Landon because it gave me flexibility so I could put my kids on the bus, work my job, get my kids off the bus that night, and go to a PTA meeting in the evening if necessary. I was a room father and a team dad when Grayson started playing basketball," I explained. I wasn't trying to toot my own horn because I was just being a parent—nothing special, really.

Leo smiled. "I'm sure your sons appreciate everything you did for them." It was damn sweet of him to say.

I kissed his lips and continued. "Over time, Jessica got herself healthy, but she never really wanted to be... well, she wasn't like *my* mom. That was fine; not many were, but when she threatened to take them away from me, I pretty much lost my mind. I thought we could co-parent, but I can't be at every game, at every science fair, at everything my younger son needs me to be at if Archie is living in Seattle." I said it out loud for the first time, grateful only Leo was there to hear it.

He wrapped his arms around me and held me because I couldn't keep the tears at bay. If she took my son... my boys... away, I didn't know if I could live through the pain of it.

I cried for the first time in a long time, having never allowed myself the freedom to let loose because I believed it made me weak and unmanly. Leo held me, making me feel like he didn't care if I cried, which I appreciated more than anything.

When I finally calmed down, Leo handed me a couple of paper towels. "I'm sorry I don't have tissues in here. I have some in the bathroom, but I don't want to let you go to get them. You go right ahead and cry until you feel better," he urged, which made me chuckle.

"How'd you get to be so sweet?" I joked as I wiped my eyes and blew my nose.

Leo full-on laughed as he took a sip of his wine. "Ask Kelso how sweet I was when we were in high school. I was such a prick to him and Kelsey when we were kids. It was more that our parents were assholes than anything, and I fought against it as much as I could. When Kelso came out and they treated him like so much dirt under their feet, I couldn't take it anymore. I left home, determined not to become the football star my father wanted me to be," Leo explained, which I found hard to believe. He just seemed to have kindness oozing from every pore of his hunky body.

"Well, we all do things when we're young that we regret. It seems like Kelso doesn't hold it against you," I surmised as I finally stopped crying.

Leo gave me a soft smile. "I woke up one day and realized that I'd pretty much abandoned my little brother for no damn reason at all, so I finally swallowed my pride and reached out to him. Our absence from each other's lives wasn't because of anything that happened between us. It was because of the shit we endured growing up, and I guess we both wanted distance from it. I'm just grateful he came down here to see me so we could get to know each other again."

It was so completely ironic how similar we were. Leo and Kelso lost touch because of their family's thoughts on Kelso's sexuality, and Cordon and I did something similar because I allowed my wife to get in the way due to Cordon's sexuality.

The worst thing, though, was that I let her push Cord out of my life because she didn't approve of him. I went along with it because I was hiding secrets of my own, so shame on me. It was crazy stupid the things we allowed people to do to us because we were so desperate for their approval.

"So, how about us getting to know each other? Will we let other people get in the way of a possible relationship? I'm not sure at all how fast you'd like things to proceed," I brought up. We'd been so caught up in denying our attraction that I wasn't really sure how to move forward. The previous night had been a great jumping off spot, or was it a mistake? I wasn't sure.

Leo picked up both of our glasses of wine and walked over to the kitchen entrance, turning off the overhead lights. "Follow me…" he tempted.

I felt we'd already established that I was weak willed, so I did as he asked, following him down the hallway and into his bedroom. He placed the glasses on the nightstand before he climbed up into the middle of the bed and patted the bedspread. "I dare ya…" he taunted as he extended his arm in a sweeping gesture over the bed.

I kicked off my shoes and climbed up next to him, settling against the huge walnut headboard where the two of us proceeded to talk about his ideas for the distillery he wanted to create at the beach. It felt as if I'd known Leo for an instant and a lifetime. There were things we didn't know about each other, but none of them were important enough to keep me from falling in love with him. We had until our dying breaths to learn the details, or so I hoped. I just wanted to have the chance to do it.

"Is this okay?" Leo whispered as he unbuckled my belt. We were going at each other... kisses, bites, moans, and groans. I was in a sex bubble where I couldn't answer clearly. I just nodded, and he quickly whisked the belt from the loops of my black chinos before he opened the button and zipper, humming appreciatively as he ran his right hand over my hard cock in my plain white briefs.

"That's definitely okay. How far..." I swallowed before I finished my thought, "How far would you want to go?" I spoke gently so I didn't disturb the lovely quiet of the moment.

Leo exhaled slowly. "I'd like to touch you—to kiss your body everywhere, if you'd allow it," he explained.

I was hesitant... Not because I didn't want to feel his touch on my body, skin to skin. I was afraid that once I was intimate with Leo Anderson, there'd be no turning back—I'd be in love with him for the rest of my days.

"If you do that, you might never get rid of me," I teased.

Leo chuckled. "Promise?"

We kissed and slowly undressed each other, taking our time until we were down to our underwear. Leo settled next to me on the bed, the two of us looking into each other's eyes.

"Tell me what you're thinking, Cam," he whispered.

I swallowed. "I think I want us to lose our underwear so I can see your dick," I replied before we both started laughing. We huddled together on the bed, both of us giggling like kids until Leo's tight body was brushing against mine. The feel of the wiry hair on his legs as they brushed over mine tickled. His muscular chest was smooth where mine had some coarse whisps of gray hair.

Leo had a very sexy trail of dark-blond hair under his navel that led to a neatly trimmed pubic area that made my mouth water a little, even though I had never sucked a cock before—I truly wanted to give it a try with his.

Leo's nipples were dark to match his golden-tanned chest, and my mouth watered to suck and nibble on them. The slide against each other was damn pleasant, to say the least.

"Okay—so naked?" Leo asked.

I nodded, and we both took off our underwear really fast, freezing when we were both naked. My dick was hard enough to pound nails. It wasn't the biggest—about six inches hard, but Leo stared at it as a slow smile spread over his handsome face.

I finally allowed myself to take in the sight of his gorgeous cock. It was bigger than mine, but I wanted to kiss the purple head in a way I'd never wanted anything in my life. I was shocked at myself, but finally, I couldn't hold my tongue—in every sense of the word.

"May I kiss him?" I asked as I pointed to his hard rod, proudly swaying as Leo repositioned himself on his back.

"Can I kiss your cock as well? Straddle my face, Cam," Leo insisted.

I didn't wait for him to ask me twice. I was on my hands and knees over him before he could change his mind, and I had his cock in my mouth—just the head—in the next instant. The smell of him wafted into my nose and took over my body.

All of my senses were engaged when it came to Leo. My eyes saw his beautiful face and body. My nose smelled the incredible musk of him, launching me into overdrive. My ears heard the sounds he made as he slurped my cock as it hung over his face. My nerves were dancing at his touch. I leaned forward and kissed the bulbous head of his cock, and I felt as if I'd died and gone to heaven. My sixth sense—my heart—knew I was already in love with Leo Anderson.

11

LEO

Friday morning, I woke to soft breaths against my left nipple and quiet snores beneath my ear. I cast my eyes down to see Cameron was sleeping peacefully. The sun was up, but barely. The previous night had been one to be burned into my memory forever.

The sensation of Cam's cock in my mouth for the first time was surreal. It was silky smooth and impressively hard, and his scent, which was delectable, was more concentrated there. The sounds he made as I sucked him off set my body ablaze, and when he came in my mouth, I froze for a moment, unsure what to do with his essence. I swallowed it down, noticing the taste of him wasn't as bad as I'd expected.

The sight of Cam bobbing on my cock had me ready to blow in an instant, but I was able to dial it back and hold out for a while longer. His tongue was talented and did very wicked things to my dick that I wanted to feel over and over again. I warned him before I let go, but he lapped at me like I was giving him cream. God, it was unbelievable.

My phone chimed, bringing me back to reality. I reached over to my nightstand and picked it up to see a message from Cordon.

Did you kidnap my brother?

I chuckled. I adjusted my arms around Cam so I could text a response.

Right now, I think I'm being held hostage. What's up?

"Why are you moving?" Cam whispered as he turned onto his side and opened his sky-blue eyes, blinking as he tried to focus, I imagined.

"Because your brother is asking if I've kidnapped you," I replied as I kissed the top of his head before scooting up to lean against the headboard. We were still naked, and I wanted to pull the sheet and blanket down to expose his gorgeous body, but I wasn't sure what his plans were for the day. If we got started, I was certain we wouldn't stop for hours. My thoughts were about how we could spend the day in bed exploring each other, but Cam might have had other ideas.

Cam finally hopped up from the bed and went to the bathroom, closing the door most of the way. "What's your schedule like today?"

"Well, uh, I have to do inventory at the bar today, which will probably take a couple of hours, but maybe you wanna go get lunch when I'm done?" I called out as I got up and pulled on a pair of sweats, leaving a pair for him on the bed before I went to make us some coffee.

I proceeded to the kitchen, feeling happy we'd cleaned up the Thanksgiving mess the night before so I didn't have to look at it this morning. I set up the coffee maker, and as I was about to turn it on, I felt warm skin against my back and two muscular arms snaking around my waist. A soft kiss on my shoulder blade sent tingles up my spine. "It's seven. Why are we up?" Cam whispered before he kissed up to my neck, setting my skin on fire.

Before I could answer, there was a knock on the back sliding door, and it wasn't just one knock—it was a slow, annoying series of knocks. I walked the two of us, still connected, over to the door and laughed when I saw Cord standing there, his face freshly shaved and a big grin shining. He was holding a coffee cup upside down as he continued to knock, making me laugh.

Cam stepped back enough to lift his head and groan. "It's *waaaay* too early for that shit. Tell him to go away."

I unlocked the door and opened it, letting in the chill of the morning before I stepped back for Cord to enter. "Good morning," I greeted.

"God, you're lazy," he complained as he took his cup over to the coffee maker. Cam followed after him, settling at the table while I got out the rest of the coffee accompaniments.

"We were up a lot later than you, jackass. By the way, how bad is my bathroom if you cleaned that shit off your face?" Cam asked as he wiggled his index finger in the direction of Cord's missing beard.

I stood at the counter watching the two of them, remembering Kelso and Kelsey when they were younger. They finished each other's sentences and did a lot of non-verbal communicating. It was sad that it all ended when Kelso told the family he was gay. Kelsey was too much like our religious zealot of a mother to accept Kelso for who he was and be happy for him to live his truth. I really wondered what the hell they'd all think of me and my current arrangement.

"I'm an adult now, unlike you. I clean up after myself. So, men, what are we doing today?" Cord asked with a big grin on his newly exposed face, which was equally as handsome as his brother's.

"Leo and I are going to the bar to do inventory. You have a car. Find something to do," Cam announced, his voice grumpy.

Cord looked at me and winked. "You sure about this? He's a little bitch in the morning—or he used to be. He can be spoiled when he doesn't get his way, and god forbid he ever gets sick. He'll act like he's losing a limb if he gets a hangnail," Cord listed off his brother's perceived faults.

I glanced at Cam and saw his frown, which I took to be his silent agreement with his brother's critique of him. I didn't give a shit. "Sorry, man, but I saw *him* first," I answered as I reached up and pulled down two coffee cups.

Cord laughed heartily, and the sound of it filled the kitchen. I really hoped someday Cam would laugh that way. I was sure he had too many things on his mind at the present to find anything funny about the day, so I let it go, but it was a goal for the future. Life should be filled with happy laughter every day.

"I'll come along to the bar and look the place over. I'm interested in your operation, and I want to see where we can put that shed and a small still like we talked about last night during dinner," Cord answered as I carried over the pot, pouring three cups of coffee for us. Cam fixed his with sugar and creamer and held the mug under his nose, closing his eyes and taking a hearty sniff.

"Oh, and he's a horrible caffeine addict," Cord added, causing his brother to flip him the bird. I chuckled at them, wondering how they were as kids. They were entertaining as hell to be around.

After coffee, Cord went over to the other apartment to dress, and Cam and I went back to my bedroom. I gave him a sweatshirt of mine to put on, and he gathered up his clothes from the previous night.

"He's not wrong, you know. I'm all that shit my brother mentioned and a lot more," he stated as he gestured toward the kitchen where his brother had pointed out a few faults of Cam's.

I nodded. "I'm sure if Kelso were here, he'd gladly give you a list as long as your arm of shit that's annoying about me, but everyone has some faults, babe," I confirmed without thinking.

Cam's breath hitched, so I turned to look at him. "What? What's wrong?" I asked.

"You, uh... Not one damn thing," he replied as he slid his feet into his loafers. "I'll get these sweats back to you after I wash them," Cam promised before he let himself out the front door, pulling it closed behind him.

Was it crazy to think I could feel the difference in the house after Cam was gone? *Yeah, you're nuts!*

SUNDAY EVENING, I was behind the bar, whistles and cheers blasting from the big screen by the stage where a true battle of the gridiron was in progress. I couldn't tell you who was playing because my thoughts were only of Cam, who'd had to return to Brownsville earlier in the afternoon, unfortunately.

The weekend had been unprecedented in my world. I knew I'd kissed and licked every inch of Cam's enticing body, and I was pretty sure he'd covered a lot of territory on mine—based solely on the love nips I found during my shower before I got to the bar. I couldn't help but wish it was something I got to do every day and night.

I was drying a flat of pint glasses I'd just taken out of the dishwasher in the kitchen when I felt a smack on my back. I glanced up to see Tanner with the biggest grin stretched across his mug that I was sure I'd never seen.

"How'd it go?" I asked, feeling like I already knew the answer. Tanner fiddled with his phone and handed it to me, a paused video of the two of them sitting in a nice restaurant.

The shot was from the left corner of the room behind Kelso. I hit the play button and saw Tanner pour Kelso a glass of wine from a bottle in a silver bucket next to their table.

I turned up the volume as the videographer zoomed in. *"You excited about goin' back to Nashville?"* Tanner had asked as he'd taken a sip of his tea.

Tanner was still under the restrictions of his parole until the end of the year, but after his obligation was fulfilled, I was taking the man somewhere fun and getting him rip-roaring drunk.

"I wish to hell you could go with me," Kelso had replied.

"After my parole is up, I'll be happy to go with ya, but Kelso, I want to go as your husband," Tanner had explained.

I saw Kelso's face freeze as Tanner stood from his chair and went down on one knee next to Kelso's chair before he turned my little brother to face the camera. *"Kelso, will you do me the honor of marrying me?"* Kelso had shot up out of his chair and jumped on Tanner, taking both of them down as their fellow diners had applauded.

I felt a couple of tears gather as Tanner had lifted Kelso and kissed him after they'd both stood to their feet, the crowd continuing to cheer for them. It was a beautiful thing to behold.

I reached for a clean bar towel and dried my eyes before I handed Tanner his phone and pulled him in for a hug, the big bastard. "I can't tell you how happy I am, Tan. Any idea when the two of you are gonna do the deed?" I asked.

"Oh, we *did* the deed a few times last night and twice today," Tanner taunted, making me groan at the thought of it.

"Fucking… No, Tanner! *Not cool!*" I protested, smacking him on the shoulder and making my friend laugh.

Suddenly, a very handsome man with the last name of March walked into On the Rocks, sitting down at the makeshift bar Landon Stenson had created for us. "I'll have a bourbon neat," he ordered.

"No gin?" I joked as I poured him a glass of the best bourbon I had in the place.

Cord laughed. "I'm not a loyalist when it comes to my drink of choice. I like to pay homage to all of the spirits in equal measure," he explained with a smirk as I placed the glass in front of him.

"Why are you still here? I thought you were headed back to Brownsville with Cam?" I asked, hoping maybe Cam had found a reason to stay at the beach. Unfortunately, I doubted he did because he had to work the next morning.

Cord took a sip of his drink and placed it on the shitty

Formica bar top. "Tell me this is temporary," he commented as he looked under the thing, returning to his seat with a smile.

I chuckled. "You don't like the décor?"

Cord shook his head. "Construction make-do isn't a décor. So, I find myself homeless at the moment. Can I crash on your couch?" he asked.

"I thought you were going to Brownsville with Cam," I inquired, wondering what had happened to change the plans.

"Jessica called him as we were leaving the duplex. She was meeting him at the house to talk, and we decided maybe it wasn't the best time for her to figure out I was in town. Cam had that pie in the sky look that maybe she was willing to compromise regarding custody of Archie, and he didn't want to jeopardize a possible truce between the two of them by having me show up. I'm not really offended because I hate that bitch, but I agreed that no good would come of her seeing me at the moment until we knew what she was up to," Cordon explained.

"Sure, you can stay with me," I agreed.

That night, Tanner, Cord, and I went over the ideas I had for the distillery, and instead of Cord going with me to the duplex, he stayed with Tanner since Kelso was gone for the week. I really had to wonder what my little brother would think about that turn of events—his new fiancé having an overnight guest! Thankfully, I was certain Cord wouldn't try anything. He seemed to be respectful of relationships.

12

CAM

I drove to my home in Brownsville and unloaded the Silverado after I'd parked it in the garage. Cord had agreed to stay on South Padre Island that night until I knew what Jessica wanted to discuss, for which I was grateful, but I didn't hesitate to threaten him to keep his hands off Leo. He'd laughed at me as I'd left the duplex before he flipped me off. *Brotherly love…*

I was busy loading the washing machine—because I damn well wouldn't trouble Naomi to do my laundry—when I heard the doorbell. I hurried to the front door, seeing a stranger on the porch holding a small plant in his hands and a legit shit-eating grin on his surly looking face.

"Good evening. I have a delivery for Cameron March," the surly-looking bastard offered.

Something inside me twinged, and my first instinct was to lie. "He's not here right now. I'm his brother, Cordon."

The guy looked at me and looked at something on his phone. "You sure you're not Cameron March?"

"I have a twin brother named Cam. Like I said, he's not here right now. Maybe come back another day. Thanks," I told the jackass before I closed the door in his face.

After he left, I called Jessica. She'd said she'd drop over about six, and after the stranger left, I saw it was nearly seven. One thing about my ex-wife—she was always punctual, so I knew something else was going on.

The phone went directly to voicemail, so I left a message. "Hey, I'm home waiting for you, so if you're not coming, call me."

I turned on the TV to catch the rest of the Sunday night football game while I waited for her to show up or call me back. I'd grabbed the basket of towels I'd left in the dryer on Wednesday and settled into the den to fold laundry, proving to myself that men could multitask.

Just as I was headed to the kitchen to get a beer and put away the kitchen towels, I heard a key in the lock of the front door. I walked into the hallway, wondering who the hell it could be. I'd changed the locks after Jessica's raid on our home when she moved out, so I knew it wasn't her.

When the door opened, I was surprised to see Archie. "Son, what's going on? How'd you get here?" I asked as I walked over to the door and looked outside to see a small blue car pulling away from the curb. He stepped inside without a word, handing me his backpack and walking straight to the kitchen, his demeanor distraught.

I dropped the backpack on the bench by the front door and followed him. "Archie, who was that? Are you meeting Mom here or something?" I quizzed as I walked into the kitchen where he was standing in front of the fridge with a cola in his hand.

"Are you hungry? I haven't been to the store since I was gone over the weekend, but I can order a pizza or something," I suggested.

Archie went to the other side of the breakfast bar and sat down, opening his soda. "I'm not goin', and you can't make me." He took a gulp from the can, continuing to study the white marble countertop.

I stepped around the counter and sat down next to him, putting my hand on his back. "Going where, Arch?" I pressed.

"I'm not going to boarding school. Mom said it was your idea, but Dad, I don't wanna go. I don't know anybody in New York, and I can't imagine why you'd want to send me away," he whispered as fat tears plopped onto the countertop.

"*Whoa... Whoa!* What the fu—What are you *talking* about? I never said anything about you going to boarding school, Arch," I barked out. My heart was in my throat at the sight of my son, who always tried so hard to project that he was an adult, crying like the little boy I still saw in him.

"Mom said you and Uncle Lan wouldn't want me around while you plan your new life, and she's moving to Seattle to be with *Dane,* so she wouldn't want me around either," Archie stated.

The fuck! I was shocked. Apparently, Jessica didn't want him around as she planned *her* new life, but she was going to do anything she could to keep him from me! I'd deal with that, but first, I needed to deal with Jessica's misinformation campaign.

"First off, I'd never send you to a boarding school anywhere unless you decided you wanted to go for one reason or another, and don't ask me what reason—we can discuss it another time. Second, Uncle Lan and I are best friends and business partners, but nothing else. We've been friends for years, but your mother never liked him, and I have no idea why," I shared with him, trying my best not to put Jessica in the horrible light she deserved.

I sighed. It was best to be upfront with the kid, and considering everything that was happening, it was best to do so sooner rather than later. "How'd you get here? Who was in the blue car?" I pressed.

"Fart got a new car for his birthday. I called him because he's home for the break, and he picked me up and brought me over. Grayson told me he'd already talked to him about some of this shit, and he didn't seem surprised when I called him," Archie explained, which was a huge relief to me.

Goddamn her! "Archie, son, I'm sorry this is happening. Your mom took the job in Seattle, and she has to move there by the new year, but I'm not in favor of you going to boarding school, trust me. I'm not in favor of you going anywhere that isn't right here," I assured, gently squeezing the nape of his neck as I moved to hug him.

"Why can't she just let me live with you? I told her that's what I want to do, and I'll come see her for holidays and breaks and stuff, but she said no. Dad, if I go to boarding school, I won't get to see either of you," the poor kid whined, but under the circumstances, I was right there with him.

"I know, son, and we'll get this figured out, okay? Do we need to go to Mom's to get your stuff for school? I think Grayson has some shirts in his closet that might work for tomorrow," I suggested as I boiled in my own anger.

"I brought my books and a change of clothes. Can we get pizza from Zappeion's?" he asked as he dried his eyes on the tail of his t-shirt before I could stop him.

"Did you tell Mom you were leaving? Where was she?" I asked.

"Great Dane came down for Thanksgiving. He tried to play like we were best friends, you know? I'm sure he's a nice guy, but he's a lot younger than Mom. Did you know that?" Archie asked. I did my best not to laugh at his nickname for the man.

"Uh, no, I didn't. I thought you'd already met him," I remarked. We didn't talk about Jessica's boy toy, but now I was interested.

"I did last summer, but Grayson didn't, remember. He stayed here while Mom and I went to Seattle. When Grayson met him, he flat out asked how old he was. 'Twenty-nine,' the guy answered, like he was proud of it or somethin'," my budding journalist filled me in. The kid was gonna be a hell of a reporter someday if that was what he wanted to do.

Archer had talked about being an investigative journalist since he watched a report on television by a journalist who had cracked a cockfighting ring in southwestern Texas near the

Mexican border. *"How cool is that?"* Archie had stated after he'd made me watch it for a *second* time.

I still subscribed to a paper copy of the Brownsville Herald because of Archie. His Saturday mornings were usually spent reading the damn thing while he sipped chocolate milk and ate his cereal, which made me laugh.

My youngest was also a cable news junkie, and he and I had some really interesting discussions when it was just the two of us because of something he'd seen on TV. I was busting with pride at my son's acuity for asking probing questions of me and really listening to my answers with insightful follow-ups. It was a great sign of the man Archer would become… if I had any say in the matter. Really listening to people was becoming a lost art unless one was being paid four-hundred bucks an hour, I was coming to find.

"Why don't you go wash your face and find us something to watch on television. I'll order the pizza—meat lovers, right? You didn't turn vegetarian without telling me, did ya?" I asked as I messed up his hair.

"It's okay, ya know," Archer said, puzzling me.

"What's okay, Arch?" I asked.

"If you like guys, too. I figure you musta liked girls 'cause you married Mom, but you can like boys, too, right?" my son asked. My dilemma… be honest with him as I'd like him to be honest with me or lie so he wasn't put in the position of keeping a secret from his mother.

I sat back in my chair and looked at my son. He had his mother's bright green eyes and oval face, but he had my hair—well, before it started turning gray. Grayson had blue eyes like me, though his were a bit lighter than mine, and his hair was light brown like Jessica's. They were a part of both of us, and regardless of how I felt about Jessica, she was still their mother.

"Archie, son, yes. Yes, it's okay to like boys or girls or boys and girls. Yes, I loved your mother when we got married, and I'll always love her because she gave me you and your brother. She and I aren't doing a very good job of being grownups right now, but I'll try to fix it, okay?" I asked, not really answering his question, but he nodded and took off, so I was guessing he got whatever he needed from my answer.

I ordered a pizza for delivery and sent a text to Leo.

Can you meet me for lunch tomorrow at my office? I want to discuss something with you. Bring Cordon along, please.

I hit send and went to the fridge to get the beer I'd intended to get nearly an hour earlier. I had a feeling my life as I knew it would never be the same. Life always brough change, but I had no idea what changes might be in store for me.

13

LEO

Cord and Landon Stenson were busy pouring concrete and discussing my needs for a shed to house the small still Cord and I were going to put together once we had all of the parts necessary. Landon had agreed to build the shed by himself to save me the labor costs, and I promised him that we'd feed his crew for free when they worked at On the Rocks.

I walked out of the kitchen to check on progress since the two of them had been at it since seven that morning. "How's it going?" I asked. I knew nothing about concrete work, but I could do anything related to hay—having grown up on a hay farm. Those memories weren't good ones for Kelso or me.

"Good. We want a level slab so we can easily move it when you're ready to build the distillery. Oh, did Cam tell you we received the approval for expansion from the Army Corps of Engineers, so we'll start pouring the foundation for the new patio next week. We can let it cure for the rest of the month and start construction after the first of the year," Landon explained. We'd been worried about the approval, but now that it was in, I felt a huge sense of relief.

"Is that what Cam wanted to discuss with me? I mean, I'm still interested in having lunch with you guys, but if it's just that, then I don't need to take up his time," I inquired. I'd been sort of dreading the lunch because of the last time I'd been to Cam's office. Once bitten, twice shy, and all that shit.

Landon chuckled. "I don't think that's what he wants to discuss with you, but you might want to call him. He called me this morning and told me you guys were coming to town, so I think he was looking forward to it," he answered.

Cord chuckled. "Great—now I feel like a third wheel."

Landon smirked. "I can meet you later for a beer if you want."

I could see a smoldering attraction between them, and I wondered if it was weird for him since Cord was Cam's identical twin brother. Did that mean Landon had feelings for Cam and was settling for Cordon?

Cord eyed Landon before he grinned. "As friends—sure. I'm afraid I'd chew you up and spit you out, my friend, and my brother would kill me."

All of us started laughing as I heard Miss Yvonne's car on the gravel parking lot. I turned to see her eyeing us before she went inside. I glanced at the two of them and shrugged. "Whoever's going to lunch with me be ready to go by twelve-thirty. Cam's expecting us at his office at one-fifteen."

I walked inside through the back door. "Miss Yvonne? You need me to bring anything in from the car?"

She stepped over to the door where I was wiping my feet and smiled at me. "Which brother is that out there?" she asked. It made me chuckle that since Cord had gotten his hair cut and shaved his beard, she couldn't tell them apart.

"Cordon. Cam's in Brownsville. We're going to have lunch with him in a couple of hours. Tanner had a meeting with his parole officer this morning, so tell me what you need me to do to help you get started," I offered.

Tanner helped Miss Yvonne in the kitchen on Sundays and Mondays because Tabitha had those days off. He was becoming a fantastic cook, and even though I couldn't cook worth a damn, I could peel anything like a champ.

"That's right. Tanner told me that on Saturday when he helped Tabitha and me plan ahead for this morning. Can you go to the walk-in and bring me those hotel pans on the far left? Today's special is roast beef and mashed potatoes, and those pans have everything ready to go," Miss Yvonne informed me, which made me feel like a useless slug.

"You know, Miss Yvonne, I can work with you to help out more. I feel like we put too much work on you," I guiltily suggested.

Of course, as I expected, Miss Yvonne began to protest. "Leo, son, you and Tanner are the working owners, and Kelso helps when he's here. I like to think of this as a family business, Leo. Are you going to tell me I'm not part of the family?" she asked, but it damn well wasn't a question I expected to hear from her. The look on her face had me worried she was going to throw a frying pan at me if I said the wrong thing.

"No, ma'am," I replied as Cordon came in through the back door, having slid off the boots he'd been wearing outside to help Landon with the concrete work.

"Hey, Miss Yvonne. Tanner mentioned this morning that you might need some help in the kitchen, and I need a way to pay for my board, so if you don't mind, I'd love to help you out," Cord offered with that slick smile of his that I was sure had been the downfall of many a young man.

"You cook, March?" Miss Yvonne asked, a skeptical look on her face. We'd all seen that look at one time or another. It was her take-no-prisoners look for anyone who ventured into her kitchen pretending to have any cooking skills at all.

"Yes'um. I've kept myself alive for twenty-seven years since I left home at eighteen. Tell me what you want me to make," Cord challenged.

Miss Yvonne looked at me, and I simply shrugged. I had no

idea if the guy could boil water or make a chocolate soufflé. "Give him a shot, Miss Yvonne," I pressed.

"Make some cheddar biscuits with adobo butter as an appetizer special," Miss Yvonne ordered.

Cord chuckled. "I'd suggest pepper jack corn muffins with honey butter, but if the lady wants biscuits, I'll make biscuits."

Cord went to work at the prep table, and I cut the potatoes into smaller pieces so they could boil for Miss Yvonne to make the mashed potatoes to go with her fantastic pot roast.

Cord was humming along as he measured out flour and grated cheddar cheese from the large block he found in the walk-in. If we ever had an emergency, it appeared Cord could jump right in and take over the cooking—well, if he was around. That was something I needed to think about. I'd have to enlist Cam's assistance to talk him into staying in Texas. One thought in particular appealed to me, but I'd have to think about it.

Cord and I walked into Stenson & March. The beautiful woman at the desk glanced up and then did a double-take, looking back to where Cam was sitting at his drafting desk in plain sight of the door.

We were a bit late because I couldn't get Cord out of the kitchen. Miss Yvonne and he were cutting up like they were long-lost friends, and Cord had garnered her approval on the flattop, making perfectly cooked hamburgers which she wholeheartedly approved of. Cord had slid perfectly into the On the Rocks team, which truly made me happy.

"Mr. Anderson, you can go in. Cameron has been waiting for both of you—I think. Who are you, sir?" the woman asked as she eyed Cordon carefully.

Cord let loose a huge belly laugh, holding onto the counter

behind which the woman sat. "Cam, you asshole! You never told your assistant you had a twin?" he shouted.

I glanced up to see Cam toss something on his desk as he walked out to greet us, shaking my hand and then punching Cord in the shoulder. "Why would I? I never thought you'd find your way to Texas. Come on into my office for a minute, guys, before we go get lunch," Cam suggested.

We followed him inside and he closed the door, wrapping himself around me and giving me a sweet kiss. When he pulled back, Cam was beaming. "Thanks for coming. I wanted to come out to the beach, but I had Archie. That's what I wanted to talk to you guys about," Cam told us before he released me and went to his desk, motioning me over.

Cord and I flanked him as we looked down at the drawings in front of him. It was the bar and restaurant with the newly remodeled front, and there was a porch to the side that connected it to another shack-looking building with a weathered sign on top of it that read, "Surfside Distillery, Proprietor—Leo Anderson." I was speechless.

"The name, of course, is subject to change, but I wanted to give you an idea of how it could look. This is just a crude drawing. I'll run it through AutoCAD to create the 2D renderings, elevations, and detailed construction plans for Landon," Cam explained.

Cord pulled out a small case, unfolding glasses I'd never seen before. He put them on, reminding me of Cam's glasses I'd only seen him wear once. "Where are your glasses, Mr. March?" I asked, placing a hand on the back of Cam's chair that reminded me of a high-class bar stool.

Cam glanced up at me and smiled. "I have contacts that I wear all the time. I only wear my glasses when my eyes are tired. That day when you saw me wearing them at the bar, I'd been up most of the night working on a project for another contractor. My eyes were too dry, but you won't catch me wearing them again," he joked.

I leaned down to his ear. "Funny… As pissed as I was at you, they looked awfully damn sexy." His body shivered against my arm that was resting on the back of his chair.

Suddenly, Cord stepped back and began waving his hand in front of his face. "Jesus, you two! Skip lunch and get a fucking room! The goddamn pheromones in here are gagging," he complained, which made me laugh.

I stepped away a few inches, moving my arm from Cam's chair. "What did Jessica want last night?" I asked. He'd hustled away from the duplex after she'd sent him a message, and I'd been worried about what had happened when they met.

"I'll tell you guys at lunch. Archie stayed at the house last night. He pretty much ran away from home, as much as I can figure. I've got a call into my attorney, Niles Church, to talk to him about strategy, and once we figure it out, I'll come out to talk to you. I don't want to have to sacrifice you in this process, Leo. It might take some time, but I'd like there to be something for us to work toward whenever I get shit straightened out with Jessica," Cam described.

Hell yeah! I'd waited my whole fucking life to find someone to plan a future with. I wouldn't allow impatience to keep me from it.

WE'D WALKED down the street to a dive called Alberta's, and Cam was greeted with a smile by an older man. "Mr. March, good to see you again. Where is Mr. Stenson, sir?" the man asked as he grabbed three paper menus and led us to a booth with red vinyl seats that were cracked and had seen better days. The table was black-painted pine, but it was clean, which was a plus.

"One of us has to work, Dan. I'd rather it was him than me," Cam joked, which made me smile.

Once we were sitting down, the man handed out the menus. "Drinks?"

"I'll have a Shiner," Cordon responded without waiting for either of us. I absolutely loved the way the man embraced life by the balls. He could teach me a thing or two about living my life to the fullest.

"I'll have a gin and tonic," Cam answered with a grin when he looked at me.

"Same for me," I ordered, which was completely unlike me to drink during the day. Maybe I needed to lighten up a bit? My parents' way of life was far too stringent, but I was committed to making On the Rocks successful. With the distillery on the horizon, I wanted it to be prosperous, as well, but everything didn't have to be so damn serious all the time, did it?

14

CAM

As I'd promised, I'd arrived at Archie's school on Wednesday evening with Cordon in tow for the mid-year science fair. I'd so wanted to invite Leo to come with me so I could introduce him to my son, but with Jessica there, it would be too distracting from Archie's accomplishment, and I couldn't do it to the kid.

"What'd he come up with?" Cord asked as we strolled through the exhibits to see the other students' projects. They all deserved attention because I knew for a fact that all of the kids had worked damn hard on their projects. They'd been meeting in the school library twice a week since school had started to plan their projects, and then going in on Saturday to test their experiments they'd been working on at home.

Most of them were your typical seventh grade science projects—spherification of juice, designing a geodesic dome, and the greenhouse effect in action. My genius took samples around my house to test for germs, and I wasn't looking forward to the results.

"Household germs. He took swabs all over my place and used them for his presentation. He said he's planning to give a copy of his findings to Naomi, proving to her that he desires to be taken seriously as an investigative journalist. I'm sure it will go over with her like dogshit in a cookie jar. Oh, I see Jessica. Don't bait her, please," I nearly begged my brother.

Cord chuckled. "Who, li'l ol' *me*?" He batted his eyes lashes and cocked his head trying for innocence, which he hadn't been since he was still in diapers, I was sure. He did know how to make me laugh, though.

We made our way over to where Jessica was standing with a handsome young guy, sporting a hell of a tan in fucking December. He had to be Great Dane.

"Jessica. Good to see you here," I greeted, biting my damn tongue for what I really wanted to say to her. *Fuck you and the whore you rode in on.*

"Why, *Cordon!* I didn't realize you were in town," Jessica stated, completely ignoring me as she glanced between us. "Wow, you clean up well," she commented as she stared at my brother. I had no idea what the fuck she was trying to pull, and I damn well didn't want any explanation.

Cordon, having the balls of a fucking Brahma bull, walked over to Jessica and grabbed her, dipping her in his arms and laying a smacking kiss on her lips. When he pulled her up, I could see sheer shock had overtaken her.

Of course, my brother laughed. "You ain't married to Cameron anymore, Jess. I know you've lusted after me for a long time, and now we're free to explore all of those kinky fantasies about me that I'm sure you've used to get off for years. Tell me, what would you think about putting on a strap-on? I'd love to have my prostate pegged by a pretty woman like you," Cordon taunted.

I wanted to fall on the floor in hysterical laughter at the look on her face, but when I saw Archie standing in front of his display, my gut turned. He deserved much better than anyone humiliating his mother in public.

I walked over to him and turned him to look at the display. "Tell me about *this*, son," I requested as I studied the three-panel display.

Of course, Archie didn't miss a trick. "Did Uncle Cord just kiss Mom?"

"Yeah, I'm afraid he did," I replied, hoping he hadn't heard what Cord had said about a strap on or his prostate. Whatever he was alluding to had nothing to do with me, that was for damn sure.

Jessica used to love to play upon my insecurities when we were younger—saying she'd bet Cord was more of a man than I. His comment about a strap on had completely blown her mind, I could tell, and I truly wanted to give the asshole a high five for all the world to see.

"You're going to let him talk that way to me?" I turned to see Jess wasn't addressing me—she was talking to Great Dane—that nickname was really growing on me.

"Hell, Jess, I don't even know who the fuck they are," the youngster announced.

I stepped away from Archie when a classmate of his walked over to talk, and I offered my hand to Great Dane, adding a glowing smile. "I'm the last son of a bitch she screwed—or should I say *screwed over*. I wish you the best of fucking luck, but please, this is my son's night, so get the hell outta here," I urged, ready to punch the bastard in the nut sack.

I'd never been in a fight with anyone but Cordon, and that prick never fought fair. He was also always on my side, though, so I had no doubt I was in good hands if something jumped off. It wouldn't, however, be because of me or mine, because I'd never embarrass my kid that way.

I turned back to Archie, who had finished his conversation with his friend. "So?" I gestured toward the display again and did my best to look interested, not disgusted.

He laughed, sounding so much like Cordon, and hell, if my youngest had to be like anyone, I wanted him to be more like my twin than me. I was a pushover. I was a man who had never stood up to anyone, not even myself. I didn't want either of my boys to be like me—I wanted them to be something more.

After my son explained to me how germ-infested our home really was, I wanted to take a dip in Lysol myself, but how would we ever explain to Naomi that maybe some different procedures might be in order when it came to cleaning our house without hurting her feelings?

"What are we going to tell Naomi?" I asked Archie.

Archie glanced up at me with that shit-eating grin that reminded me too much of my twin. "I'd say we don't tell her anything, or she'll quit and then we gotta clean the damn house by ourselves," he stated. I couldn't chastise him for his swearing, and I couldn't help but laugh at the kid's comment. He was truly a treasure.

"Do you still have to stay to help everyone clean up? I'll hang out with you and take you home after if you do," I suggested.

I glanced around to see Jess and Great Dane were in a heated conversation near the gym doors, and Cord was talking to a young lady and her father about how the girl had used eggs to show the effects of sugary drinks on one's teeth. I was sure Cord had some choice things to say about it, but currently, I was quite interested in Jess giving Dane a huge piece of her mind that would likely leave him raw as hell. I wondered if the guy was second guessing himself regarding a relationship with her. If he had a fucking brain, he was.

"Naw, Dad. I'll go home with Mom and Dane, but when are you gonna talk to her about boarding school? I don't wanna go," Archie reminded in a loud whisper.

It was my time to step up for my kid, so I patted him on the shoulder. "I'll start the conversation right now."

I walked over to Jessica and her boyfriend, and I cleared my throat. "Sorry to break up your lovefest, but I need to talk to you about Archie, Jess."

Apparently, she was more pissed at him than me, so she headed toward the exit door, and I followed. Once we were outside in the cool air, I took a few breaths to gather my nerves. Finally, I was ready to meet her head on.

"You lied to Archie," I snapped at her for likely the first time since we'd met. *Candyass* came to mind as I stood there seeing the expression on her face at my criticism. It wouldn't be the first time she'd called me that.

"About what, Cameron?" she grumbled, appearing to be totally bored with our short conversation.

"You told our son that I was the one who had suggested sending him to boarding school so I could have time for Landon, and you know none of that is true," I stated, squeezing my fists until my nails made half-moon cuts into my palms. Losing my temper with her wouldn't do anything to sway her in my favor, but I wanted her to see I wasn't backing down.

Jessica swept her brown hair over her left shoulder, a tell that she was going to try to intimidate me and berate me into believing I was the one at fault. "You mentioned it to me a year or so ago, Cameron, and I dismissed it at the time because I thought it was harsh. Under the current circumstances, it seems to be the best path for us to take with him. Archer doesn't want to move to Washington with me, but he doesn't want to stay here with you and whatever the fuck you're up to, either. There's a wonderful boarding school in Upstate New York that specializes in STEM, which Archer has expressed an interest in pursuing. I say the sooner we get him on the path, the better for him," she insisted.

I laughed. "One, I never mentioned boarding school to you… *ever*. Archie has no interest in STEM. He's a great student to be sure, but he doesn't want to specialize in science, just like he doesn't want to leave Texas, Jessica. You're the one who wants to move away and leave this life behind, not Archie," I replied.

I saw her bristle, so I braced myself for her ire. Suddenly, the door opened and Archie walked out. "Mom, you better go save Dane. Miss Fisher has him cornered," Archie informed, referring to the middle school guidance counselor who was a huge flirt. Jessica knew her reputation from when Grayson was in that school and Miss Fisher came after all the dads of his friend. She didn't hesitate to rush back inside.

"Where's Uncle Cord?" I asked my son.

"He's watching my booth. What did she say about it?" Archie asked. He looked so damn worried that it tore me apart.

I sighed. "She didn't say anything, really. I'll talk to her again, son. This isn't over," I promised as we walked inside the school. I hoped to hell I was able to keep my word. Archie's trust in me was everything.

"Is the temperature okay?" I asked my passengers—Archie, Cordon, and Leo. It was the third weekend in December, and we were on our way from Brownsville up to College Station for the Wisconsin-A&M basketball game. Grayson was still riding the bench, but he was at the game to support his team, and we were on our way to College Station to support Grayson.

"Dad, you've asked us that about ten times since we left the house," Archie reminded. I could hear Cordon laughing from the back seat where he and Archie were riding, Leo on my right with a grin as I glanced at him.

We'd gone out to On the Rocks the previous week when Archie was with me so I could introduce Leo to my youngest son for the first time. Cord was still staying at the beach, offering a plausible explanation for us being there in the event Jessica had someone following us, as Cordon and Niles had suspected. Leo, bless him, hesitated to comment on anything that had to do with my ex-wife.

"I just want to be sure we're all comfortable," I defended to the little smartass who was playing a video game as Cord seemed to be nodding off.

Leo grinned. "Uh, I could use a bathroom stop, Cam. I'll drive for a while if you'd like," he volunteered, which was sort of a relief. My body was so tense that I knew I'd be sore when we got to A&M. I kept second guessing myself about bringing Leo along for the trip, but how much more time could I let go by before I came clean with Grayson?

"Uh, yeah, sure. You guys hungry?" I asked as I glanced into the mirror that reflected my backseat passengers to see Archie toss his game onto the seat as he elbowed Cord. The two of them were like two peas in a pod, aggravating each as much as Grayson did Archie.

I thought back to the previous Wednesday when I took Archie out to South Padre Island for dinner. Thankfully, him meeting Leo, officially, had gone smoother than I'd anticipated.

"Can I get a milkshake?" Archie asked as we pulled into the parking lot, finding a spot near the front of On the Rocks.

"I'll ask Leo to make you a small one. It's already six, so you don't need all of that sugar," I replied.

"Jeez, Dad," Archie complained, which I'd expected. Everything with the kid was a negotiation.

We went inside, and Tanner approached us with his big grin. "Guys, good to see ya again. You wanna sit on the bar side or in the main dining room?" he asked. I glanced to Archie to see he was studying Tanner, concentrating on the eye patch.

"Uh, where's Leo?" I asked.

Tanner grinned and grabbed two menus. "Follow me. Archie, have you been eating your vegetables?" Tanner quizzed, making me laugh at my son reaching up and touching his eyes as if to make sure they were both still in his head.

"I, uh, I ate green beans last night when Mom made dinner," Archie replied.

I chuckled. "Your mom made dinner?" Jess hadn't been the cook in our relationship at all.

Archie chuckled. "She heated stuff up. That counts as vegetables, right?"

I glanced at Tanner, who laughed as he seated us at a table near the makeshift bar where Leo was talking to an older man. When he glanced up, I gave him a little wave and he grinned before he stepped from behind the top and walked over to our table.

"Hi, Cam. Who's your friend?" he asked as he glanced at Archie.

I appreciated his prompting. "Archer, this is my good friend, Leo Anderson. He and Uncle Cord are working together on a project, and he's partners with Tanner. His brother is Kelso Ray from The Tex-Sons," I introduced, prodding Arch from under the table so he reacted properly.

My sweet son stood and extended his hand. "Mr. Anderson, it's nice to meet a friend of my dad's. You can call me Archie," he replied as he and Leo shook hands.

"Nice to meet you, Archie. Call me Leo. What can I get you guys?"

The night was incredible, and I was beaming proud of Archie for how nice he was to Leo. I prayed it was a sign of good things to come.

"Can I sit up front if Leo drives?" Archie asked.

I glanced in the rearview mirror. "We'll see," I answered him, happy he was eager to get to know Leo better.

I saw the pout on Archie's face at my answer, and I chuckled. I pulled into the first burger place I found, and we all got out, stretching from being cooped up in the truck for four hours. Once we all went into the restaurant, Arch actually grabbed Cord's hand. "You'll sit with me, right, Uncle Cord?"

I looked at my brother, who came to a dead stop in the fast-food place. "I swear to god, Cameron, it's painful to watch whatever this is," he spouted, waggling his finger between Leo and me. "If the kid and I don't push you along, you'll be ninety before Leo ever gets to first base," my brother announced, getting the attention of everyone in the building. Hell, people were coming out from the back, one kid even carrying the damn grease-dripping fry basket with him.

Then, of course, my progeny turned to the other customers. "Kiss! Kiss! Kiss!" he chanted, pumping his arm in the air like we were at the damn Super Bowl. It only got worse when others joined in, and before I knew it, even Leo was chanting with them.

I surrendered. "I guess we're comin' out, huh?" Then, I grabbed him and kissed him like a sailor home on leave. The crowd's reception at our public display of affection was definitely mixed, but above all of this hissing and booing, I could hear cheers coming from my sweet Archie. I never imagined he'd be happy to see me kiss another guy.

15

LEO

I PULLED into Cam's driveway, nervous as hell. Grayson was home from college for the Christmas break, and Cam had invited me to come over for dinner the week after we went to A&M for the basketball game. The Aggies won the game in a nail biter, 96-99. The Hail Mary three-point shot at the buzzer was outstanding, bringing everyone to their feet. High fives were being shared with strangers, and I found myself having a great time.

"You're awfully quiet, big guy. Somethin' on your mind?" I glanced up, forgetting that Cord was in the car with me. I didn't dare go anywhere with Cam when Cord wasn't with us. Cam's attorney had notified him that Jessica had requested a meeting with the judge on December 23, coming clean that the plant delivery guy was actually a process server trying to serve Cam with a new custody agreement.

Her attorney had sent it over to Mr. Church, who was pissed about it, so we were being extra careful not to be seen in public alone. If someone at that Burger Barn the previous week had taped the kiss Cam and I had shared on the way to College Station, it would be hard to figure out which March man I was kissing, thankfully.

"I'm nervous. When I was introduced to Grayson, he didn't

seem to be impressed," I admitted as I turned off the ignition of my Chevy Trailblazer. Cord had decided to lease a car while he was in South Padre Island, but he wouldn't be picking it up until the following Monday, not that I thought it was necessary. I had no problem loaning him my SUV if he needed it.

Cord chuckled. "Yeah, well, that's because my brother's a chump. I'd have introduced you as my hot piece of young ass, but that's not Cam's style."

I couldn't help but laugh. "*You* would, Cordon. Oh—Landon told me he's coming to build the shed on Monday, so we should go shopping for still parts, don't you think?" I suggested.

"I've already got the list made up," he assured as he patted my hand. Cord had been working at On the Rocks, refusing to take money from us as payment. He claimed he just loved hanging out with all of us, and everyone at the restaurant had embraced him as a member of the family. It was nice having him around.

He and Tanner kidded each other like old friends, which was nice. Kelso was in Nashville for the charity thing they'd been rehearsing for, and Tanner was bummed he couldn't go along. He still couldn't leave Texas, but his parole was up in January, and I was planning to send the two of them off for a month to go wherever the hell they wanted. With Cord there to help out, it would be the best Christmas gift I could give them.

Cord cleared his throat. "Ya know, we could start making mash in the kitchen if you think Miss Yvonne wouldn't kick our asses. Oh, this came for you, and I forgot to give it to you earlier," Cord told me as he reached into a duffel he'd brought with him, producing a package addressed special delivery to me.

The left top corner had a return address—L. Lawson, Maryland Distillers Guild, 6247 Falls Rd, Baltimore, MD 21209. "It's from Luke Lawson," I read out loud.

"Yeah? What is it?" Cord asked as he unbuckled his seatbelt.

Just as I was about to open the large manila envelope, there was a knock on both of the car windows. We looked up to see Cam on my side and Archie on Cord's. I opened my door and stepped out, feeling Cam pull me closer and whispered as he patted my back in a bro hug. "Missed you. Come inside," he insisted as he stepped back and started for his beautiful home in Brownsville.

"Are you sure you want to do this? I mean, Archie made me nervous enough, but he seems to like me. Grayson? He's a grown man, and he might not take too kindly to his father dating a guy," I pointed out.

Of course, Cam chuckled. "I think your hype guy already prepped him for something. I heard Archie saying he really likes you. He thinks you can teach him to surf," Cam explained.

I laughed. "Well, I haven't done it in a while, but that gives me some ideas about Christmas."

I walked around and shook Archie's hand before the four of us headed into the house. There was some Christmas music playing in the background, and when I glanced to the left, I could see boxes strewn about the room, a colorfully lit Christmas tree standing in the corner just waiting for its glitz and glitter. "Ah, trimming the tree, I see. Looks nice," I commented.

Grayson popped up from beside the tan and beige couch, actually smiling at me. "Hey, Leo. Uncle Cord, will you tell Dad the tree should be in front of the windows," Grayson insisted.

"Cordon, tell your nephew that people can see the tree through the windows with it in the corner, and it's much less trouble than having to move the furniture around," Cam replied, placing his hand on his back for emphasis.

"I'll help move furniture," I offered.

'There, old man. Leo and I can move the furniture around. Arch, get your butt in here and help me move these boxes out of the way," Grayson ordered.

"Come on, Cordon. You can help me make the pizzas," Cam directed. Cord and Cam left me with Archie and Grayson. Thankfully, Archie looked my way and winked. I was sure there was something hatching in that egghead's brain, so I went about helping him move the boxes, which were filled with ornaments that looked like they were family heirlooms. There were some glass balls, but a lot of them must have been made by the boys when they were younger.

"I made that one," Archie pointed out when I picked up an ornament that resembled—loosely—a sleigh and reindeer.

"It's cool. What's it made of?" I asked as I gently placed it on the end table before I moved the rest of the boxes around so I could move the couch out of the way.

"Flour dough. We made them in kindergarten. Mom hates it because it sheds glitter. She has a fancy tree in all white at her house that she hires some lady to come put up every year. I like this tree better," Archie announced as he moved the coffee table, which was on casters, out into the entryway to give us room to move the tree into place.

I glanced in Grayson's direction to see him staring at a family picture in a frame on the other end table. It was the four of them, their mother sitting in a chair with Cam sitting on the floor next to it. The boys were standing on either side, but Archie had his hand resting on Cam's shoulder. It was telling of the relationship Cam had with Jessica—her in the throne and him beneath her to the side. I didn't like it at all.

"Grayson, I'll lift the tree if you'll just guide me to where you want it," I said to break the silence, pulling him from his thoughts. He discreetly wiped his eyes with the cuffs of his long-sleeved t-shirt and turned to me with a nod, a fake smile in place.

We moved the tree, and Grayson opened the sheers that hung beneath the ivory drapes on the living room picture window. When he did, there was a man with a camera pointed at us. "Who the fuck—" Grayson hissed.

I put the tree down and booked it out of the house as the guy ran down the street. He was a quick little bastard, even with all of that camera equipment hanging off him. Luckily, I caught sight of the license plate of the white Ford Fusion he'd jumped into, "Fotoman."

Fucking idiot! Way to be covert…

I hurried into the house and closed the door, seeing Cam and Cordon standing in the hallway. "Uh, peeping tom, I think." I winked at Cam to confirm—I hoped—that Jessica was, indeed, having him followed. That certainly put a pall over the festive mood at the house.

I went back to the living room to help rearrange the furniture, noticing the picture of the family that had been sitting on the end table was tossed into a box where a number of Ziploc bags had been placed, likely having held the light strands to keep things organized. I didn't say anything about it because I was sure it was Grayson's way of ridding himself of the past. The kid was probably dying inside, and it honestly broke my heart.

Archie was on his belly under the tree, spreading the skirt around the base, so I stepped over to Grayson. "It'll be okay, you know. It's hard now, but you guys will figure it out together because you're a family and you love each other," I attempted to assure him, thinking how much better things were for Kelso and me. It took a while, but we were finally there, supporting each other and caring about what happened to the other, like I believed family should do.

"I'm hoping it'll be better for all of us," he whispered, pointing to the box where the family picture had likely found a final resting place. "I know she didn't appreciate Pop, and I know she thought of me and Arch—seemed like we were always in the way. You care about him, right? Our dad?" Grayson asked, standing taller and facing me with square shoulders to show me he was speaking as the oldest and he was to be taken seriously. I would never disrespect him by laughing or treating him like a kid.

It was clear he loved his father and didn't want the man to be hurt any more than he'd already been by a careless woman who didn't seem to know how lucky she'd been to get him in the first place. I would rather be alone for the rest of my life than hurt Cameron.

"On my life, I will do everything in my power to keep him from being hurt by anyone, ever again—including me. I care about him deeply, Grayson. He's a wonderful man, and I know he loves the two of you very much. Will it bother you if I date your dad?" I asked, feeling my gut tie itself into a knot as I awaited his answer.

Archie crawled out from under the tree and stood, walking over to stand next to me. He reached up to touch my shoulder in silent support, seemingly having heard my discussion with his brother. "Dad's happy when he's with Leo, Grayson. He hasn't been like that in a long time," Archie said quietly, sincerely.

Tears welled in my eyes, so I swallowed around the lump in my throat and rested a hand on each of their shoulders, looking at Grayson with all the sincerity inside me. "If you think I'm not treating your father the way he should be treated, you have my permission to bust me in the mouth, and I won't say a word," I promised.

"Man, don't say that. He hits hard," Archie informed, a crooked smile on his face to lighten the heaviness of the mood. Grayson broke out into a loud laugh, and both boys actually hugged me.

Cord walked into the living room and grinned at me from his place by the entry. "I've got a better idea than all of us moping around here. Why don't I take you guys out for dinner and a movie, and your dad can burn—I mean cook—pizza for the two of *them*. We'll eat like kings," he suggested.

Archie glanced at the tree before he turned to look at me with worry on his face. "We can all decorate it together when you guys get back," I assured.

Both boys hustled upstairs, and I followed Cordon into the kitchen where Cameron was sitting at the breakfast table in the bay window, his head in his hands. "Trade clothes with me—or just give me your sweater," Cordon ordered as he slipped off his flannel shirt and draped it over the back of a kitchen chair.

Cord then looked at me. "There's some wine in the freezer to chill. Don't let him time the pizza, or it'll burn. Do it yourself. We'll be gone for at least three hours," he determined.

I sighed, "You don't have to leave, Cord. Hell, I'll leave if I'm the problem."

Cam stood and walked over to me, pulling his sweater over his head and leaving his hair a crazy mess before he handed it to Cord. He wrapped his arms around my waist and rested his head under my chin.

"You're not the problem, Leo. Jessica is and will likely remain the problem. I'm going to get this over with when I go to this meeting next week. Please don't leave tonight," Cam whispered. I hugged him tightly, not even letting go when we heard the boys clomping down the stairs like a herd of cattle.

"What's wrong, Daddy?" Archie asked as he walked over and wrapped his arms around both of us. For a kid who seemed so mature, it was a stark reminder that he was only thirteen. Knowing how my childhood had gone, I was determined not to let anyone ruin Archie's.

I stepped out of Cam's arms urging Archie forward. There was a discussion that needed to be had between a father and a son, and even though I loved Cameron with my whole heart, I had no place voicing an opinion.

I POURED MORE wine in Cam's glass, limiting myself to one glass with dinner because I had to drive back to the island. We'd eaten one pizza, wrapping the other to put in the freezer. "You have a better selection of wine here than I do at the restaurant," I joked as I emptied the bottle and placed it in the recycling bin under the kitchen sink.

Cam chuckled. "I got in the habit of buying it when Jess and I were married, and I've just kept buying it since. I like some of it, but most of the reds are her taste," he admitted.

I grinned. "Box it up and give it to her. Maybe if she drinks a few bottles, she'll be less of a bi—less disagreeable," I suggested, tempering my language and feeling only a little catty with my response.

Cam chuckled. "I don't think you've seen the whole house. Come on. Let me show you around."

I nodded and let him lead me upstairs. "Grayson's room, and as you can see, he's *home*," Cam commented. There were clothes scattered everywhere, but I only laughed, having done much the same when I was in high school before I left Tyler for a chance at a better life on South Padre Island.

"What kind of relationship does he have with his mother?" I asked.

"He doesn't talk about it much, but he stays here when he comes home instead of staying with her," Cam replied.

I shrugged my shoulders. "Maybe you should talk to him and ask him why? He's very protective of you, Cam. He wanted to make damn sure that I wasn't planning to hurt you. Maybe Jessica already knows she's lost Grayson, and she's afraid she'll lose Archie if she moves to Seattle without him. If Grayson doesn't want to see her now, what are the chances he'd ever go to Seattle to see her?" I asked, thinking how I'd left the farm and never looked back, returning only once when Kelso and Kelsey graduated high school.

That day, I'd had another fight with my dad about playing football, and I'd never talked to anyone in my family again. It had been a lonely existence before Kelso came back into my life. I'd always be grateful for reaching out to him when Tanner was getting out of prison and asking him to come see me. I'd been even more grateful that he'd done it.

"That's a good question, Leo, but I hesitate to speculate. Here's Archie's room," Cam said, stopping in the doorway. The room was meticulous, which wasn't really a surprise. Archie struck me as a perfectionist—more like Kelso than me.

We reached the door at the end of the hallway, and Cam opened it and stepped inside. It was a beautiful pale blue with a large mahogany king-sized bed that faced a huge window looking out onto the backyard. There were nightstands on both sides of the big bed, which was covered in a blue and brown plaid comforter. There was a dresser with a television and a blue armchair in the corner. It was exactly as I'd expected Cam to want for his private space.

"This is really nice. You've seen mine—not so stylish," I remarked as Cam stood in front of me and touched my face.

"It was comfortable, just like you. All of the furnishings in your home are no-nonsense, and they're not fussy. They're functional and comfortable. I lived with Jess too long, and I don't know how to not be fussy or comfortable here. Maybe it was a mistake to keep the house, but it was the only home the boys remember, and I wanted them to have those memories to get them through all of the turmoil in their lives. With the divorce, I didn't want to disrupt them anymore by me moving, as well, which was why I asked for the house instead of anything else. Lan let me take out a loan against my half of the business to pay her the cash she wanted so I didn't have to sell my piece of the business to someone else. Now I'm not so sure it was the best idea," he continued.

I took his hand and led him to the bed. He needed to feel love and affection more than anyone I'd ever met.

I had him sit down, and I knelt in front of him, taking off his shoes and socks before I stood and took his hand. "Can we lay down together so I can hold you for a little while?" I asked as I kicked off my shoes, not waiting for him to agree. Sometimes, I believed other people knew what was best for us when we couldn't think for ourselves.

Cam sniffled as a tear fell down his right cheek, but I took it as agreement before I unbuttoned his jeans and slid them down his legs. I then quickly undressed myself, tossing our clothes into the chair next to the window.

I pulled back the comforter and sheet, taking his hand to help him into the bed before joining him there. I pulled the sheet over us and then slid closer to him, hovering over him to kiss the tears away.

"I feel like such a failure, Leo," he whispered as more tears slid down his temples due to him on his back.

I cradled his head in my arms and kissed his forehead, hoping I was making him feel like the treasure I believed him to be. His sons absolutely adored him. He had a lucrative business, and a partner who believed him to be the best architect in the country, as Landon had told me a few times when he'd brought one of their employees out to measure for the shed and finish cleaning up the trash from the demo.

The future held a lot of promise for the two of us if we worked out, but at the moment, I had a wonderful man in my arms who was in dire need of TLC. I leaned down and kissed his wet cheeks again. "You, sweetheart, are the furthest thing from a failure as I've ever met. Look, this might not be what you want to hear, Cam, but I've fallen in love with you very easily. I didn't tell you this because I wanted you to say it back, but I think you need to hear it right now. Those boys love you, too. You're far from a failure," I whispered before I continued pressing kisses to his handsome face.

Falling in love with him had been quick as lightning. Getting him to love me back was the challenge. The man had a lot of hurt that needed to heal before he could trust his own feelings, I was sure, but I could love for the both of us in the meantime.

16

CAM

LOVE? Did he say he loves me?

I gently pushed him onto his back and placed my knees on either side of his hips, straddling him. "Did you say you *love* me?"

The shock on my face must have been something comical because Leo struggled not to laugh. In all the time I was married to Jessica, not once had she told me she loved me. The boys said it to me when they were younger, but my parents were the last adults to say it to me over the phone on my birthday before they were killed in a car accident on their way home from the grocery store.

It was two weeks after Archie was born, and my mother had been asking if I had Cord's last phone number. They were planning to come to Texas to see our newborn, and they wanted to see Cordon, as well, if he was anywhere nearby—which I would later find out he had been somewhere in Berlin training with a dominatrix, or so he told me when he came back to the states for our parents memorial a month later in Denver after he'd finally checked his email and called me. Yep… Cord and I were different as night and day.

"Yeah… That's what I said. I love everything about you. I'm

not sure if that's good news for you but please understand that I don't say it lightly. You told me you've never done anything with a guy besides what we did the other night. Have you thought about going further?" Leo asked.

Had I...? Holy shit! Only since I'd met him! Fuck, I'd thought of nearly nothing else!

I leaned over to the nightstand on the left side of the bed, turning on the lamp before I opened the drawer. I pulled out my vibrator and a bottle of lube—Tush Cush—which was getting low. I'd need to order more for sure.

I handed both to Leo, sitting on his groin where his hard erection felt warm along the crack of my ass—even through the fabric of both of our underwear. "This lube has been in that drawer unopened since my divorce was final eighteen months ago. I bought the vibrator right after I met you, and the day it came in the mail, I finally opened the bottle. It's been getting a lot of use lately," I admitted, seeing Leo's sheepish grin.

"Do you, uh, do you enjoy it? The vibrator, I mean?" he asked quietly.

"A lot," I answered honestly.

I leaned forward and captured his soft lips in a searing kiss, feeling his hands reach up and pull my hips forward so our cocks rested against each other. "I wanna be inside you so badly, Cam. I've fingered myself a few times, so you can do me first if you want, but being inside you will be like a dream come true for me," Leo stated, his low voice sending tingles down my spine as his hands slid inside my boxer briefs, gently squeezing my ass as he thrust against me.

"We can't do anything with our underwear on," I reminded him.

Leo picked me up and moved me, whisking off his blue boxer briefs before I could take a breath. There, resting against his toned belly and leaking a trail of precome on those sexy abs, was his thick cock. I hurriedly slid off my underwear, trying to look sexy but probably failing miserably.

I started to lay down next to him when Leo stopped me. "You control the speed, sweetheart. I don't wanna hurt you," Leo insisted as he pulled me to straddle him again.

I reached for the lube when Leo stopped me. "I definitely want to get you ready," he sweet-talked, the sexy devil.

I handed him the lube and leaned forward, kissing along his neck and jaw as the lid *snicked* open and the *squish* of gel being squeezed out of the bottle filled the quiet room. The flex of Leo's abs brought goosebumps to my skin before the warm slick of his fingers caught my attention as they slid down my crack. He'd been so kind to warm the lubricant between his fingers so the cold liquid wouldn't cause me to tense up.

"Will it be okay if we, uh, if we make love like this. I wanna see your face so I know if I'm doing something wrong. I've watched porn, but I've never done it. Is that okay?" Leo asked, his handsome face scrunched up a little with worry.

I was a bit tongue-tied at his concern. Here I was, a forty-five-year-old *virgin to male intercourse*, and there he was, a twenty-eight-year-old *virgin to the same*, and we were about to embark on our first time. It was almost laughable, but he was really sweet about it.

"I, uh… Yeah, that's fine with me. You don't want to try it from behind?" I asked him. Much of the porn *I'd* watched had depicted the men just fucking, no emotions ever coming into their interaction. I guessed every guy had a preference to what they wanted out of sex. I just knew I wanted Leo Anderson inside me, and I appreciated how gentle he was about it. I couldn't imagine Cordon being so kind to one of his sexual partners as Leo was being with me—which was kinda gross for my brother to pop into my head at that moment.

I bore down and his finger slid in to the second knuckle. "It's nice and warm in there," Leo whispered as he kissed my neck, biting my earlobe as he pressed in deeper, moving in and out of my channel and revving my motor in a hurry.

"God, *Leo*," I groaned as he added another finger. I kissed him, our tongues dancing together. Leo continued to slide his fingers inside me as I writhed on top of him, the sensation of his digits as they continued to stimulate my body into a frenzy had me nearly losing my mind. When the fat tip of his middle finger bumped my prostate, I groaned at the heady sensation.

"More," I begged, sounding like a slut to my own ears even though I hadn't slept with anyone else since Jess and I stopped sharing a room when Archie was three. I didn't hate having a room and ensuite to myself, and I'd had celebrity fantasies when I wanted satisfaction, but none of them could compete with what Leo was doing to me.

"Wait—we don't have condoms. I, uh, I haven't had anything resembling sex in a long time, but I did get tested last year for my insurance. I was negative," Leo assured.

"Yeah, uh, I get tested for our insurance once a year as well, and I haven't been sexually active with anyone but my hands for about nine years. I think we're fine without condoms," I agreed.

"Good, good. You ready to give it a try?" Leo asked, our cocks rubbing together to add to the party.

"God, yes," I hissed at the incredible sensations coursing through my body as I reached behind me to lift Leo's hard cock and rub it against my rim to get it slick.

"Wait. Don't hurt yourself," he ordered, picking up the lube where he'd dropped it and squeezing more into his hand. He reached under my balls and slicked up his cock a bit more before he held it for me to work it into myself.

When the thick, bulbous head pushed inside, I gasped in pain for a moment. His cock was a lot thicker than my vibrator or my fingers. I froze for a second before I relaxed. "You're a big boy," I teased as I slid down a millimeter at a time.

It took a bit, but finally, I was settled on Leo's groin as I looked into his eyes. "I'm really glad it's you," I whispered to him before I rose up and slid back down, the burning sensation decreasing as the pleasurable tingles zinged up my spine. The heat from his hands on my waist did funny things to my head, but I wouldn't trade it for anything in the world.

"Glad it's me what?" Leo asked as he began thrusting up into me slowly.

"Glad it's you who's my first, but more important, I'm glad it's you who loves me. This is completely the wrong time to say it, but I love you, too," I told him.

"*Fuuuck!*" Leo moaned as he thrust with more force. Having Leo inside me was unlike anything I'd experienced with my vibrator, that was for damn sure.

I took his hands from my waist and forced them on the bed by his head, leaning my weight against them as I began riding him in earnest. "*God…* that feels fucking good," I gasped as I continued sliding up and down his shaft, the sensation of his hard cock tickling the nerve endings inside me and making my heartbeat quicken with every move.

Leo moved us, sitting up and dislodging the vice grip I had on his hands. He pulled me with him and leaned against the headboard, watching me as I lost my mind because the shift in position had allowed him to go deeper inside me and peg my prostate. It absolutely took my breath away. It was so much better than when I used that stupid vibrator. If Leo and I worked out, that thing was hitting the trash. The real deal was so fucking much better.

"Oh, god, Cam… I don't think I can last much longer. Tell me again," Leo grunted out as we moved in opposite directions in the most pleasing way.

The sounds of our groans and skin slapping skin as Leo thrust up into me echoed in the bedroom like our own sexy tune. "Tell you what?" I gasped as we both sped up, breathing hard against each other's lips as I rested more forehead against his while continuing to impale myself on that incredible cock. The scent of our combined sweat and musk filled my lungs, making me lightheaded—or it could have been the intense pace we'd set. At that point, who gave a damn!

"Tell me you love me again," he whispered as he reached for my hard prick, providing opposite friction to what his cock was doing to my ass until I couldn't hold back any longer.

"*Yesss!*" I hissed as I shot off all over his abs. Leo pulled me to him, kissing me hard as he continued his brutal pace, finally freezing as his warmth painted my insides. We halted right there together for what seemed like forever and nothing at all before Leo began gently thrusting and retreating, sending lightning through my body as the aftershocks, which were just as intense as the orgasm, subsided too quickly for my liking.

"I do love you," I murmured between kisses and nibbles. I latched onto his neck and bit down gently, hearing him groan from the depths of his soul it felt like. I'd never forget it.

We were both a panting, sticky mishmash of fluids, but god, I felt alive for the first time in a long time. "We're... we're a... Jesus, we're a mess," I wheezed, unable to hold in my smile as I looked into his shining eyes.

Leo reached his hands up to my face and pulled me down, kissing me as if it were our last kiss. When he backed away, his face was glowing. "Your shower big enough for both of us? I'd love to help you clean up," he offered with a sincerity in his eyes that shook my heart. *Never in my life...*

I nodded, so he slowly angled his hips until his cock slid out of me, as his come trickled out of me, ticking my balls on its downward slide, the loss of part of him inside part of me left me feeling empty.

Before I could focus on the void, Leo chuckled and reached out for me. "Come on, sweetheart. Cord and the boys will be back soon, and this might be a little hard to explain to Archie and Grayson." He did have a point, but I hated the idea of leaving the bed. It had been the single-most incredible physical experience of my life.

"On the Rocks, this is Kelso." The phone was answered on the second ring, and I could hear lots of noise in the background.

"Hi, Kelso. This is Cam March," I replied, speaking loudly as if I was at the bar with him.

"Hey, Cam. How are you? I'm sorry, Leo's not here right now. Maybe try his cell," Kelso suggested, raising his voice as well.

"Thanks, I will. How was your holiday concert, by the way?" I asked when it got quiet on Kelso's end of the line. I wanted to be polite because he was Leo's brother, and I hoped to get to know him better. Hell, I hoped to know the singer for many years to come.

"It was great, actually. The concert raised a few hundred thousand for the children's hospital in Memphis. I was sorry Tanner couldn't come with me, but he only has a few more weeks… Uh, that's something we can discuss some other time when we get to know each other better," Kelso backpedaled a little bit. I had no idea what he meant by his comment, but whatever it was, I could wait until he or Tanner was ready to include me. Absolutely nothing could scare me away from Leo's family. I was invested—case closed.

"I look forward to getting to know you better, too. I hope I'll see you over the holidays. Leo and Cord are coming over for Christmas Day. Won't you and Tanner join us? My sons will be here as well," I invited.

Kelso chuckled. "We'd love to come. What can we bring?"

"Some white wine, please? Do you happen to like red?" I asked, thinking of the varieties of red I had in the wine rack in the kitchen.

"I do, as a matter of fact. I'll bring a few different kinds of white along. Can we bring anything else at all?" Kelso asked again.

"I'm making Italian, I think, so maybe some cheese and salami so we can make an antipasti platter?" I responded, thinking of something easy to make for a group. The boys loved Italian, and so did I.

I recalled a recipe I'd found earlier that day for an Italian dish that had looked delicious. It was beef, sausage, and ricotta stuffed pasta shells with a vodka cream sauce, and the sight of it made my stomach grumble hangry as anything. I hoped to hell I could pull it off because I wasn't the best cook, but I'd kept my sons fed as they were growing up, so I guessed I wasn't a complete fuck up when it came to food prep… though, I was the absolute worst at setting a timer and not burning the food. I'd have to be careful.

My meeting with Jessica was the next morning, and then I had planned to go to the grocery to pick up ingredients for our dinner and some oven-ready appetizers with a loaf of garlic bread for Saturday, Christmas Day. For Christmas Eve on Friday, well, we'd figure something out. I just had to get through the meeting tomorrow on the twenty-third.

I spoke to Kelso for a few more minutes, and then I hung up to call Leo. Unfortunately, it rang through to voicemail, so I asked him to call me, and then I added, "Love you," before I hung up, my heart singing with my new reality. Being in love was absolutely unbelievable in the best possible way.

I'd finished wrapping the boys' gifts to put under the tree that morning, having finally received the packages at the office the previous Friday from where I'd ordered them online after Thanksgiving. As Grayson and Archie got older, it was harder to shop for them, but I'd tried my best after a conversation with Leo one late night on the phone.

"*I really miss you,*" I sort of whined. "*After school's out next summer, I'm going to rent a place at the beach for me and the boys. God willing, I'll get to have them for the summer, at least,*" I worried.

"*I miss you, too, babe, and that reminds me. I'd like to give the boys surfboards and surfing lessons for Christmas, if that's okay with you,*" Leo explained. I was truly touched by his generosity.

"*Are you sure? That seems like an awfully expensive gift,*" I replied, not adding, "*for two kids you don't know well at all.*" I wanted to change that in the worst way, so I wouldn't give it space in my head. They would get along fine, I was certain.

"It'll be worth it if they like me," Leo joked, making me laugh as well.

"Okay, then I'll get them wetsuits to go with your gift. How's that sound?" I asked.

"Perfect. I can't wait to start the lessons," he whispered. I fell more in love with him in that moment.

I moved to my drafting table to work on a new proposal for the City of Brownsville when Nichele knocked on the door and opened it, carrying in a little Christmas tree. "You got a cute little plant delivered," she teased.

"What? From whom?" I asked her.

Before I could move, Nichele put the little tree on my desk and pulled out the small card attached to the plastic pick in the soil. It seemed to be a bonsai evergreen with tiny little ornaments on it and a gold heart at the top. It was cute—and like nothing I'd ever received before.

"Hmm... *'Don't forget I gave you my heart for Christmas. Love you, Leo.'* Damn, Cameron. That's absolutely adorable," Nichele remarked. I felt my face flush at her words, but it didn't take away the fact that my man sent me a little Christmas tree for my office.

"Isn't that the lyrics from a Wham! song?" Nichele speculated.

I could hear the song in my head, but it wasn't a positive one. "You're showing your age, Nichele. Plus, he's too young to remember the song, and I don't believe he'd ever give my heart away," I replied.

Nichele giggled as she grabbed a pitcher of water from my credenza and gave the tree some moisture. "You're in love, aren't you?"

After she watered it, I placed the little tree on the windowsill in my office and turned to Nichele. "I am." It was actually a little scary to admit it out loud in light of the looming disaster of a custody battle I was facing, but Nichele had proven time and time again that she was loyal to a fault. She'd never betray me—that I knew for certain.

I opened the desk drawer and pulled out the envelope for her that Landon and I had put together. "Merry Christmas, Nichele," I offered as I handed her the card.

Nichele had worked for us for nearly twelve years, and we'd all grown the business together. Lan and I paid her a fair salary with good benefits, and at the holidays, we gave her a share of the profits. The three of us worked hard, and we shared the fruits of our labors, as well.

"So, where are you off to for the holidays?" I asked. Every year, Nichele took the week between Christmas and New Year's to travel. Her mother and father had passed while Nichele was in her twenties, but she had two sisters who she took on trips. They usually took a cruise to somewhere in the Caribbean.

"Actually, this year, we're going to Hawaii instead of taking a cruise. We've rented a house on the Big Island. I'll bring you back some pineapple, Cam," she teased. I hugged her and sent her on her way. Lan was off to Costa Rica to see his parents—which I'd only learned about a couple of months earlier—and we had no jobs in process. We were set to begin the remodel of On the Rocks in January, and I couldn't wait.

An hour later, my cell rang. I checked the number to see it was Grayson. "Hey, Grayson. What's up?" I asked as I finished the draft for the Brownsville Chamber of Commerce building which we were submitting a proposal to remodel next year.

"Dad, Leo and Uncle Cord are in jail," Grayson rambled out faster than I could understand.

I felt light-headed as the words sunk in. *"What?"* I was pretty sure I hadn't heard him correctly. It couldn't be possible.

"Archie called me, Pop, while I was with the guys at the park playing basketball. He said Mom had Uncle Cord and Leo arrested for trespassing. What should I do?" Grayson stated clearly.

"I'll be—where are you?" I asked, trying like hell to wrap my head around what *exactly* he'd said.

"I'm at the park by Fart's house. I got the call from Archie a few minutes ago that Mom had Uncle Cord and Leo arrested, so I called you. We're on the way back to Fart's house now so he can give me a ride home—to your house," Grayson explained.

Archie had asked me if it was okay to go to On the Rocks to spend time with Leo after school was out at three for the holiday break, and I'd given permission for Cord to pick him up and take him out to the beach until I finished for the day. I was going to drive out to pick up Arch and Leo when I finished work, and Cord was supposed to come over to my place in Brownsville on Christmas Eve morning to spend time with us since the bar would be closed until the day after Christmas.

"How the fuck did they end up in jail?" I asked as I began to clean up my shit so I could get to the police station to bail out my brother and my lover.

Grayson sighed. "Archie forgot his homework at Mom's after they picked him up from school. He has that project… well, anyway, Leo drove him and Uncle Cord to Mom's so he could get his materials, and Mom walked in when they were there. She called the police and had them arrested for trespassing, from what I could make out from Archie," Grayson explained.

I wanted to scream, but mostly, I wanted to get to Archie since Grayson hadn't mentioned where he'd ended up. "Where's your brother?"

"He's with Mom. I have the feeling she's gonna take him to Seattle tonight, Pop. During the phone call, Archie mentioned that he loved me, and he hoped he'd see me after he got settled, and then the call cut off," Grayson detailed.

"Oh, hell no," I stated. "I'll be at your mom's in fifteen minutes. You get home, Grayson. I'll call you when I know more," I promised as I disconnected the call.

I quickly scrolled through my contacts and hit the one for Niles Church, my attorney. I should have had him on fucking speed dial with all the shit going on with Jessica. "Church & Associates. Mr. Church's office," the receptionist answered.

"It's Cameron March. Is Niles available? It's an *emergency*," I emphasized, trying to keep my impatience at bay.

"Oh, Mr. March, he's on a conference call at the moment. May I have him call you back the minute he's through?" she asked.

I walked to the closet in my office and grabbed my jacket, pulling it out before I responded. "Tell him to get to the Brownsville Police Department on East Jackson. My brother Cordon March and my boyfriend Leo Anderson were arrested for trespassing at my ex-wife's home. That's where I'm headed. I don't have any details about the situation but make sure he understands that he better get to the police station. Hell, I might end up in jail, too," I snapped at the woman, immediately feeling guilty for taking out my frustrated anger on her. I knew Leo would never put up with that attitude.

17

LEO

"Are you sure you don't mind? I can call Mom and ask her to drop it off at Dad's house," Archie insisted from the backseat of my Chevy Trailblazer. I'd taken Cordon to the school to pick up Archie so we could bring him out to the restaurant for the day. We were closing at six until the day after Christmas, and Cameron was coming to get us so we could all spend Christmas in Brownsville. I'd already hidden the surfboards at his place earlier that morning after I picked them up at the surf shop, and I was excited to give them to the boys on Christmas morning.

"I don't mind. You'll be able to work on it today while I'm busy at the restaurant, and if you need help, you'll have me, Uncle Cord, Miss Yvonne, Kelso, and Tanner. Oh, and Richie, the busboy is home from college, so he'll probably be able to help you the most," I informed him, hoping to set him at ease since his father wouldn't be there.

Archie nodded and put his mom's address in my phone so we could have the directions, and then the three of us took off. "How's your confidence level that your dad will be able to make this Italian feast for us on Christmas Day?" I asked my companions, wondering if we should think about something to have on hand as a backup, based on what Cord had said about Cam's inability to use a timer.

Cord turned to look at me before he started to laugh. He then turned to look at Archie in the backseat. "I'm at about a twenty-five percent. How about you, Arch?"

"I'll help him watch the time, and you'll be there. You've been helping Miss Yvonne at On the Rocks, so you hafta know some stuff about makin' food, right? It means a lot to Dad. I talked to him last night, and he read the recipe to me, so we can all help him," Archie decided. He really was a sweet kid.

"Yeah, we'll all help him," I agreed.

We pulled into the driveway of Jessica's house, a rambling ranch-style home on a large lot. The outside was beige stone with dark blue trim. It was nice, but nothing like Cam's two-story stucco home across town.

"You have a key, Archie?" I asked, seeing nobody appeared to be home.

"I know the code to go in through the garage. Oh, since we're here, we can get the presents Grayson and I bought for everybody. Can you come help me?" he asked.

"Yep," I answered as I unbuckled my seatbelt. Cord did the same, and the three of us went to the double-car garage door. Arch stepped around the side of the house and came back with a stool, placing it under the keypad on the left side of the garage entrance. He punched in a five-digit code, and the door rumbled to life, lifting slowly to reveal the garage was filled with stacks of boxes.

There were empty moving boxes stacked against a wall and a few bundles of collapsed ones in the middle of the painted concrete floor. "That's a lot of boxes," I whispered to Cord as we slowly walked through the mostly empty space.

"Yep. Looks like someone is moving," he responded as Archie let us into the house.

Cord and I followed Archie through the laundry room into the kitchen, seeing dishes, pots, pans, and cooking utensils stacked on the counter. "What, uh, what's up with this?" Cord asked. I stopped next to him, seeing what he was seeing. Someone was definitely moving.

"Mom says we're moving to Seattle right after Christmas. She said we can stay until Monday so I can spend the weekend with Dad," Archie explained. Anger overtook me, but I wasn't about to throw a fit at her underhanded behavior. It wasn't my fight, really.

Cord stepped forward, a deadly smile on his face. "Where's your mom right now?"

Archie looked at the clock. "She had a Christmas party. She won't be home until later tonight," he responded.

Cord nodded. "Can you call her and tell her the keypad didn't work, and you're locked out? I'd really like to talk to her, but if you tell her I'm here, I don't think she'd drop by. I'd *really* love to tell your momma goodbye," he stated, no humor evident.

The tone in his voice was a bit sarcastic, but based on the sweet, innocent smile on Archie's face, he didn't pick up on it.

"Sure. You want somethin' to drink? I think there's beer in the fridge from when Dane was here. Mom has wine, too," Archie offered.

Cord went to the fridge and pulled out an open bottle of wine. "You'll drive us back to the island. I want to enjoy this a little buzzed," Cord joked.

"Is this wise?" I asked him, feeling nerves in the pit of my stomach. I knew whatever happened wouldn't be good, but I also knew how destroyed my love would be if Jessica took Archie away without his knowledge.

We'd been making plans, the two of us, and I was covertly shopping for a house near the beach for Cameron and me to live in together on the weekends. I loved that man, and I wanted him to be happy. He seemed to like being at the beach as much as me, so I wanted to make sure we had a place that was just ours.

"Probably not, but that bitch ain't taking Archie away

without a fight," Cord replied as he took off the cap of the bottle and chugged.

Archie reappeared in the kitchen with a messenger bag and smiled. "You guys want some popcorn?" he asked as he walked to a box in the kitchen filled with dry goods and pulled out a microwave pack of popcorn.

"We, uh, are we gonna be here—" I started to ask.

"Mom will be here in fifteen minutes, and I'm hungry for a snack. I had this really great popcorn at my friend James's house. His mom showed me how to make it. You wanna try it?" he asked, looking so happy that my heart broke a little at the idea of him being taken away from Cam. Their meeting with the lawyers was the next morning, and I was worried about how it would go.

"I'd love to know how to make it. Sounds great," I agreed.

Archie went exploring through a few boxes on the floor until he found oregano and rosemary. He went to the fridge and pulled out a green can of parmesan cheese. "You want a soda?" he asked me.

"Yeah, sure," I answered.

Archie was the perfect host. He filled a glass with ice and retrieved a cola from the fridge for me as the popcorn popped away. When it started to slow, I walked over to the microwave and pulled out the bag. "You have a bowl?" I asked.

He went to another box and produced one, so I rinsed it out and dried it before dumping the hot snack into it. Archie poured the cheese and spices into a small bowl to mix it before pouring it over the popcorn and tossing it with two forks, going to a box and pulling out two snack bowls to put on the table.

"It smells incredible," I replied as I dumped some into a bowl for him and me. It really did.

"So, tell me about your project," I suggested.

Archie and I ate the popcorn he'd made—which was really delicious—and talked about his English paper, a history of his family. "So, how are you supposed to frame it?" I asked. Cord continued to drink the wine.

"First I have to do an outline. Mom told me about her parents, but she never knew her grandparents. I need to interview Dad about his family so I can do both sides, then I have to do a timeline of my heritage with a story about everyone in my family," Archie explained.

I nodded. "I'm sure your father will be happy to tell you everything he remembers about his parents, but you're lucky. Your Uncle Cord can talk about things your Dad might not know or remember. Everyone carries memories differently. My brother, Kelso Ray, has different memories of growing up than me. I have a sister, Kelso's twin, and she has memories that are different from either of ours. You can talk to everyone and not get the full story, but the thing about everyone's story is how they remember it," I offered.

"What do you remember about your parents? Are they still alive?" Archie asked.

As I was about to respond, we heard the garage door open. "That's Mom," Archie announced. I looked at Cord to see he'd finished the half bottle of wine, and he was cocked and ready. I was now really fucking worried.

I first set eyes on Jessica March in the kitchen of her home. She was a beautiful woman, which accounted for the physical attributes in the boys that weren't like Cameron, but she had an ugly soul that shined through her scowl. "Archer, what the fuck are you doing with these people in my house?"

I started to protest against the nasty attitude she seemed to hold for her son when Cord stood, a smile I didn't recognize on his handsome face—Cam's handsome face. "Well, well. You haven't changed a fuckin' bit, have ya?" Cord stated. The sound of venom in his voice really surprising me.

I turned to Archie. "Where's your Switch? Let's go play a game," I suggested. Jessica chuckled, and the laugh that came from her? It was evil as fuck.

"Aw, what's wrong, Cordon? You sad you never got to hit this?" she asked, smacking herself on the ass as she tossed her purse on the table. She was spoiling for a fight, and I had every reason to believe Archie didn't need to be there for it.

"Come on, Archie," I prodded, grabbing him by the back of his shirt.

"You wait right there, pervert. You're not going anywhere with my son," Jessica announced as she dialed a number on her phone.

"This is Jessica March. I need the police at my home. I've caught two trespassers here," she announced. I had a very bad feeling about what was coming next, but if it kept her from taking Archie away, I'd do it for Cameron.

"Leo Anderson. Cordon March," the police officer called out. Cord was snoring incredibly loud on one of the two metal benches in the cell, and I really wondered how the fuck he was able to do it. That wine must have hit him harder than I thought.

"*Here!*" I answered, grade school flashbacks ricocheting through my brain as I walked over to the bars. I'd never been in jail in all my life, not that I hadn't done some shit that should have landed me there. I was guessing I'd been lucky.

"Come with me. You're lawyer's here," the officer stated flatly.

I stepped over to Cord to wake him, pushing against his arm until his eyes popped open. "Come on. A lawyer is here asking for us. Tell me one thing—did you fuck Jessica?"

Cordon sat up and pushed his hair off his face. "Good god, no. I only met that bitch when Cam and she got married in Colorado after she got knocked-up. She lost that baby two weeks later, and I told Cam to get the fuck away from her, but he didn't listen. Besides, Leo, I'd never do anything to betray my brother," Cord responded. The look in his blue eyes and the tenseness of his body at my suggestion that he might do something so awful convinced me that he meant it with everything inside him.

He stood from the bench, stretching enough that his back crackled and popped like rice cereal. I chuckled as he stalked over to the door and laid a smacking kiss on my cheek before he winked at the cop. "When we get out of this mess, I might give you a call, hot stuff."

Cord then turned to me and chuckled. "Don't worry, Leo. We're gonna build that damn still and start making some prime liquor. I'm coming to like it here," Cordon announced, winking at the cop again as the poor man opened the metal bars and stood behind them as if he was scared of my companion. I laughed as we walked down the hallway behind another policeman.

We followed the other officer down a short hallway until we were led into a room with a large table and two-way glass exactly as I'd remembered from television. I walked over and checked my hair in the mirror, hoping the cops were watching me.

The door opened and a man in a suit stepped inside. "I'm Niles Church. I'm Cameron's divorce lawyer. I'm not well versed in criminal law, but I'll make sure your civil rights aren't violated until I can get you proper representation if this goes any further. Can you tell me what happened?" the fancy man asked.

Mr. Church was definitely a no-nonsense sort of character. He flipped open his briefcase and pulled out pad and pen before he reached into the pocket of his grey suitcoat to retrieve his cell. He was slender and pointy—his cheeks and his nose were very angular, which contributed to making him look strict—like a headmaster at a boarding school, much like the one where Jessica wanted to send Archie.

"We'd picked up Archie at school to bring him to Cameron's house, but he needed to get his homework from Jessica's—"

Mr. Church interrupted me. "Mrs. March. Always say *Mrs. March*. She's a stranger to you," the lawyer informed me harshly.

I nodded, worried about what the fuck I was facing. We hadn't done anything wrong as far as I could tell, but I wasn't a lawyer. We were at her house without her knowledge, but we'd meant no ill will. I was going to be roped into a hell of a fight because of the man I loved, but I was ready to go into the fray. I'd do battle for Cameron until the end... of whatever was coming.

Cordon slid forward, bracing his forearms on the table and clasping his hands. "Mrs. March has never been *Mrs. March*, counselor. Jessica took Cameron's last name, but she made it her own and tried to make him grateful for sharing it. You need to know the person you're dealing with," Cordon informed the lawyer. I was eager to hear what else he had to offer.

"Jessica Hanley was an opportunist who found a man struggling to find his identity. We came from money—though our parents worked hard to make it. They loved us more than anything, and Cameron sought their approval. I just wanted to live my life in a way that made me happy, so college was out for me, but our parents supported us both," Cord stated with indignation that the man would question him.

Niles sighed. "I'd love nothing more than to hear the family story of the March brothers, but right now, I need to know how you ended up in Mrs.—Ms. Hanley's house with Archer. He's a minor... not able to give consent for you to enter his mother's home, and since you were there without her permission, she has a good case."

I glanced at Cord to see a grin on his face. "No. She's looking to erase the guilt she has for not wanting to take Archie with her. Did you notice none of Archie's things were packed?" Cord asked, turning his head toward me.

"I didn't go out of the kitchen, remember. Did you?" I asked him, to which Cord nodded.

He turned to the lawyer. "So, what now?"

Niles stood from the battered metal chair with a look of concern written on his face that made me uneasy. "I seriously have no idea, but I'll try to get you bonded out. I know I sound like a bastard, and I'm sorry. Cam caught me on a bad day and being out of my comfort zone makes me nervous—and that makes me crabby. Please don't do anything to piss off anyone, okay? I'll see what I can do," the man stated before he extended his hand to shake ours as if offering an apology for his straight-forward attitude, which I actually didn't mind.

He knocked on the door and was let out. After he left us, I turned to Cordon. "So, what do you think?"

Cord chuckled. "I think we're fucked, but trespassing is the most she can charge us with, and that's not a felony. Fine? Probably. Community Service? Maybe. I'm not really worried about it. What I'm worried about is Jessica's intentions. I really want to talk to Cam. Wait—that bitch told that cop not to let us have our phone call, didn't she! *We're owed a goddamn phone call!*" Cord announced—fuck, he yelled it and then started spouting about our civil rights being violated. I was far too nervous to consider what he was saying. I felt like I was going to puke at any moment.

AN HOUR LATER, we were back in our cell, still not having been allowed to call anyone when the same cop returned—Officer Cox. "You two are free to go. Your lawyer said somebody will be here to pick you up before he left, so you didn't need that phone call after all, did ya?"

The guy opened the cell door, and Cord and I walked out. I had no idea what to do next, but I was grateful to be out of that box with bars—the bologna sandwiches and bottle of water we'd received around five that evening wasn't a gourmet meal, either.

We followed the cop until we were in the lobby of the police station where Officer Cox pointed toward a corner for us to sit and wait, yet again. Suddenly, Cam came in with Grayson. They both looked panicked, but when Cam saw us, he seemed to sigh in relief.

"Where's Archie?" I asked, suddenly worried that everything had taken a turn for the fucking worst. Could Jessica really get away with taking Archie to Seattle without Cam's permission? I prayed it hadn't happened already.

18

CAM

I BROKE land-speed records on my way to Jessica's house. I couldn't fucking *believe* she'd had Cord and Leo arrested, but who was I kidding? It was truly typical behavior for her, especially since we'd divorced and were caught up in this bitter custody battle.

I parked on the street and walked up the drive to the front door because Leo's Trailblazer was parked on the driveway. I continued onto the porch, pressing the doorbell and not taking my finger off it until the door opened.

There stood Archie, his face red with tear tracks. He flew into my arms, and I picked him up to hold him tightly, relief settling into my gut that he was still there.

"Shh. I got ya, bud. Where's Mom?" I whispered to him when we both heard a crash. I set him on his feet, and we both hurried to the kitchen to see a box on its side on the floor with a pile of broken glass next to it.

I reached out to grab Archie's arm because he was only wearing socks. "Stay right here. Where's the broom?" I asked both of them.

Archie pointed toward the hall closet, and I hurried over to grab a broom and dustpan to clean up the mess, returning to find Jessica with her back to us. She was holding her hand under the steam of water from the faucet, not saying a word, though her shoulders were shaking.

"Jessica, are you okay?" I asked as I righted the box, seeing all of the dishes that had been our wedding set from my parents were shattered.

"Why do you care, Cameron? For what possible reason could you give a damn about me?" she snapped back at me, which was quite familiar behavior from her where I was concerned.

I turned to Archie. "Go up to your room until I come get you, please. This is adult conversation that you don't need to hear."

"And pack up your things like I've been telling you all week. We're leaving in the morning after our meeting with the judge. I'm sick of this attitude from you," Jess chastised the boy, which went down the wrong way for me.

Suddenly, Archie stopped and turned to us. "I'm not going. I'm not going to boarding school, and I'm not going to Seattle. I wanna stay here with Dad and Grayson. *If you make me, I'll just run away!*" Archie yelled at her.

"Arch, don't talk to your mother like that. Go ahead to your room, please," I insisted.

Archie didn't say anything else, rushing out of the room and down the hallway where I heard the door slam in confirmation that he'd at least listened to *me*. I began sweeping up the glass as Jessica turned off the water and wrapped a paper towel around her finger.

"Do you need stitches?" I asked her as I worked.

"No. It's not bad. Cameron, why do you care?" she reiterated. I dumped a dustpan full of glass in the box and broadened my efforts around the kitchen when I saw light reflecting off some of the shards that littered the travertine tile.

"I care because you're the mother of my sons, Jessica. You gave me two of the most important things I've ever received in my life, and for that, I'll always be grateful and care about your wellbeing. Grayson and Archer are my finest accomplishments, and I thought they were yours, too," I responded as kindly as I could muster.

I so wanted to rail against her and scream, breaking a few things of my own, but what good would it do? It would only put us further at odds, and that wouldn't solve anything.

"I don't want this life. I love them, of course, but they're not really *my* boys, are they? They're yours, Cameron, and I'm tired of playing second fiddle to you in the parenting department," she admitted. Suddenly, it dawned on me that she was bitter with jealousy for the relationship I had with our sons. I couldn't imagine doing anything that would have kept her from cultivating that kind of relationship with them, too.

I stood and rested the broom against the counter near the box the broken dishes had fallen out of. "Jess, you weren't playing second fiddle to me. You were ambitious and wanted your career, and I was supportive of you, but there was nothing stopping you from having a better relationship with the boys if you wanted it. You were in favor of me taking over the role of primary caregiver years ago so you could concentrate on your practice when you first started working after Archie was born, and I was happy to do it. My job had more flexibility, and I thought it worked for us. What's really going on?" I asked her.

Jessica's attitude toward me had changed since our divorce, and there was something more urgent and definitely more bitter about her recent behavior that I couldn't understand. She had gotten everything she wanted from me since the divorce, except I refused to let her move Archie so far away. That was something I couldn't allow. I hadn't tried to take him away from *her*, but I wouldn't let her take him away from *me*.

Jessica finally turned to look at me, tears shining in her green eyes. "Mom and Dad are pissed about all of my choices, including our divorce—even though they weren't in favor of us getting married in the first place. At Thanksgiving, they said some horrible things to me, confirming every fear I ever had… that I'm a terrible mother to the boys, especially Archie, and until I get my shit together, they don't want to see or talk to me," she whispered before she started to cry.

As much as I disliked the woman Jessica had become, I knew her parents' approval was the main driver of her ambitions. She'd grown up with a brother who was the golden child—Trent had a decorated naval career and was well respected by the troops he served with until his death in a training accident in Japan when Jessica was a sophomore in college at the University of Colorado-Denver. The loss devastated Jessica's parents, and Jess took a semester off to be with them, working online to take a few classes to stay on track.

I knew her parents put her on a pedestal after they lost Trent. I guess I never considered how hard it was for her to stay up there, or what it would mean if she didn't have their approval. I couldn't help but feel pity for her situation, even though I knew she'd likely stab me in the eye if I ever said it out loud.

I opened my arms to her, offering a shoulder to cry on. She stepped closer and wrapped hers around me for the very first time in years. "Jessica, your parents have always put pressure on you to achieve all the things they felt should be accomplished by their children, and when Trent was killed, they shifted all of their expectations to you. You're no longer that twenty-year old girl who could do no wrong in Mom and Dad's eyes out of fear of disappointing them. What do you *really* want out of life?" I asked her. It was something we should have talked about years ago, but yet, like everything else, I let her steer our destiny and went along for the ride.

Some might argue that the demise of our marriage was all her fault based on the events as they'd unfolded, but I'd allowed her to push me around and always get her way. I owned part of the problem, too, and it had to stop.

"I don't know, but I don't want the life Dane has planned for us, either. He wants kids, for god's sake. He wants to get donor eggs because I've already started menopause, and he wants me to carry them. I'm forty-fucking-five years old, Cameron. I don't want more kids. I have two wonderful sons that I don't know how to mother, and I just can't go through it all again," she conceded, not that I didn't already know it.

I took her hand and led her to the table so I could look at her finger. "Why are you really fighting me about Archie?" I asked as I unwrapped the paper towel. I reached into the pocket of my shirt for my glasses, having discarded my contacts earlier in the day because my eyes were overly dry—and maybe because Leo had said once that my glasses were sexy. Who knew why I did some of the shit I did?

I slid them on and examined her finger, taking up my old role in our marriage—caretaker. I checked to see it was a clean slice and not deep, which was good. "How'd you get this?"

"I broke a glass and cut it before I dropped it on the floor, and when I went for the towel to clean it up, I didn't notice the box corner was resting on the towel on the counter. When I pulled it, the box fell on the floor and the dishes scattered and broke. I didn't intend to destroy our wedding dishes, Cameron. I feel like all you've seen of me for so long is the worst, and I hate it," Jessica admitted.

I pushed my glasses up from the tip of my nose and offered her a cautious smile. "I think that's all we see in each other. Maybe we should have called it quits sooner so we didn't wreck each other so horribly. It's really too late to cry over spilled milk, isn't it? We just need to change the pattern going forward because we're still parents to Grayson and Archie, and they still need both of us. So, are you moving to Seattle, because I have to tell you, I'll throw everything I have in your way to stop you from taking Archer with you?" I announced, scooting back from the table. It was time for me to change as well.

"I have no idea what I want anymore. I just… When I was in Seattle, it felt like a fresh start was just waiting for me. Maybe I could do things differently this time? I don't know, but I wanted to try anything because I'm so damn unhappy here," Jessica lamented, looking into the distance with nothing to focus on that I could see.

"I have a suggestion, if you'll listen," I offered. Jess nodded, so I continued. "I want to live my life here in Brownsville. This town is the only home Archie and Grayson have ever known, so let me be home base for them. I might sell our old house and move to South Padre someday because that's where my… Shit! Why did you have Leo and Cordon arrested?" The anger was welling again, but this time it was at myself. They were sitting in jail, and I was worried about *her* problems. *I was an idiot.*

"Archie told me he couldn't get inside because the keypad didn't work, so when I got home and he wasn't outside, I got pissed at him. He wasn't supposed to be here anyway, Cameron. He was supposed to be with you. When I saw Cordon, I thought he was you for a second. When I figured out it was your idiot brother, I just lost all reasonable thought. I couldn't believe he brought a stranger into my home. I had no idea who that guy was. Is he Cord's boyfriend or something?" she snapped. I supposed our détente was over.

I swallowed any fears I'd been harboring, preparing to be honest for the first time in my life. "No, he's not Cord's boyfriend. He's mine. I'm bisexual, Jessica, and Leo is *my* boyfriend. He and Cord picked Archie up from school today, and Arch said he'd forgotten his project here, so they came by to get it for him to work on for the next few days. Would it have killed you to ask a few questions before you reacted so harshly and had them arrested? Jesus…"

"How the hell was I supposed to know? That answers a lot of questions I've always had, though…" Surprisingly, Jess didn't lose her shit at my confession. She reached into the pocket of her slacks and pulled out her phone. "May I speak to Officer Cox, please?" she asked the person on the line, holding the phone out from her ear enough that I could hear noise. A few seconds later, I heard a deep "Hello?"

"Hi, Tracy. It's Jessica March. I'll be dropping my trespassing charges against Cordon March and Leo…" She glanced at me.

"Leo Anderson," I supplied his last name.

"Leo Anderson. Seems it was a misunderstanding but thank you for coming when I called you. I've found out why they were here, and it was all an innocent mistake. Thank you and say hi to Annie for me." She ended the call, and my heart finally started to slow down. Now, I just needed to get to him to ensure he was okay.

"Who was that?" I asked her.

"It was a co-worker's cop husband," she answered, supplying nothing more as far as information, which was typical.

I rolled my eyes. "Well, I can't speak for Cord or Leo, but I hope they can forgive you. I've got to get going. *Archer James!*" I called out.

I stood and looked at her, trying to quell the blazing anger I felt at her actions. Unfortunately, my fury wouldn't get me anywhere. "Look, let me be home base for the boys. Archer can stay in school here, and Grayson has somewhere to come home to on weekends and breaks, and you can come see them anytime you want," I suggested.

She looked away, so I kept talking. "You got a good deal of money from the settlement, so why don't you take a leave of absence from your job and travel? Get a feel for what you think you might want to do with your life if it's not the plan Dane seems to have in mind for the two of you. Was he really in the Navy?" I asked as I waited for Archer.

As I thought about the bullshit story she'd told me about Dane after our divorce, things didn't seem to add up. Unfortunately, I hadn't given enough of a shit to question her at the time, but I had a minute while I waited for Archer.

"I, uh, I might have exaggerated his accomplishments just a bit. His father is a fisherman, and Dane went into the Navy to get away from his overbearing parents after he graduated from high school. When he got out, though, he ended up going to work for his dad on the boat he always despised anyway. Claimed the life of a fisherman was all he ever knew and was all he really wanted," Jessica explained. *What a fucking putz!*

I chuckled. "Wow—now I see the attraction. The two of you have a few things in common," I commented, surprised at her giggle.

"Fuck you for that, but if I leave them here with you and go in search of myself, does it mean I'm a bad mother?" I wasn't sure it was a question she wanted answered, but I swallowed my smart-alecky retort and offered an olive branch. "Honestly, I think it means you're a great mother by putting Archie's needs ahead of your own."

Jessica looked around at the mess in her kitchen. "I guess I'll spend my holiday unpacking."

I had an idea. "Or, you know, if you're not sure you want to stay down here, why don't you put it all in storage. It would be cheaper for that than maintaining the rent here. You can put the big furniture in my garage if you'd like, until you figure out what you want to do and where you want to do it. I don't want us to be enemies, Jess. I want the boys to see that we can behave like adults and be loving parents for them. Can we try to do that?" I prayed she had a modicum of compassion and love in her heart for our sons and would agree.

Jess looked out the windows in her kitchen at the impending sunset, her face a blank slate. Finally, she turned to me and smiled sadly. "Cameron, you were always far too good for me, you know. I'm so sorry for how truly awful I was to you during our marriage. I wasn't worthy of you then, but I can honestly say that you're going to be the best ex-husband a girl could want," she joked, making me laugh out loud.

I heard Archie running down the stairs before he came bursting into the kitchen where I was waiting. "Mom? Dad? Is everything okay?" Jess held open her arms for him, but he didn't move. She looked at me because of his hesitation, and I could see she was hurting.

"Things are going to be fine, Arch. I need to go right now, but I'll be back to get you. I gotta go pick up Leo and Uncle Cord, but I'll be back as quick as possible. Get your things together while I'm gone. We'll be going home when I come back," I told him before I looked at his mother. "Why don't you explain things to him while I'm gone?"

I rushed out of the house, extremely relieved at her change of heart, but I needed to get to Leo and fast. It had been an hour since I'd arrived at Jess's house, and I was sure every minute Leo was locked up was like a lifetime.

I called Grayson on the way across town to tell him that Archie wasn't going anywhere, and he asked me to swing by and pick him up before I went to the police station. I was going to have to take Leo back to Jessica's house because his Chevy was parked in her driveway. I'd get Archie and his things then and bring him home with Leo following behind us.

When we walked inside the police department, I saw Leo and Cord sitting in a corner, both looking agitated. "Where's Archie?" Leo snapped at me.

"Fuck that—what took so goddamn long? We've been here all fucking afternoon, Cameron. I hope you gave that bitch a piece of your mind," Cordon griped, and I knew my answer wasn't going to make either of them happy.

"Archie's at his mom's house packing his stuff. Jess and I have finally reached a custody agreement," I informed them, feeling relief settle in my chest, loosening the vice that had been tightening at the idea of going to meet with the judge the next day. Thankfully, we'd settled things without the lawyers.

"Where'd Niles Church go? He came here, right?" I asked as I glanced down to see Leo holding his sneaker shoestrings in his hand, along with his wallet and cell phone. He looked completely beaten down, which broke my heart.

We started walking out of the police station, but Leo hadn't said a word. My brother, however, had no problem speaking up. "Church left when we got released, the little weasel. They didn't let us make a call, you know, or I'd have called a dungeon master I know and sold your ass, making sure he knew you liked a lot of pain with your pleasure for letting her lock us up. That fucking..." I looked at Cord and then glanced Grayson's direction. Yes, she was a bitch, but she was still his mother.

"She told that jackass cop not to let us call a lawyer, you know," Cord hissed under his breath. *Great! What a fucked-up situation!*

"I'm very sorry," I apologized. I'd have to figure out how to make it up to the two of them. They were just doing me a favor by picking up Archie, after all.

ON THE WAY to Jessica's house, I explained what had transpired that afternoon, leaving out shit Grayson didn't need to hear about his mother. "Archie's going to live with me full time and go to school here, and Jess is going to do a little soul searching," I hedged. I could fill in Leo and Cord later.

"What about that idiot she wants to marry?" Grayson asked from the backseat where he was sitting next to Cordon.

Cord chuckled. "Stupid son of a bitch." It was under his breath, but we all heard it.

I shrugged. "She'll have to figure it out, but hopefully, she'll do what's right for her. She's not moving to Seattle—well, at least not right away. Archie is going to move in with me, and Grayson, I guess if you have anything at Mom's you want to hang onto and not put in storage, you better grab it, too," I suggested as I pulled up in front of the house.

Grayson bailed immediately, but as I was getting out, Leo grabbed my arm. "I'll stay in the truck," he stated quietly, having been completely silent the whole ride. I reached over and touched his hand, feeling it trembling. *Had something happened that I didn't know about?*

"I can't tell you how sorry I am that this shit happened," I tried to apologize. I heard the backdoor slam, looking up to see Cord was out of the truck, standing at the back of it. The way he was pacing let me know I'd be hearing an earful from him soon enough.

I looked at Leo, taking his hand. "Are you okay?" I could see he was affected by what had happened, and I couldn't blame him. I'd been selfishly riding the high of Archie staying in Brownsville that I'd neglected to pay as much attention as I should have to the man I loved. I was a fucking jackass.

"I, uh, well… Jail wasn't fun. Now I sort of know how Tanner felt, though I was with your brother, so it was a lot better than his experience, I'm sure. I think I just wanna go home and take a shower," Leo stated.

"I'm so sorry, honey. Let me get Archie and his stuff, and we can go. I'll take care of you when we get home, okay? I owe you some TLC," I suggested. He'd been kind to me when I'd had a bad day, and it was my turn to do the same for him. I wanted to hold him and show him how much I loved him. He certainly deserved it for what had happened that day.

Leo reached into his pocket and pulled out his keys and the white shoelaces I'd seen in his hand at the police station. "No, Cam. I mean *home. My home*. I'm sorry, but I think it's best if I skip the Christmas celebration you're having. I need some time… Yeah, I need some time. Goodbye."

Before I could say a word to stop him, Leo hopped out of my truck and slammed the door. I didn't really know what he meant, so I sat there, completely stymied. That feeling of euphoria I'd had earlier at reaching an agreement with Jessica over Archie staying in Texas floated away, quickly replaced with a dark cloud. Was Leo saying goodbye forever?

19
LEO

I sat on the couch in my side of the duplex, staring at the black television screen as if I were watching a show. I had no idea what time it was or how long I'd been there. I didn't even remember driving home or coming inside.

Everything was like a blur of activity around me and I was moving at half-speed. For one moment, I was laughing in the SUV with Cord and Archie after we picked him up from school. Next thing I remembered was sitting in the back of a police car with my hands cuffed behind my back like I'd assassinated the president. Then, I'd been shoved into a cell after being *thoroughly* searched and was sitting next to my friend—though Cord had made me laugh when the cop had instructed him to drop his pants and underwear and bend over.

"*I'm usually the one giving the orders, Officer, and I definitely don't put out on the first date, but are you going to buy me dinner after I'm sprung? What kind of lube do you use? I have some allergies,*" Cord taunted Officer Cox.

"*You'll get the finest cuisine this jail has to offer, and sorry, princess, I don't use lube,*" the cop stated as he snapped the wrist band on a clean rubber glove.

The snapping sound the glove had made would be seared in my brain for eternity.

My phone buzzed next to me on the couch, so I glanced down to see it was Kelso. I debated for a split second, but I ended up answering it. I needed to tell him I wasn't going to Cam's house for Christmas so he could decide if he and Tanner were still going.

"Hello," I answered.

"I've been calling you since you left here. The place is dead. Think we should go ahead and close up? It's almost ten," Kelso suggested.

I felt like I was underwater. "Yeah, whatever."

I was suddenly exhausted, but before I could shower and go to bed, I had to tell Kelso about Cam. "I, uh, I won't be over at Cam's for Christmas. I'm not sure if that messes with your plans, but I'm staying home. Cam and I—well, I don't know where we stand, but I need time to figure things out. Bye."

I disconnected the call and tossed the phone toward the coffee table. It missed and glanced off the side, ending up on the floor somewhere. I truthfully didn't give a shit. I was suddenly too tired to move, so I slid off my unlaced sneakers—the laces were still in my SUV; they'd taken them away at the jail—and I grabbed a throw pillow to cover my face while I reclined on the couch. Sleep took me immediately.

"LEO! LEO! LET ME IN, MAN!"

I opened my eyes to see the sun was up. I was on the couch—still in my clothes. I couldn't remember what had woken me, but a quick glance out the window, the stiffness in my body telling me I'd slept for a long time. I hoped to fuck it wasn't an Ebenezer Scrooge situation playing out in my head like a bad movie.

I glanced at the coffee table, not seeing my phone, so I got up and started for the kitchen to make coffee when the door was pounded on again, this time in real life.

"Leo! Let me in or I'm breaking down the door!"

"Fuck," I groaned as I turned to head toward the door. I looked out the curtain to see Tanner standing there, and he looked fit to be tied.

I quickly unlocked the deadbolt and the knob, opening the door. "Yeah, yeah, don't break down the door. It's not mine," I ordered as I turned to go to the bathroom.

I hurried down the hallway, glancing in the mirror over the sink to see I looked like hell. After I drained my bladder and washed my hands and face, I stripped off my dirty clothes, making a mental note to buy disinfectant at the store to spray the couch.

I pulled on the sweatpants that were hanging behind the door and stepped out to see Tanner pacing the hallway. I walked into the kitchen, hearing the coffee maker sputtering on the counter even though I hadn't set it up before I'd crashed. "Thanks, man. I can't find my phone, so if you called, I'm sorry I didn't answer," I volunteered as a preemptive strike.

"Yeah, you're gonna have a lot of angry texts and voicemails when you find it. We've been trying to get ahold of you for nearly two days, Leo," Tanner advised. That was surprising to hear.

"What time is it?" I asked as the coffee maker hissed its finale. I went to the cabinet and retrieved two mugs, pouring us each some coffee.

"It's six in the morning on Christmas Eve, Leo. Kelso was still asleep when I left, but he was really pissed at you. Have you talked to Cord?" Tanner asked, studying me carefully.

"I guess he's with Cam. After we got out of jail on Wednesday night, he stayed at Jessica's house while Cam was picking up Archie, and—"

"*Whoa!* Back up. What were you doing in jail?" Tanner asked, taking a seat at the table.

"Cam's ex-wife, Jessica, had Cord and I arrested for trespassing," I answered, not really wanting to go into detail about the worst night of my life.

"I think I need a little more, Leo," Tanner insisted. *Of course, he does!*

I sighed, the weight of the world on my shoulders. "We picked up Archie at school and took him to his mom's house to get some homework he needed to finish over the break. He asked us to come inside with him so we could help him carry shit out, so we did. We were eating popcorn while we waited for his mother to come home after he called her, and when Jessica came in to find, she called the cops to have us arrested. We finally got out Wednesday night… I have no idea what time it was. What day is it?" I questioned my friend.

"I see. It's early on Christmas Eve, Leo. You suffered a severe adrenaline drop," Tanner answered, though I wasn't sure I'd heard him properly.

"Say what now?" I pressed, my head still pounding from when I'd been sitting on that bench next to Cordon at the jail.

"Your body's sore, isn't it?" he asked. The ache in my muscles reminded me of high school football practices at the beginning of the season.

"Like I just got done with the first drill at summer camp," I answered.

Tanner nodded. "Headache?" he responded.

"Like a marching band at half-time. I slept on the couch last night, which likely didn't help anything," I assessed.

"Yeah, you slept on the couch longer than that, my friend. When you got arrested, your adrenaline climbed and stayed high while you were in jail. When you got out, it dropped, which is like coming down from a drug high. It's hell, trust me," Tanner explained. Yeah, if anyone would know about something of the sort, it would be Tanner.

"God. Did you have that every day?" I asked, hating that I was reminding him of his time in prison, but thankfully, in a matter of days, he'd be free to go anywhere in the world that he wanted, and he happened to be the resident expert on all things incarceration at my disposal.

"Only the first year. After that, it just became part of the fucking routine. Lots of cons become adrenaline junkies while they're in, fucking around with some of the monsters inside for the high of it. I was never one of those guys," Tanner explained.

Bzz! Bzz! Bzz!

His phone danced across the table before Tanner picked it up. "Hey, babe… I'm at Leo's… He's fine… I'll ask him and explain it when I get home. Stay in bed. I'll be there soon. Love you, bye."

"Kelso?" I asked. Tanner's face turned a bright red, and his smile was undeniable. He was the picture of a man in love.

"What's up with Cameron? Why aren't you going to his place for Christmas dinner? That's what you told Kelso the other night?" Tanner pressed.

"Cord and I sat in a fucking jail cell while Cam worked out his custody agreement with his ex-wife. What if he decides it's best for them to work shit out with each other? What if he decides maybe he's not as bisexual as he thought, and the best thing for his sons is to get back with their mother, huh? I'm in love with him, Tanner. Where the fuck does that leave me?" I worried.

He didn't say anything for a moment, but finally, Tanner nodded. "What else?"

I swallowed down some coffee and continued. "Maybe we're just not meant to be, okay? It's better if I initiate the breakup so he doesn't feel guilty about it. The kid's just a teenager, and I remember what a scary time it was for me. He's going to need his father's full attention. I'd just be a distraction," I stressed to Tanner.

My friend sipped his coffee and studied me for a few long

seconds. "I think that's bullshit that he's going to get back with his ex, so let's say you're wrong. What about Cameron? He's gonna need someone, too, Leo. Don't you know that man loves you? Your ducking out on him right now makes it look like you were only in it for the good times, and when things got rough, you just packed up your toys and went home," Tanner seemed to rant, which wasn't anything I'd heard from him since high school.

Without waiting for me to respond, he went off again. "Do you really want to be considered a flight risk by him forever? Believe me, I tried to do what I thought was best for Kelso, and you remember how fucked up that became. Thankfully, your brother is a relentless little shit when he really wants something, and I'm just glad he wanted me. Don't you want Cam?" Tanner reasoned, which I hadn't seemed to be able to do.

It had been a dark time for both of them, and it wasn't that long ago that it happened. They were both a huge mess while all of that was going on.

"He has Cord and even Jessica if they reconcile." It was my shitty response, and even I didn't buy it.

Tanner chuckled. "For some things, it's good to have family, sure. When he needs someone to hold him after he has to yell at Archie and feels guilty or when Archie has something great to celebrate, who do you think Cam's gonna want next to him? I don't think it'll be Cordon, Leo, and based on shit Cord's said about her, I damn well don't think it's gonna be Jessica, either."

I had no idea how to answer him. Of course, Tanner made good points. He always did, the goddamn beast. Would I be the bad guy for running away? Was I running away because his life was changing? Did I want to be considered a flight risk?

Tanner fucked around with his phone and then stood and walked into the living room, lifting the couch and reaching down before he returned, handing me mine. "I never figured you for a coward, Leo. You didn't run out on me when I went to prison. You stuck by me, even coming to see me when I was at my lowest after I lost my eye. You gave me hope for when I got out. Without you, I don't know if I would have made it out alive. You need to think about how Cam feels right now. Ask him flat out if he's trying to reconcile with his ex-wife before you make any decisions you'll regret, my friend," Tanner stated before he left me alone with my thoughts as time seemed to stand still again.

A minute or an hour later, I walked into the living room to stop Tanner and ask him what I should do, but he was gone. When I opened the door after seeing shadow through the window, there stood Cameron and Archie, who was holding a bag.

"Merry Christmas Eve," Archie greeted with a big grin.

"Come in, please," I invited. I stepped aside to allow them entrance, suddenly aware I wasn't wearing a shirt.

"Excuse me for a minute," I said as I hurried to my bedroom and rifled through my dresser for a t-shirt.

The door snicked closed as I pulled the shirt on, and when I turned around to leave the room, there stood Cam, looking very upset. "I'm so sorry if I made the wrong call on coming over here this morning, but I've been…" he began apologizing.

That was the last thing I wanted to hear from him, but I needed a definitive answer to one thing. "Are you trying to get back together with your ex-wife?"

Cam looked at me as if I'd lost my mind. "Oh, my god, *no!* Is that what you thought? If I gave you that impression, Leo, I'm so sorry—"

I stepped closer and put a finger over his lips. "No, sweetheart. I'm the one who's sorry, Cameron. I was freaked out about the jail thing, and then I worried about maybe you wanting to get back with Jessica. I pulled away because I was afraid I'd be left behind. Now, I see it was a mistake," I began my explanation.

Cam took my hand and held it. "I realize this is a lot for you all of a sudden, what with Archie living with me full-time, but I want you to talk to me about what has you so worried so we can figure things out, you and me… together. Please don't run away from me," Cam pleaded, his eyes filling with tears that made me feel absolutely like the lowest creepy-crawly thing on earth.

"Oh, god, no. That wasn't my intention. I just panicked, Cam. I mean, Tanner came over here and talked to me because I didn't answer the phone. It fell under the couch. He and Kelso were also pissed because I'd told them I wasn't going to your place for Christmas dinner tomorrow," I admitted.

Cam knelt down in front of me, his hands holding mine to his forehead like I was his master or something, which was unsettling. "Please, I need you, Leo. I can't lose you; I only just found you," he whispered before he began sobbing silently.

I knelt with him and wrapped him in my arms. "Shh. I'm so sorry, babe. I mean, raising a kid is a lot of responsibility, and I worried I'd take you away from Archie. I was afraid you'd need to give him more time, and I'd be left out. I'm a selfish asshole, Cameron, but I don't want to be. I'm so sorry," I whispered to him, remembering the walls were thin and Archie was in the living room doing something.

"I want you to do this with me. I want you to be there *with* us, Leo. Archie loves you, and I love you. We want you to share our life. Tell me what I can do to help you see I'm sincere," Cam whispered. I felt like the most horrible person on the face of the good earth.

I leaned forward and kissed his forehead… his nose… and finally his soft lips, tasting the tears I put there and wishing I'd made a better decision when Cam picked us up from jail and took us back to Jessica's house for me to get my SUV. I could never say I was sorry enough for my actions.

"Before I fuck this up so badly that we can't fix it, what does Archie know about why I didn't come over the last couple of nights?" I implored.

"I told him you were giving us privacy so we could talk about his mom and what she's doing. We had a good discussion about it, and I think he understands and wants to support her while she figures herself out," Cam explained, taking that worry from me.

"Good; I guess that's good for Archie to have that understanding. What about the guy who was following you? The one who was outside your house taking pictures?" I asked, trying to understand everything so I could ask important questions. We only got one shot to do things right as far as making a family when a kid was involved. I wanted to make sure we did right by Archie.

"She admitted to hiring him. Desperation wasn't a good color on her, but she's got issues with her parents that will take a team of shrinks to help her reconcile. Fortunately, that's got nothing to do with us," Cam reported.

"Okay. What's going to happen to her now? Is she moving to Seattle?" I asked Cam.

"She's going away for however long it takes her to figure her shit out. That's what I wanted to tell you the other day, but not in front of Grayson when we were in the car.

"I had the chance to talk to Grayson last night when he came back home from his friend's house. He's worried about you, too, which I was happy to hear. I sent him to Jess's house with his buddy, Alan, yesterday to get the rest of his stuff," Cam explained to me.

"I appreciate his concern," I replied.

Cam then continued. "Cord's stayed with me the last couple of nights because he thought you needed time to yourself, having mentioned that you seemed to be particularly upset about being locked up. I'm guessing that was because of Tanner's situation, which Tanner told Cord about at some point and my brother related to me. Cordon wouldn't let me come over to check on you after Archie went to sleep last night or the night before. The crazy jackass threatened to tie me to the bed, which I think he was serious about, but I was able to talk him out of it," Cam told me, chuckling a little. At least the tears had stopped.

I sat down on the floor of my bedroom and pulled Cam with me into my lap. "I'm very sorry, sweetheart. I lost my mind for a minute, but it will never happen again. I'll talk to you first, but you have to promise to do the same with me. I love you, and I think your boys are incredible. I want to get to know them much better, and I want to be there for the good times and the bad, okay? Can we agree to be a team?" I asked him.

Cam wrapped his arms around my neck and lunged, knocking both of us over, me on my back with him on top of me on my bedroom floor. I started laughing at our precarious position, just as there was a knock on the door. "Come in," I called out, still laughing as Cam kissed all over my face.

"Yuck! Is this a sex thing? Can I eat the donuts we brought or do I gotta wait for you guys?" Archie asked from his place by the door.

I looked at Cam's beaming face, seeing he was startled. "Not it!" We both laughed, thinking the same thing—there was an uncomfortable discussion to be had with a thirteen-year-old boy to explain what he'd walked in on, and it was definitely not sex.

Cam and I scrambled, helping each other up from the floor. My muscles were still aching, so I decided to go ahead and shower while Cam talked to Archie. "Tanner made coffee, and somehow, I have fresh milk. I'll be out in a few minutes. I need to shower the jail off me," I commented with a chuckle.

Cam winked at me and turned to Archie. "Come on, smartass. Let's have some donuts and a discussion I don't think I'm going to enjoy about the many kinds of love that people can have for others." He then placed his hand on his son's back and guided him out of the bedroom, pulling the door closed behind them.

Life was never going to be dull with Archie around, I was sure. I found I wasn't dreading the idea at all.

20

CAM

END OF MAY...
Clomp... Clomp... Clomp...
"Archer James!!" I shouted from the kitchen.
Clomp! Clomp! Clomp!
"Pick it up, Archie!" I shouted again.
"*I got it!*" That was my partner, Leo. He had become the love of my life, and the man I wanted to share the rest of my days with.

It was the first day of summer break, and the three of us were moving to the beach. We'd bought the duplex where Leo had lived, and we'd been working to open it up to make it a single-family home. There were four bedrooms in all, so Archie and Grayson could have their own rooms, and I could have an office in the fourth bedroom to work there, even though Stenson & March was only about forty-five minutes away in Brownsville.

I wanted to be with my guys at the beach as much as possible, but I wasn't too far away to go into the office if I was needed. Landon was on board with my idea to work from South Padre Island since he'd still be working at On the Rocks for the summer, so Nichele could transfer the phones to her cell and work from home. It was a win for all of us, I felt sure.

"Pop, where are you?" That was Grayson, who was home from school for the summer and would be working for Landon during his break. He was helping us move some things to the beach, but he was going to stay in Brownsville at the house most of the time because that was where his friends were, all of them at home on break.

It was a good solution to my problem of what to do with the house while Arch and I were at the beach with Leo. Grayson would give the house the lived-in look the neighbors would need to see, and I'd accepted it would be a pig stye all of the time, and I'd need to call before I dropped by. A boy of nineteen needed that independence, but knowing his family was nearby if he needed us would be good for him, too. We'd talked about it, much to Grayson's dismay.

"So, no guests," I stated as we sat on the back deck one evening before Archie and I moved to the beach for the summer. I was having a glass of wine and Grayson was drinking one of his energy drinks, having just returned home from a pickup game of basketball at the park near Fart's house.

"Oh, come on, Pop! We won't burn the house down," he replied to my edict. Leo was inside with Archie playing a video game. We were staying at the house in Brownsville before for the end of school, and I was in the mood to give my oldest son a little shit.

"How do I know that?" I challenged, seeing his face contort into impatience. He looked like his mother when I'd first met her. I hadn't heard from her since she'd left town, but I hoped she was doing well.

"Well, you never burned it down," Grayson pointed out, the smartass making me laugh. It was true—if anyone was going to burn the house down, it was destined to be me.

"Okay, I'll give you that one. Seriously, though, Grayson—no parties. Mrs. Preston won't hesitate to call the police, and you know that for sure. We've had enough time with Brownsville PD," I reminded.

Grayson exhaled loudly. "Can Fart stay over sometimes? His folks are going on a European cruise this summer, and he doesn't like to be home alone, Pop," my oldest explained. *I finally relented, not really surprised. Alan was a good kid, in spite of that dreadful nickname.*

"In here, son," I answered, stepping out into the hallway so he could see me. He had a guitar strapped to his back and was headed to the door from the second floor. Leo was loading the truck and his Trailblazer with all of the essentials we wanted to take to the duplex, which included the surfboards Leo had given them for Christmas.

Every weekend, Arch, Grayson, and I went out to the island when the weather had begun to warm, and Leo made good on his Christmas gift to teach them to surf. He was a man of his word, and I loved him for it.

Grayson dropped his things by the door just as Leo stepped inside. "That it?" he asked Grayson with a friendly smile.

"Leo, he can take those out there himself," I ordered. Leo spoiled them both with attention and love, and the boys were thriving with his help. My heart swelled with pride when I saw them hanging out or working on a project together. It was like he was the missing piece to our puzzle.

The first part of the expansion at On the Rocks was nearly finished, and the place was looking amazing, if I did say so myself. I'd put down the ideas on paper, and Landon had, once again, brought them to life.

My heart leaped with joy every time I went by to check on the progress, but the most gratifying thing to see was how happy Tanner and Leo both were with the results. Kelso had been gone through most of the construction phase, but he was back on South Padre Island now, and he'd been astounded when I'd shown him around one afternoon when I was there. It was why I was passionate about my profession—knowing Lan and I had made something from nothing was incredibly satisfying.

We'd doubled the size of the bar area and added sliding doors that could be closed in cooler temperatures without blocking out the view of the beach and the water. The back patio that led to the sand had also been doubled in size with more tables for patrons outside. Four volleyball pits had been added at the back of the vacant lot where ground had broken for the distillery, and a large barbecue pit area was in the process of being built with a shaded picnic pavilion they could rent out for occasions or seat an overflow crowd.

When it was all finished, it would be one of the larger beach bars at the southern end of South Padre Island, and Kelso had talked to The Tex-Sons about doing some charity concerts at On the Rocks over the summer and fall. Excitement was in the air for all of us, but I was the most excited of all—I got to sleep next to one of the owners of the fine establishment every night—and do a hell of a lot more than sleep.

"Babe, I got it. Grayson, I took the surfboards out there over the weekend. I made a stand on the back deck for you guys to store them, so find the box with your wetsuits. We can leave them out there as well," Leo suggested.

"I will, Leo," Grayson agreed. Leo nodded before he and Archie went outside with some of Grayson's stuff to put in the truck.

I turned to Grayson as he opened the fridge. "If you want something, it's probably in that box. You'll have to go to the store and stock up for yourself. I left condiments for you, but as far as food and snacks, you're on your own," I told him as I pointed toward the large wax box where I'd emptied much of the refrigerator's contents into to take with us to the island. It was time for Grayson to understand he was responsible for himself, and that included grocery shopping.

"Have you talked to Donovan Gullett lately?" Grayson asked as he rooted through the box.

"Uh, I saw him outside the other night with Mitzi when she did her daily dump in the yard. Thankfully, he cleaned it up for a change, why?" I asked.

"I just wondered. I think Uncle Cord has a thing for him," Grayson advised as he pulled out an energy drink bottle that was Leo's favorite when he was at the house, twisting off the lid before gulping half of it.

I chuckled at him. Seeing my son as a man had been a hard pill to swallow, but it was good to know my little boy was still there under the surface. Grayson had always downed any liquid like it was going to be taken away from him at any moment.

"I think Uncle Cord has a thing for any guy who breathes," I replied as I finished packing some of the herbs and spices to take with me that I was certain Grayson would never use and would go bad over the summer.

I'd been spending a little time with Miss Yvonne in the kitchen at On the Rocks, and she'd given me a few pointers, Cordon offering his two cents when he was around, the prick.

The half-dozen timers I'd received as Christmas gifts the previous year hadn't hurt anything, either. Leo had even written a note in my Christmas card that he promised to always be my backup timer anytime I was making food, and so far, the new system had been working out. Nobody had died, which I counted as a win/win.

"I also noticed Archie staring at Donovan the other day. Have you had *The Talk* with your youngest yet?" Grayson asked, glancing over his shoulder to see if "my youngest" was within earshot.

I stopped what I was doing and stared at *my oldest*. "Which talk? He's only thirteen," I reminded.

"He'll be fourteen in a week, Dad," Grayson whined, as if I didn't know how old my son was going to be.

"Grayson, your mother had a general sex talk with him a few years ago, and I talked to him about Leo and me at Christmas," I assured, remembering how that conversation had gone.

Leo had gone to shower after Archie walked into the bedroom to see me laying on top of Leo while we worked out how we'd handle Archie coming to live with me full time and Leo's worry about where that left the two of us. Leo was right—I needed to have a discussion with Archie about my relationship with Leo going forward.

I'd walked down the hallway with him and walked over to counter while Archie was pouring himself a glass of milk. "Leave that out, son. I want some in my coffee," I remarked as I picked up my coffee cup, placing it in the microwave to heat. After a minute, I sat down at the table where the sugar bowl was always sitting since Leo and I had started seeing each other in earnest.

"So, what you walked in on back there, that wasn't sex, Arch," I broached the subject.

"Ah ho," he mumbled around a mouth full of kruller.

"Don't talk with your mouth so full," I chastised as I pinched off a piece of the cake donut I'd picked for myself.

"Don't ask me questions when I'm eatin' then," he responded, bringing a snicker from me.

I put down my donut and stood to get napkins for us. I handed one to Archie and sat back down. "I love Leo, Archie. Does that bother you?"

Archie grinned. "I know, Dad. Grayson told me that's what he thought was going on. I'm glad. I don't wanna know what you do for sex, though. I think I'm too young for that. Don't you?" *Arch suggested.*

A huge belly laugh echoed around the kitchen, so we both turned to see Leo standing there with us, feet bare and hair wet. He was dressed in a pair of jeans and a t-shirt, a duffel bag with him and a pair of socks over his shoulder.

"I think that's probably right, Archie. You can tell us when or if you want to know, and we'll sit down with you and have a discussion. Don't listen to your school friends because they'll just make stuff up and scare the crap out of you. You come ask your dad or me, and we'll tell you the truth," *Leo vowed. Archie looked at me, and I winked. That was the extent of the gay sex talk we had with him, and I'd never been more grateful about it in my life.*

"I know you're just worried about Archie, Grayson, but let's let him come to us when he has questions or wants to talk to us about it, okay? What would you think about all of us going to family counseling?" I suggested.

There was no way all the changes we were living through wouldn't have impacted all of us, including how they might feel about Jessica. A good airing of the of feelings could be helpful, I was sure.

"What, like you, me, Archie, and Leo?" Grayson questioned.

"And maybe Mom if she's around? It might help you and Archie if you could talk to her about how you feel with the changes in your life if you're in a safe space with someone who can help us hear each other," I suggested, shocked to hell when I heard my mother's voice coming out of my mouth. It actually made me laugh. I missed my parents immensely in that moment.

Leo came into the kitchen, looking around. "Any of this ready to go, babe?"

Grayson walked over to him, taller than Leo now since he'd had a growth spurt, which made me smile. "What do you think about therapy?"

"Do you mean like for an injury, or to help process things you might not know how to process on your own?" Leo asked him.

I was actually eager to hear his thoughts on the matter. We had never discussed therapy or mental health, which I felt we needed to do. How could we love each other if we didn't love ourselves?

"Mental health?" Grayson replied.

Leo smiled. "When I was trying to figure myself out—whether I was gay or bi or ace or demi, I went to a therapist to help me process it. The best thing I learned is I don't gotta have a label. I can just be me and love your dad, and I don't have to put myself in a box for anyone. So, yeah, if anyone wants or needs to go to therapy, I'll go just to support you or to actively participate. Tell me when and where," Leo told us.

I walked over to him and took his hand, pulling him closer to me to kiss his sweet lips that had just said the most beautiful thing I'd ever heard. I was proud to be with him, and I was beyond happy for my kids to know him. He was an extraordinary man.

"When we redo these bathrooms, I want a big tub for us so we can relax in it together," Leo insisted as we showered in the bathroom on his side of the duplex. The boys were in the other apartment, but Lan had opened the wall for us and roughed in a large doorway. We'd taken out the small stove and capped off the gas, but the rest of the second kitchen was intact, which made it awkward for us to spend time together, but we were making it work.

"Yeah, good idea. Tell me, Mr. Anderson, how would you like this place to look? Tell your favorite architect what you want so he can work on plans," I quizzed.

Leo stepped from under the spray and moved me under so I could rinse my hair. We'd both grown short beards during the spring to keep the other from getting beard burn when we got frisky, which we had been doing quite a lot lately, though now that all of us were living at the beach, I wasn't sure how much time or privacy we'd have.

"I definitely want to keep both bathrooms, but maybe make them a little bigger if that's possible. A powder room off the deck so people can pop inside to pee if they've been outside or maybe walked down to the beach. Hell, maybe we should just keep this as two rental units and get a place closer to the beach for ourselves," Leo seemed to be thinking out loud.

"Or we can fix this place up and sell the Brownsville house. We can add onto this if we want, but Grayson will only be here sporadically, and hell, Archie's gonna be fourteen next week, so in four years, he'll be going off to college. The beach is less than a mile away, so it's nice and quiet here, which it wouldn't be if we lived right there," I reasoned.

Leo nodded as he soaped up my body while I shampooed my hair and then rinsed, just as there was a hard knock. "Dad, Uncle Cord's here," Archie announced through the door. I was grateful he didn't barge in as he'd been known to do, especially with Leo and I both sporting wood, just from our proximity to each other.

I opened the shower curtain and stepped out, cracking the door. "Tell him to make himself useful and light the grill. There's beer in the fridge," I called out to whoever was listening. I closed and locked the door as my brother's raucous laughter echoed through the place. I knew he'd keep Archie occupied while Leo and I took care of business.

I got back under the spray and braced my arms on Leo's broad shoulders. "Now, where were we?"

Leo giggled, which I'd heard a couple of times, but never with any regularity, so I hadn't mentioned it. Of course, I couldn't avoid it since he was three inches away from me. "What was that?" I teased as I played with the back of his bright blond hair.

"It's the Anderson curse. When we're happy, we giggle. I can't help it. Surely, you've heard Kelso do it all the time," Leo replied as he pulled me closer and his big hands landed on my ass. He gently squeezed and jiggled my cheeks, fueling the simmering passion that ricocheted between us.

"*Mmmm*. I'm glad you're happy. I want you to be happy all the time. It makes me feel like you enjoy being around me," I confessed.

Leo slowly circled his index finger around my hole before he kissed me, then gave me soft kisses across my cheek to my ear. "I want in here tonight, but we don't have time right now. Could I interest the handsome gentleman in mutual hand jobs?" Leo asked, reaching up to the dispenser on the wall where shampoo and bodywash were available.

He pushed in the one marked shampoo and reached down, grasping both of our cocks in his strong fist before he slowly moved his forearm up to brush his hand over the tips, squeezing just a bit as his thumb circled the rim of my cock while he kissed me.

His mouth tasted like the mint toothpaste he liked to use, and when it mixed with my cinnamon toothpaste, we both moaned at the flavor as the sounds were swallowed up by the heady steam in the bathroom. "I love feeling your hands on me," I whispered as I offered my neck for Leo's nips and kisses.

He brought out the gooseflesh on me like I'd never experienced as he continued to stroke us together. I moved one hand off his shoulder to join his, both now stroking us together. "God, it feels so fucking good," Leo whispered as he bit my earlobe, sending a spark down my spine to where he was still massaging my entrance.

I wanted him inside me so badly, but in a slick shower, the possibility of injury was too much for me to risk at my age. I wanted to be able to sex up Leo well into my eighties, and a broken hip would throw a wrench in the plan.

I began pushing back onto his finger and sliding forward into his fist, seeking the friction he was giving. "Do you—have you played with your ass? Would you let me play with it sometime?" I whispered as I felt my heavy balls begin to draw up into my body.

"What do you want to do to my ass?" Leo tantalized as his finger inched in and out of me, not going deep because he didn't have anything to use for lube. I'd remember that the next time I went to the store.

"I want to fuck it with my tongue," I gasped, feeling my blood begin to boil at his unrelenting assault on all my senses.

"*Mmmm*," Leo groaned as my body released. The heat from my come was like fire on my hand and then I felt his cock erupt, raining down more hotness as I continued to pump into his strong fist.

I leaned forward and kissed him softly, absorbing the warmth of his wet skin and the feel of his hand gently stroking my deflating dick. I realized then that he was washing the jizz from my body and his own before he kissed me once more. "Oh, and we need a bigger hot water tank. *Son of a bitch!*" he yelped before he hit the plunger on the spigot to stop the shower and turned off the burst of cold water. I chuckled as I opened the shower curtain to see Cordon leaning against the door while the toilet emptied.

"What the fuck, Cordon? I locked the door," I complained.

The jackass had used to do the same thing to me when I was a kid, standing outside the shower as I rubbed one out more than once, flushing the toilet to rain down cold water over me at the least opportune moment.

"I'll give Leo points for not screaming like a girl when I flushed the toilet. Oh, and there's not a lock made that I can't pick. Remind me to tell you about the time I was fucking a Beefeater in the Tower of London, and we were about to be discovered by one of his fellow Yeoman Warders on patrol. I was magnificent that night. So anyway, I started the fire, drank two beers, and I had to pee. Archie has locked himself in the bathroom on the other side with some sort of testing kit I'm not asking about, and I doubted you'd want me to pee in your kitchen sink or off your back deck," Cord added as he stepped forward and opened the door.

"You were peeing while we were…" I stopped speaking as I reran our conversation in my head while handing Leo a towel and taking one for myself.

"Yeah, I just finished about the time you said you wanted to eat Leo's ass. I held off for a second so I could hear if he's into it, which he didn't answer, but please, don't let me get in the way. Think about what you want for side dishes. I'll run over to On the Rocks and pick them up," Cord insisted before leaving us.

I turned to Leo, worried about what he was going to think of my brother's rude behavior. "I'm very sorry about him. Well, actually, I shouldn't apologize for his behavior. You've known him for a while, so you know how he is," I said as I wrapped the towel around my waist and opened the door while Leo did the same.

"Yeah, I get it. He's into kinky shit, isn't he?" Leo asked.

I nodded, chuckling as I walked to our bedroom. "He trained to be a Dominant in Berlin. He's traveled everywhere and lived a very bohemian lifestyle," I assessed, then added, "Sometimes I envy him his knowledge of the world. I moved down here from Colorado after college because this is where Jessica is from," I replied.

"Colorado? How did I not know that was where you grew up?" Leo inquired, as he dropped his damp towel and hung it on a peg by the door, placing mine over it.

"Well, I think there's probably a lot of things we don't know about each other, yet. I don't really have any outstanding memories from living there, and I haven't been back since we closed out our parents estate. I mean, ask me questions and I'll answer. I look forward to learning about you, too," I responded.

After we were dressed, Leo took my hand and kissed the top of it. "Cameron, I can't wait to learn more about you. I know some people are too afraid to make a commitment to one another until they know everything, but I look forward to the surprises we'll learn about each other along the way. I love you, sweetheart."

The warmth of his gaze washed over me, and in that moment, I knew Leo Anderson would be careful with my heart. I knew he'd love me and my sons, and there was no doubt in my mind that Leo would fill every day with love and family. It was like being granted a wish I never dared to make, but I was holding onto it with both hands.

21

LEO

I STOOD on the new back deck of On the Rocks watching Archie and Whiskey playing fetch on the beach. We were having the grand re-opening of the new tiki bar, patio, and the new picnic area later that day. Work had begun on the distillery, which was going to be called Ima-GIN-ation Distilling. We'd worked hard to get everything done, and I was ready to celebrate.

The previous fall, Luke Lawson had sent me a letter that I'd completely forgotten about, and when I finally got around to opening it weeks later, I'd been stunned at its contents.

I'd been cleaning out my Trailblazer one day because somewhere during the shopping trip I'd taken with Cordon earlier that day, I'd lost a large bag of juniper berries, and I'd been taking the damn SUV apart to find them. I'd bought out the only bag they had at a big ass grocery store in Corpus Christi, and I didn't want to lose them.

Cord and I had decided we liked the unique taste of the wheat and molasses added to a simple corn mash and distiller's malt. We'd made a batch at the restaurant on Saturday morning that we had been ready to put into the fermentation bucket, so we were ready for the next steps to add the yeast and some other flavors before we put it in to ferment, and the berries needed to go in the mixture as well.

As I'd been rummaging through everything and throwing away trash, I'd come across the letter from Luke Lawson, and I'd opened it.

Dear Leo,

I hope this letter finds you well. I truly enjoyed meeting you this fall and talking to you about my passion for distilling. It took me back to the days when I was my happiest before my Susan passed, so thank you.

I've found out I don't have long to live, and as I considered my legacy and what I wanted the world to know about me, I thought of the excitement on your face when I told you my stories. I've enclosed three COMPLETE secret recipes from my creative years—one for gin, one for bourbon, and one for absinthe that are my favorites.

I hope you'll enjoy the recipes and make them your own. Someday, when you meet a young man like yourself, pay it forward and give him some of your recipes. That will be the best legacy I can think to leave behind.

I wish you much happiness in your life, Leo. Live every day like it's your last and have stories to tell of your adventures to your special someone like I had with my Susan.

Much success, my young friend,

Luke Lawson

I'd folded the recipes, having wiped my eyes of the tears that had gathered, and had hurried into the restaurant to show them to Cord. We'd immediately dumped out the mash that we'd made and had started over, using Luke's recipe and doing as he'd suggested, adding a few touches of our own.

The slamming of the back door of the tiki bar's glass enclosed porch caught my attention. I turned to see Kelso stroll out with a big grin. "I wondered where you'd run off to with my dog. Those two get along very well," he remarked as he watched Archie and Whiskey playing in the surf.

"Yeah, I'm jealous. I wish I could be so carefree to just run in the surf all day," I offered, sounding like a true dreamer.

Kelso laughed. "It's hard to be that way when you have goals and passions to pursue. You ready for the party?"

I nodded before I whistled for Whiskey, who brought Archie running with him. Grayson and Cam had gone to see the therapist we'd been going to with the boys. Jessica was in town and had asked Cam to attend the session with them, so I'd stayed at the beach to allow them to work on the relationship Cam hoped Grayson could rebuild with his mother. It remained to be seen.

Archie was doing quite well, but it seemed Grayson had some residual anger at his mother he was working out one girl at a time, and Cam was worried about him, just as any good father would be.

"As ready as I can be. How about you?" I asked. Kelso's bandmates were in town to help us celebrate the grand re-opening of On the Rocks, and we'd sold out tickets for the show. The proceeds were going to a no-kill animal shelter in Brownsville, and the evening promised to be a fun one.

Cord walked out of the screen door just as Whiskey rushed up the back stairs where I had a towel ready for him. I handed it to Kelso to clean Whiskey's paws, and I walked over to Cord, taking the drink in his hand to taste. He'd been behind the new bar, working up signature cocktails for the party, and I was anxious to try one out.

I held the liquid in my mouth, allowing the sweetness of the mixer to coat my tastebuds. "What… It's orange blossom," I recognized, making me smile. It reminded me of the first gin I'd tasted at McClintock Distilling Company.

Cord grinned. "And…"

I took another sip and let it linger on my tongue again. "Cardamom," I declared.

"Cardamom syrup. It's an Orange Blossom Special," Cord stated, making me laugh. I'd found that Cord loved naming cocktails.

"I was able to mix up pitchers of them so Gina won't have to mix them. This is a great way to introduce Ima-GIN-ation's top-shelf liquor, Lawson's Finest Gin. Have you heard back from the lawyer about the trademark work? Any problems with the licensing for the Whiskey Dreams name for our bourbon?"

We were licensing the name of Kelso's song for our Ima-GIN-ation brand top-shelf bourbon, and Kelso's manager, Brant Essex, was working with our lawyer, Lance Church—who happened to be Niles' husband—to license the name so everything was on the up and up. Cord and I still had to firm up our deal regarding the distillery, and I'd already discussed it with Tanner, Kelso, and most importantly, Cameron. We were hoping Cord would take me up on my offer to partner in the distillery.

Kelso walked over to Cordon, Whiskey wagging away at his feet. "What's that?" He took the drink from me and sipped it, smacking his lips which made me grin.

"Orange Blossom Special," I answered as Archie finally came up the stairs from the beach and stopped next to me, brushing off his bare feet.

"When's Dad coming back?" Archie asked.

I put my arm on his shoulder, "As soon as their session is over. You hungry?" I asked. Archie nodded.

"Come on, let's go see what Miss Yvonne has that we can taste test. You, too, Whiskey. Time for your bacon fix," I joked, remembering that Miss Yvonne sneaked bacon to the dog which pissed off Tanner because the dog could clear a fucking room faster than anyone I'd ever met with the gas bombs he laid.

We went into the kitchen to find Miss Yvonne taking a tray of potato skins out of the oven as Tabitha stirred a pot on the stove. "Ladies, there's a young man in need of sustenance—oh, and Archie's hungry too," I joked as Whiskey sniffed the air.

Miss Yvonne walked over to a restaurant pan next to the flattop and picked up a piece of bacon, folding it in half before she walked over to the dog. She held out her hand to the mutt. "Shake?"

Whiskey lifted his paw and Miss Yvonne shook it before giving him the bacon, which the dog devoured in one swallow. She patted Whiskey on the head and shoved him out of the kitchen as she went to wash her hands before turning to us. "What's your pleasure?"

Before Archie answered, Tanner came into the kitchen, his sickeningly happy smile plastered on his face. "Hey guys. Archie, how are you doing?"

I glanced at Archie, seeing him swallow before he looked at Miss Yvonne. "You got any broccoli?"

WE WERE STANDING on the back patio, Cam in my arms as we swayed to the music the Tex-Sons were playing. The surprise was that Tanner was sitting in with them, and they were playing one of their new songs with Tanner and Kelso singing in perfect harmony. It was a love song, of course, but instead of being repulsed by it, I could understand why people loved the damn things.

Imagine if we'd never met,
I wonder where we'd be today.
I'd have my nights out on the town,
And wonder why I live that way.
Now I don't have to wonder why,
The sky's a deeper blue,
It's the color of your eyes,
It's not my imagination… it's you.

I turned my head and kissed Cam's cheek. "Look at that—my brother's plugging the distillery in his next hit song," I whispered, and we both started laughing as the tune ended and everyone clapped.

"Babe, I think now's a good time to talk to Cord about the partnership. What do you think? Oh, where's Grayson?" I asked.

Cam turned to look at me, smiling as he wrapped his arms around my neck, and the two of us danced some more. "He's at home in Brownsville. He was upset after the session and didn't really want to celebrate. Please don't take offense. You remember teen hormones, right?"

I nodded. "Archie hasn't walked away from the buffet since Miss Yvonne and Tabitha put the food out," I pointed out as I turned Cam to see the kid stuffing his face.

A hand on my shoulder caught my attention, so I turned to see Tanner with a big smile as he danced with Kelso. "You guys doing okay? We, uh, we have some news," he stated.

Kelso was about to bust, so I looked at my little brother and cocked my eyebrow. "We got married today at the courthouse. Will you be okay to handle the bar without us for two weeks? We're going on a honeymoon," he announced, both of them holding up ringed fingers.

Cam and I separated, and I hugged each of them as Cam did the same. I hurried over to the bar where Gina and Cord were holding down the fort. "Can you get sparkling wine for everyone? I want to make a toast," I asked, looking at Gina. She nodded and hurried off before I looked at Cord.

"I have a proposition for you," I suggested to Cord.

Of course, he smirked. "Sorry, Leo, but I'm not about to help fulfill your March brothers sandwich fantasy. That's even too weird for me."

I nearly doubled over with laughter. Of course, he'd take it to the gutter. "I can't tell you how relieved I am to hear that," I replied, still chuckling at his comment.

"Then what can I do for you?" he chortled.

"Would you consider going into business with me? Would you be my partner in the distillery? After Tanner and Kelso get back from their honeymoon, they'll be able to run this place without me always here, and hell, I'll just be next door at the distillery when it's finished. I'd like to have you as a partner, Cordon. What do you say?" I asked, feeling bats in my stomach.

Cord hopped the bar as I'd seen him do more than once, and picked me up, spinning me around in a circle as he shook loose my damn fillings. "What are you trying to do to my partner?" Cam asked.

Cord finally stopped spinning me and put me down as the room continued to move. "He's my partner now, so you'll have to marry him to have priority over me," Cord stated, which made me smile. I took it as a yes to my proposal—well, it wasn't *the proposal*, but I had that one in my sights, as well.

Once Gina and I handed out the glasses, I stepped on the stage, Ant, Kelso's bandmate, turned on the microphone for me and I nodded in thanks. It buzzed and shrieked for a second until Jinx, the band's drummer, adjusted some knobs and it stopped.

I smiled out at the crowd. "Hello! Thanks for coming to help us celebrate the renovations to On the Rocks. Tonight, I have an embarrassment of riches to share with everybody, so I'm glad you're all here to be the first to know. My little brother, Kelso Ray, and my best friend and business partner in the restaurant, Tanner, ran off and got married today!" I announced.

The applause was deafening for a moment as Kelso and Tanner joined me on stage, holding hands. I looked out into the crowd to see Archie standing between Cam and Cord, a big smile on his face, and everything just seemed perfect.

I held my hand up and everyone quieted. "I got more. You've seen the March brothers around here during the remodel, but I want to introduce the man of the hour who designed the remodel. He and his business partner, Landon Stenson—Lan, where you at man?" I asked, knowing I'd seen him in the crowd, and I wasn't really surprised to see him with a good-looking guy and a beautiful woman, his arm around both of them.

He released his hold on them and grabbed Cam and Archie, pulling them onto the stage with us. "This is Landon Stenson, the builder, and his partner—and my boyfriend—Cameron

March. This is Cam's son, Archie, who you'll see a lot more of from now on. Let's give them a round of applause," I insisted.

People clapped, and then I held up my hand again. "When we gonna drink?" someone yelled out.

A ripple of laughter skittered over the crowd. "One more thing, and you can drink to your heart's content. Gina's a great bartender, and she's hell on the register as well," I joked.

Once the next wave of laughter died down, I looked around seeing lots of friendly faces in the crowd. There were regulars and locals and new faces that I hoped would become regulars. It was more than I ever thought I'd had when I'd headed to the beach from Tyler, Texas with about a grand in my savings account and an old beat-up Chevy Impala that quit me the day before I found the job working for Billy Kelly, the man who gave me my start and later sold this bar to me. I couldn't have imagined life would lead me in the direction it had, but I was grateful.

"Last thing. That lot next door where we just started to break ground will be the future home of Ima-GIN-ation Distillers, and Cordon March, my future brother-in-law, has agreed to run it with me. Now, let's all drink up to all of the good news! Cheers!" I called out.

I turned to Cam, seeing the surprise on his face. "In the not-too-distant future, we'll toast our good news, okay? Let me get Ima-GIN-ation off the ground before we start a new adventure. I love you and never want to be without you," I whispered in his ear as the crowd continued laughing, cheering, and drinking.

It was a wonderful night I'd never expected to celebrate, but that just shows you—with a little Ima-GIN-ation, you can accomplish anything.

EPILOGUE
CORDON MARCH

I was sitting at the kitchen table in Tanner and Kelso's apartment, enjoying the lovely quiet of the space. On the Rocks wasn't open yet, and the construction workers, who were my favorites to watch, hadn't yet started their workday. It was just after dawn. To me, who didn't sleep much at all, it was the golden hour.

Tanner Bledsoe and Kelso Ray had left for their honeymoon, asking me to stay at their place to watch their sweet pooch, Whiskey, a rescue mutt who seemed fucking intuitive as he rested next to my chair in the early mornings, his paw on my bare foot to be sure I didn't go out for a walk without him. I found myself loving the company.

Tanner and Kelso had gotten married two weeks ago on the morning of the grand re-opening of On the Rocks, the beach bar the two of them owned with my friend, Leo Anderson. The couple had decided to limit their honeymoon to two weeks, but Leo, being the romantic at heart, had insisted they take a month. They were supposed to return to the beach at the end of July, and I hoped they had a wonderful time—I didn't hate having the privacy for a while, though.

Kelso and Tanner were loud when they fucked, and with

Kelso traveling a lot for his career, they copulated like rabbits when they were together. I'd had the misfortune of staying at their upstairs apartment over On the Rocks while my brother and Leo were living between two homes—one in Brownsville and one about a mile from the beach, and most nights, I felt like a goddamn third wheel as I jacked off to Tanner and Kelso going at each other. The break provided by their absence was definitely welcome.

I'd met Leo Anderson the previous October when he was on a distillery tour in Maryland, where I'd lived and worked at the time. We became fast friends, and when the woman who owned the distillery where I was working as the master distiller closed it down to help out a family member, I hauled my ass to Texas for a couple of reasons.

I'd found out, quite by mistake, that the real reason Leo was on his little sabbatical was because he had the hots for my twin, Cameron, and the two of them had been fucking up things in Romancetown.

Leo took off to give himself some breathing space to get his head together, which was smart at the time. Thankfully, they'd gotten their shit straight and were currently living a sickeningly romantic lifestyle with my nephews, Grayson and Archie.

I'd gone to the restroom to get ready to take Whiskey on his morning stroll when I heard those size thirteens of Leo's on the stairs. Whiskey was in the kitchen, ready to attack, but not in the way any dog ever did. That sweet dog didn't bark and growl as any other mongrel would have done. No, he whined and groveled until Leo opened the apartment door and baby talked to him, which was totally undignified, in my opinion.

"Hewwo wittle Whiskey dog… How's my boy?"

I stepped around the kitchen doorframe, raising an eyebrow at him until he finally looked up, his face flaming red. Leo was one of the best friends I'd ever had, and I loved catching him off guard. It always made me smile.

"Aww… good mowning, Weo," I mimicked him. He

chuckled at my mocking and flipped me the bird, just as I'd expected.

"Oh, good. You're up. I, uh, well, *Tanner* needs a favor. You got coffee on?" Leo asked, trying to recover from showing Whiskey affection because all he ever did was bitch about the dog as he slipped the dog treats when he thought nobody was looking.

Leo stepped inside, but he wasn't alone. He clipped a leash on Whiskey and turned to a skinny red-haired kid behind him with a black eye and a busted lip. "Take him for a walk, will ya?"

The young guy nodded and took the dog, but not before Leo placed a plastic bag in his hand from the basket just inside the door. The dog and kid plodded down the stairs slowly, the young redhead mumbling as he went.

I nearly swallowed my goddamn tongue when a huge, gorgeous mother fucker stepped into the apartment behind Leo. I needed to check the goddamn calendar—was it my fucking birthday and Leo was bringing me the best present ever?

"Oh, hello there. Are you my prize for putting up with the bullshit around here?" I greeted, making a joke so nobody noticed my cock swelling in my pants.

"Easy Cord. He's married," Leo seemed to scold.

He then grinned as he turned to the man, extending his hand like a fucking spokesmodel. "Raleigh Wallis, this is Cordon March. He's my boyfriend's twin brother and my business partner in Ima-GIN-ation Distillers when it finally opens next door. We are, however, mixing up fantastical spirits in the meantime if you're interested," Leo introduced.

Leo then turned to me and offered a nervous grin. "Cord, this is Raleigh Wallis and that kid was Bailey Marsden, Tanner's *other* best friend. Bailey got to town a little sooner than Tanner expected, and Tanner wondered if you'd could keep an eye on him until they return from France in a week or so," Leo asked, seeming nervous as hell.

"And how does Tanner know that kid?" I asked, watching

the other man, Raleigh Wallis, who looked like he carried trucks off the assembly line in Detroit. He had a steady smile that didn't waiver in the slightest, no matter how many quick, jerky moves I made in an attempt to freak him out.

Leo looked at Wallis who stepped forward and offered his hand. "Hi, Mr. March. Nice to meet you, sir. Bailey and Tanner had a mentor/mentee relationship when they worked together. Bailey recently graduated from his program, and Tanner invited him to come stay here for a while to visit," the man explained vaguely, never losing that fucking cap-toothed smile. He was a real knockout, though.

I looked at Leo, resorting to the old "staring contest" strategy until he flinched. God, he was easy.

"Bailey and Tanner are good friends from when Bailey was just a kid. He got into a little trouble, but he's learned his lesson. Can he stay here with you until the happy couple gets back in two weeks or not?"

I sighed. "How old is he?" I asked them. I was nobody's babysitter.

"He just turned twenty-two," Wallis answered as the door opened and the kid walked inside, kneeling down to unfasten the leash of the mutt.

"There's a towel by the shoe tray to wipe his paws because of the sand," I informed.

The young guy looked up and nodded, grabbing the towel and wiping Whiskey's paws. "Sorry, Sir," he responded, staying on his knees with his head down.

I gulped in air as if I was being choked. He had perfect form as his hands rested on is thighs, palms up. I looked at Leo and crossed my arms over my chest. "Okay, what's the joke? My asshole brother put you up to this shit, didn't he?" I asked, looking between the two men for an honest answer.

"I, uh, I... *What now?*" Leo stammered a bit.

Mr. Wallis walked over to the young man, who was clearly a well-trained submissive or maybe a slave, and took a knee next to him, whispering to the guy. He took the young man's hand and helped him to his feet, but Bailey never looked up at me.

I stepped forward. "Bailey, call me Cord. You have permission to speak," I stated, seeing Wallis scowl at me and hearing Leo hiss.

I turned to them. "You can like it or you can hate it, but he's been trained. He won't speak to a Dom until he's given permission. You wanna bet me on it?" I challenged Wallis.

Nobody uttered a sound, so I turned to Bailey. His red hair was short, but there was some curl to it, which would likely be stunning if it was longer. His stature was small, but he was muscular. He was one of the most beautiful men I'd ever seen.

"Bailey, please look up," I stated politely, my voice firm. The young redhead lifted his head and looked straight forward, his eyes clear, but his expression dead. Someone had hurt the young man, and I couldn't help but wonder how badly.

I stepped in front of him without touching him, happy when he finally met my gaze. "Hi. Will you be okay staying here with me until Tanner returns? Was Tanner your master? Answer," I asked.

"There's no fucking way—" Leo began complaining behind me, but I expected it. Knowing Tanner had been to prison and the boy was his friend led me to some conclusions I wanted to explore so I didn't overstep. Every Master/slave relationship wasn't sexual, so I couldn't rule it out.

"No, Sir. Tanner saved my life." The young man volunteered no more information as a tear fell down his peach-colored cheek. My heart seized in pain as I looked at him, remembering why I'd walked away from the lifestyle a few years earlier. There were a lot of bad actors in the community, and I'd met my fill of them. I had a bad feeling the kid had as well.

I had to wonder how long it had been since young Bailey had given away his free will, but more importantly, had it been consensual? Something in my gut told me there was a lot more to the story, but I was immediately protective of the young man.

I didn't know his story, but he was in a vulnerable state, and in the wrong hands, he could be hurt badly—likely already had. If I stepped up to protect him, how much of my free will would it cost me?

If you enjoyed **"Ima-GIN-nation, On the Rocks, Book 2,"** get ready for -
Absinthe Minded, "On the Rocks, Book 3".

Coming in December 2022. An "On the Rocks" spinoff holiday story. Read on to know more about Mabry's Minor Mistake!

Mabry's Minor Mistake
Christmas 2022

Mabry Caldor

I STARTED across the parking lot behind my residence hall where I saw Grayson March pacing nervously. He was hard to miss. "Oh, dude, I was just coming to see if your shitty car was on the lot. Greek parties are tonight, and you've got a car, so you gotta come with me," Grayson insisted.

I slammed the trunk of my old beater car to head to Schuster Residence Hall. It was my senior year, and I'd taken a position as a Resident Assistant at Schuster instead of sharing an off-campus apartment with Grayson and another guy on the basketball team, Quincy Thompson.

I'd turned down Grayson's invitation to live rent-free and split costs three ways when he'd called me over the summer to extend it, but as an RA, I was getting free housing and a meal program, and I knew he wasn't exactly thrilled at my choice to decline. My job allowed me to defer my athletic scholarship for a year to recover from a meniscus tear I'd suffered over the summer when I was home in Iowa. I'd been redshirted for the year, having actually seen playing time my freshman year because I was damn good at the game.

Grayson had redshirted his freshman year, and he was eager to indulge in all of the fun he'd missed because he was riding the bench the previous year, an unknown to all the pretty girls, though from what I'd noticed and heard from other team members, the guy seemed to have done just fine without the jersey. I had the feeling he was going to get the notoriety he so hungrily sought without much effort at all once the season started. I just hoped to hell it wouldn't be his downfall as I'd seen happen more than once in my time as an Aggie.

"Can't. I've got freshman dorm orientation, and after, I gotta pick up my books from the bookstore. I also gotta have someone come fix the damn Wi-Fi in my suite. I put in a call to Campus IT, but I haven't heard back yet. Anyway, I gotta get going, March. I'll see you at Cox-McFerrin in the morning for weight training," I said as I carried a cloth grocery bag with food to have in my dorm room.

I'd inherited the small fridge from the RA before me, so my choices for having healthy food on hand had expanded this year. The previous year I'd had to share with two other guys, and space was at a premium—which probably explains why we never became friends. They were two of the dirtiest guys I'd ever met, and I wanted nothing to do with them. The girls they bedded in our dorm room had extremely questionable taste in what they wanted in a relationship if they thought those two assholes were the cream of the crop.

"If I can find someone to help with your computer issue, will you be our designated driver and go with us? Quincy really wants to go, and I want to start the year off with a bang or two, ya know?" Grayson offered.

There was no way Grayson March knew anyone who could fix my computer issues. There had been an invasion of mice in the Schuster building over the summer when the dorm was empty and it was hot as fuck in Texas, and they'd chewed through wires while enjoying the cooler temps in the dorm than outside in the sun. The college superintendent had dropped by the day I arrived a week ago and said they'd get someone on it. I'd been spending my time using the Wi-Fi in the cafeteria, and it was okay because the place wasn't busy—yet. Once the school year started, things would definitely pick up. I needed the quiet to concentrate—I wasn't a good student athlete like March, and I damn well wasn't going to get it in the cafeteria.

"You got someone who can fix my problems, send 'em over, and I'll go with ya to the party and introduce you around. Come get me at eight—if you can get someone to get my Wi-Fi going," I challenged. No way did he know someone who could fix my problems. After I'd settled in my freshmen students that night, *I'd* be settling in with the textbook for my taxation class. At least I wouldn't have a headache the next day—from alcohol.

LATER THAT AFTERNOON, I was busy tucking the navy sheets around the hard mattress, which was about a foot too short for my tall frame. There was a quick knock on the door before it opened and Grayson stepped inside with a really cute guy trailing behind. "You should've taken me up on the apartment. You can't bring chicks here you know. You'll get demerits, big guy," Grayson laughed as he glanced around.

His companion, who seemed to be very shy and very cute—based on the glowing pink cheeks upon which tortoise shell glass frames were resting—kept glancing up at me through his dark brown lashes which actually brushed the lenses when he glanced at me. His hair was short, but he had bangs, which he continued to brush off his forehead. *Maybe it was a nervous tick?*

"Hi. Excuse March for his bad manners," I greeted. "Mabry Caldor," I stated as I waited for him to shake my hand. He was slender, probably about five-ten if I was guessing. Before he reached out to shake my hand, he wiped his palm on his khaki pants, which was unusual for a college student to be wearing before classes even started.

"Jimmy. Uh, Jimmy Lewis," he introduced before he quickly jerked his soft hand from mine and rested both palms on his cross-body bag.

I glanced down to see he had on a pair of vans with the checkerboard top that was so popular with skateboarders. "You like to skateboard?" I asked, trying to make small talk as Grayson rooted through my small closet. Jimmy looked at me like I was dumb as a rock for my observation.

I glanced behind my back where March was holding a blue plaid button down. "Are you stealing my clothes while this guy offers a distraction?"

Grayson chuckled. "You've got a long fucking torso. How damn tall are you?" March asked. He was shorter than me, but my height was what made me a good shot guard, or so everyone always said.

"Taller than you. So, Jimmy Uh Jimmy Lewis, what brings you by? March hire you as a personal assistant to manage his dating calendar?" I joked.

A small smile appeared on Jimmy's face, and his neck flushed. "I don't have that kind of time between my job with IT and my studies," Jimmy Lewis joked, which made me grin. *Cute and a sense of humor…*

Jimmy didn't seem to be a man of many words, either. He looked around before walking over to my desk, kneeling down without a word. I turned my attention to March. "What's he doing?"

Grayson March offered a smile that I was certain charmed the panties off many a woman. "He works the help desk in Campus IT. There are about a billion other students who are on the list for some sort of technical shit, but Jimmy, here, was kind enough to move you to the top of the list and personally take the work order to get you all fixed up," Grayson explained.

I looked over to see the kid sitting on his feet, completely engrossed in whatever was happening under my desk, so I stepped closer to March. "And what was he promised to get him to do such a selfless thing," I pried. Nobody was that nice at the beginning of the semester when everyone was trying to settle in and get organized for the start of classes—especially not a freshman who was probably away from home for the first time and scared shitless at the mere size of the campus.

"He's going to the party with us tonight. He's from California and doesn't know anyone, so I'm taking him under my wing," Grayson admitted, confirming my thoughts that the kid was promised something.

"Fake ID," we both heard from the corner of the room.

"What? What's that?" I asked as I stepped closer to him.

"He's hooking me up to get a—"

"*Shh!* We keep some things to ourselves, *Jimmy*," Grayson chastised, glancing my way.

"Jimmy, how old *are* ya?" I asked. It reasoned that he was eighteen if he was at college, or so I believed.

The kid crawled out from under the desk and looked at me, his brow furrowed in concern. "Seventeen. I finished high school at sixteen, but my parents wouldn't let me come in person until I turned seventeen, so I took classes online for a year," the kid—who I now knew was *really* a kid—answered. I heard Grayson hiss next to me, so I turned to look at him, not hiding my disappointment.

"You're corrupting a minor," I sighed, not really surprised March would do something of the sort, which was confirmed by his shrug.

"I'm just helpin' the kid get the lay of the land. So, come on,

Caldor. Hit the showers. We're pregaming at my place in an hour, and then we'll head out for the night. I'm counting on you to know where all of the best parties are and take us to them where you'll introduce us as your friends and then sit quietly in a corner with a nice soft drink," Grayson said as he pulled out a pair of jeans from the shelf in my closet and handed them to me, along with the blue shirt.

"It's too damn hot for pants," I complained as I went to the dresser and grabbed a pair of navy shorts before I went into my ensuite—which was a perk a lot of RA's didn't get. I assumed I got it because I'd willingly volunteered for the RA program as an upperclassman, but then one of the other RA's told me coach was fucking the Director of Housing. Whatever the reason, I had my own bathroom that I didn't have to share like years past.

I took the world's fastest shower and got out, brushing my teeth and doing a touch-up shave before I combed my hair and pulled it up into a bun. It was long from the summer break. I hadn't taken the time to get it cut before I got to campus, so I'd need to find somewhere tomorrow morning before Coach Maw saw me and threatened to cut it himself as I'd heard him do more than once. He didn't like long hair on his players. He was really a prick about us representing the university when we played. I guess the administration wanted a straight-laced image out there for public consumption. The people I knew on campus were far from role models, in my opinion.

I hurriedly dressed in my briefs and shorts before stepping out of the bathroom to see March flipping through his phone without looking up, sprawled all over my clean bed, the dick-head. I spread my damp towel on the closet door and tossed my dirty clothes into the hamper in the corner of my room before I took my shirt off the hanger and hung it on the bar in my closet. I damn sure wasn't looking forward to going to a party, especially if I was the DD, but if the kid was going, I felt it was my responsibility to see that he didn't get into any trouble.

"Eep!" I glanced behind me from where the squeak came,

worried it might be a damn mouse. What I saw was Jimmy Lewis, face as red as a tomato and eyes as large as Oreo cookies.

I scanned down to see I was still without my shirt, so I turned my back and pulled it on, buttoning it as I considered what to do about him. The kid was seventeen. He was quiet. He shied away from looking me in the eye, and apparently, I was thirst trapping him without even knowing it. Not a position I ever thought I'd be in.

"When did you turn seventeen, Jimmy?" I asked out of curiosity.

"Last Thursday," the kid replied, making my stomach flip.

March quickly spoke up. "You surf?" I turned to see him giving me the up and down, which was totally unexpected as well.

For an instant, I almost asked if he wanted to teach me personally—and let me teach him a few things, as well. Grayson March was damn good looking. He had brown hair and green eyes, and he was muscular in all the right ways. I wasn't fat, but I wasn't as firm as I'd been before my injury. I couldn't do cardio because of my knee, and while I did as much exercise as the doctor would let me do, I had put on a few pounds. My mother showed her love with food, and she loved me a lot. She was also a great cook, and as an only child, I liked being spoiled.

I turned to the kid, seeing he was back under my desk with a laptop doing something. I looked back at March. "Not in land-locked Iowa. You?" I responded.

"Yeah. My dad's… A friend of the family taught me and my little brother to surf over the summer. I'm not very good at it, but I like to go out when I'm home," March explained.

"Done." I looked to the right to see the kid slide out from under the desk and pull up my desk chair. He turned to me and offered a shy smile. "Can you log into your account so I can check the connection?"

I did as he said, and then his fingers, which were long and

slender, flew over the keys. Screens were popping up and moving off so quickly, I couldn't keep it all straight.

Five minutes later, he turned around with a triumphant grin. "Its working just fine." Jimmy then grabbed a sticky note and wrote on it quickly with a pen he'd retrieved from his bag. He peeled the note from the pad and stuck it to the bottom of my desktop.

"Fake ID?" Jimmy seemed to question.

"Yeah, I guess we can do it now. Get your shit together, and we can drop it by your dorm room as we head to the parking lot. I'll pop for food so we don't get too hammered. It's your first night, and newbie's tend to overindulge," Grayson announced. My friend had a point, and I questioned the logic of taking the kid to a party, much less a frat party, but I remembered being the eighteen-year-old kid, away from home with my first taste of freedom from parental scrutiny. It was a goddamn dumpster fire.

"Okay, but, Jimmy, you go nowhere without me. I'll make sure nobody slips you something, but when I say that's it, you leave with me without argument," I insisted.

I stared at Jimmy until he finally relented. "Fine." He pouted, his mouth puffed up so his pink lips looked so inviting, and his knows scrunched up like a little bunny. I needed to slam my dick in the door to get my head right. *Seventeen… Jail is bad… He's the age of consent, though… Knock it off!*

We walked Jimmy over to Haas Hall and he ran upstairs to dump his crossbody bag. As he walked away, I noticed a retractable keyring hooked on his black belt. There were at least ten keys on it. "What's he do again?" I asked Grayson as we stood on the grass under a tree to wait for the kid.

"He works for IT. He's some computer genius, according to my source. He's on work-study. If he's smart, he'll work those computer skills into a lucrative business by charging to… Well, the kid has options," March explained, making me feel even more uneasy about Jimmy's future if his only source for morals was Grayson March or people like him.

A couple of minutes went by before the door opened again. Jimmy stepped out wearing a white button up shirt—buttoned all the way up. He was still wearing his khaki pants and Vans, but the navy jacket slung over his arm had me looking at March.

"Is he Mormon? You can't get a Mormon kid a fake ID! My god, Grayson, what—"

"Relax Caldor," my friend interrupted before turning his back to where Jimmy stood on the stairs adjusting his shirt before pulling on the jacket.

"He's a nerd. They dress that way," Grayson whispered before he continued, "I've got one at home who's just a few years younger than Jimmy, here, who dresses just like that. I hope to fuck Archie has someone like me in his life when he goes to college in a few years to show him the ropes and keep him from killing himself. Now, let's go," March insisted.

"I'm sure I'll regret this," I mumbled as we stepped from the shade of the tree. Jimmy's face relaxed when he saw us, a smile slowly blooming that made him just that much more adorable. God, why me...

I PARKED down the street from the Sigma Chi house, seeing the party had already spilled out onto the lawn and it was only six in the evening. There were scantily clad guys and girls playing lawn darts, which I thought was completely illegal by now.

Jimmy stopped on the sidewalk, quickly removing his jacket and tying it around his waist, which didn't make him look any older. "Yo! Jimmy," Grayson called out. The kid, who was about five feet ahead of us, stopped and turned around before he trotted back to us.

"Yeah?" he asked, looking like an eager puppy. I felt like I was leading a lamb to slaughter.

"Rules, young Padawan. Don't take a drink you didn't pour

yourself. Don't put your drink down and go back to it. These Greeks like to fuck with freshman, and you damn well don't want videos circulating around campus of you in a compromising position," March schooled.

I sighed. "This is a bad idea," kept circling my brain, but Grayson had a point that if the kid was going to be on campus, it was best for him to learn the ropes from those who'd already hung themselves, then maybe it was my good deed for the year.

I turned to Jimmy. "*Do not*, and I mean unless you want to be carried out over my shoulder like a sack of grain, do not drink more than one beer," I ordered.

"I don't like beer. I snuck a taste of my uncle's one time. It's gross. Is that all they have?" Jimmy asked, his face scrunched up again in distaste, which made me chuckle.

You're so going to hell…

We walked up to the lawn, Jimmy safely tucked between us, and Grayson greeted a few of the guys and girls he knew. I waved to a few guys I knew, but the Greeks weren't my favorites, a lot of them self-entitled douche bags—especially the legacy members.

We went inside, and goddamn, I was getting old. I was surprised the plaster wasn't peeling off the walls at the deep vibration of the bass on the sound system. The pictures were definitely dancing from their precariously hung spots along the stairway to the second floor, which reminded me.

I leaned forward to Jimmy's left ear and touched his right shoulder. "Don't go up there with anyone. It's not a place for you," I mandated as we made our way to the large dining room where a makeshift bar had been assembled on a side table.

I looked at Jimmy. "Don't drink any of that. You don't know what it really is. It could be grain alcohol with a little soda for color to make you think it's whiskey or rum, and trust me, it's not. That shit will have you puking for a week," I instructed.

Suddenly, a girl I recognized from my Economics class the previous year walked by with a tray of flavored gelatin shots in plastic pill cups like they used in the hospital. She was wearing a coconut shell bikini top and grass skirt, a ring of flowers around her neck and wrists. She had a silk-flower lei around her neck and a bit of a drunken smile on her pretty face. "Mara, right?" I asked the girl.

She nodded and then her eyes lit up. "May, honey, how ya been? I heard you're sittin' this year out," she mentioned, but small talk wasn't on my agenda.

"You make these? They look great," I shouted over the noise of the music I didn't even recognize. It wasn't in English.

"Yeah, want one, honey?" she asked with a friendly smile. I glanced at Jimmy to see him staring at me, not the pretty girl, and I had to wonder…

"You first," I suggested, attempting to sound chivalrous. I reached over the tray and circled my finger for a minute, picking up a green cup and smirking at her. "Head back," I instructed.

Mara tilted her head such that her flower crown fell off. Jimmy quickly retrieved it and held it as I squeezed the sides of the cup into her mouth. She chewed it and smiled brightly. "Lime. My favorite."

I leaned forward and kissed her cheek, snatching a red cup for Jimmy. I also lifted the lei from her neck and winked, sliding it over Jimmy's neck as he handed her the flower crown. "Thank you, ma'am," he answered.

We didn't stick around long enough for Mara to ask his age. I'd dissuaded the fake ID card adventure for another day when we showed up at the rundown house just off campus to see the line of students already waiting. How the fuck the cops didn't shut it down, I'd never know—It was where I got my fake ID a few years earlier.

I escorted Jimmy through the kitchen and out to the back yard where there were considerably less people. After we found a bench to have a seat, I studied him, seeing him examining the cheap lei I'd put around his neck.

"Yeah, I think they were going for a hula theme or something, but I think their loose interpretation—mostly naked—makes it hard to pick up on at first glance," I joked. Jimmy let go of the lei and looked around the back yard where tiki torches were plunged into the ground, obviously waiting for sundown to add a festive light to the weed infiltrated, mostly gravel back yard. It was truly a fucking mess.

There were broken chairs that barely offered a seating space, and a metal barrel like most would see on a street corner up north during the winter where fires were lit in an attempt to keep warm by the homeless—or maybe they didn't do it any longer, but I remembered seeing movies.

"Anyway, this is a Jell-o shot. It can be made with anything from Everclear, which is flavorless and colorless and deadly, to vodka, to white rum," I explained.

I leaned forward and sniffed it, noting no smell but the strawberry gelatin. I took a little bite of it and held it in my mouth for a moment to determine the liquor, relieved when I felt the familiar taste of vodka on my tongue. Assuming they'd been made in a big batch, I was pretty sure the alcohol content was low and likely safe for the kid. I pretended I didn't know his age to assuage my own guilt, and I handed over the little cup.

As he reached for it, something popped into my head. "You're not allergic to strawberries, are you?"

Jimmy gave me a little giggle. "Nope. No allergies," he announced triumphantly, so I handed him the cup and watched him sniff it. The tip of his pink tongue darted out, nearly giving me a fucking heart attack with the rush of thoughts in my mind. I felt like a goddamn creep.

I looked away from him, studying the others outside with us, most drinking beer and hard seltzer. There seemed to be a corner of the yard where they were "recycling," as in, tossing all of the cans in that spot, and I could only imagine how that part of the yard smelled with the sun baking the cans. The idea of it made my stomach want to heave.

I glanced to my left to see Jimmy studying me while still

holding the shot. "Well, go ahead. You might as well try it," I urged.

Jimmy laughed again before he slurped the thick gelatin into his mouth and chewed, dipping that wicked tongue out to lick the remnants from the little cup before he sat it down on the bench between us. As I glanced around at the gravel littered with the damn things, I realized he was the only person who had ever been to that frat house and respected littering laws.

"So, you graduated high school at sixteen? What's your IQ?" I asked as a joke.

"One-sixty-two," the kid announced matter-of-factly. I quickly bounced it around my brain and remembered something from an anthropology class I barely skated by in my sophomore year. An IQ of over one forty was high. If the kid was at one-sixty-two, he was a damn genius.

"Wow, so college is probably going to be boring as hell for you," I remarked, not sure what else to say on the matter.

"Do you imbibe in alcohol regularly?" Jimmy asked.

"Not when I'm driving or training. Never drink and drive," I tossed out like a PSA. Jimmy nodded and then a little giggle slipped out.

"I don't have a driving license or a car. I have a bike, but you don't need a special license to ride a bike in Texas, but you must adhere to the same traffic laws as drivers," he explained before he held up a finger.

"One, bicyclists have the rights and duties of other vehicle operators. Two, ride near the curb and go in the same direction as other traffic. Three, At least one hand on the handlebars (two are safer). Four, use hand and arm signals," the kid recited, obviously from memory. Those long fingers kept popping up.

I let him continue until he'd recited all eight of them and put his hands in his lap. I glanced around to see more people were showing up. I wondered if Grayson had scored a girl or was ready to move on. "Should we go find March?" I asked.

Jimmy nodded and followed me inside where the place was a

mob scene. We managed to wade through and found Grayson waiting by a beer pong table on the front sidewalk. "You ready to go, or are you staying?" I asked.

"Yeah, this bites. Let's go," he turned around to look at Jimmy. "How you doing, Jimmy? You have a drink?" March asked.

"Shello jots," the kid announced. I glanced down to see him holding the one plastic cup from when we sat in the back yard, plus three more in his other hand, still looking for a trash can.

"Fuck…" I complained. I was definitely in for a long night.

We lost March when we got to a party off campus, so I took young Jimmy, who seemed to be getting drunker by the minute, and we headed back to his residence hall. It was ten after midnight, and I was tired. I'd had a long day, and I was ready to crash.

Just as we were getting ready to go into the building, Jimmy darted to the bushes on the right of the main entrance and blew. I had no idea when he'd kept sneaking drinks, but I was so fucking full of soda and water that my bladder was about to burst.

The kid stood up and wiped his mouth on his jacket sleeve that he'd pulled on at some point. The front of his shirt was a mélange of things I didn't want to consider, so I took his arm and guided him toward the door.

I couldn't just leave him in the hallway—he'd pass out—so I led him to the elevator, finally deciding it was easier to pick him up and carry him like a blushing bride who'd just booted all over the front of her wedding dress.

"What floor?" I asked him.

"Suite 222. I have a single room all to myself," he announced.

My knee was killing me after all of the walking I'd been

doing, but the elevators in Haas were notoriously slow, so I took the stairs, two at a time, and when I finally arrived at his room, I glanced down to see he'd passed out. "Son of a…"

I remembered that key fob on his belt, so I put him on the floor for a minute, taking the keys to try each one until I finally found the one for his room. After I opened the door, I picked him up and carried him inside. He woke up when I put him on the bed.

"I don't feel very good," he whispered. I wanted to laugh, but I'd been in that position a few times myself, so I didn't.

"Yeah, how'd you sneak drinks?" I asked as I sat on the edge of the bed.

Jimmy started giggling. "All of those places we went to had trays of those Jell-O things, so I had a few when you weren't looking. I like you a lot, May."

I laughed quietly. "Right now, I bet you like *everybody*," I joked.

Jimmy sat up and began scrambling around until he was on my lap—pukey breath and clothes far too close for comfort. "Do you have a girlfriend?" he asked.

That was a landmine I didn't want to begin to go into with him. I hated that his tight ass was making my dick hard. Hell, if he was just three years older… "I don't have a girlfriend. I don't have time for one," I answered him, quasi truthfully.

"I don't want a girlfriend. I want you for my boyfriend," Jimmy stated, staring into my eyes. His were a light blue I'd never seen before, and I was captivated for a moment. He was a beautiful guy someone would be lucky to have someday. It definitely wouldn't be me, but some lucky prick was going to have his hands full.

Jimmy ground in my lap, and I quickly picked him up and plopped him on the bed, standing quickly to adjust myself. My hands flexed with the desire to pick him up and put him right back where he'd been, but my sober brain kicked in and reminded me of all of the reason he was off limits.

"Kid, someday, you're gonna make some guy really happy. It won't be me, sorry," I stated as I rushed out of his room like I was on fire, which wasn't exactly wrong. Thankfully, I had a room to myself because I was about to abuse the hell out of my dick to get Jimmy Lewis out of my head.

The next morning, I woke and turned on my computer to check my schedule for the day. When I tried to log into the student portal, I kept getting a message, "number unknown," which pissed me off. I hadn't printed off my class schedule because I'd left with March and Jimmy and hadn't hooked up my printer.

As I glanced down at the sticky note on the right side of my monitor, I saw a name that made me smile.

Jimmy Lewis
415-555-8292

I smiled and left it there. I wouldn't call him unless my computer acted up again, but then again, was I leaving myself open to temptation? I decided the number was glaring at me, so I took the sticky note and shoved it into the address book my mom had given me to bring with me to school. It held all of the important numbers she thought I might need while I was away. I stuck the note into the front cover of the book and put it back on the windowsill.

I dressed to go over to the Student Services Building across from Simpson Drill Field to see what the hell was going on with the portal. I was lucky it was early enough that the frantic freshmen hadn't shown up yet with screeching panic at not being able to get into the network.

I waited in line and smiled at the attendant, mostly likely a grad student of some sort. "I'm Mabry Caldor, and I can't get into my account to find out what time my first class starts. I'm not new here, just too lazy yesterday to connect my printer. Can you help me?" I asked, handing her my student ID.

For fifteen minutes, she tried to find my account. Then, her co-worker tried. Then her boss tried. Then they called the Director of Student Services, and he tried. Finally, they called IT.

The Director put the phone on speaker so I could hear what the unknown IT geek on the other side of the line was saying. "Uh, looks like the scholarship was revoked and the account closed. Oh, here it is. The student dropped out," the unknown woman's voice stated.

"No, I didn't!" I yelled, drawing a lot of attention from the gathered crowd.

It took me three weeks to get things reinstated. The bottom line was that their computer system was hacked and my student account was the only one compromised. They claimed there was no way to trace it, but I had a feeling I knew *who* happened to it… *Jimmy Lewis*. He was the devil incarnate.

Enjoying it? Look for these Easter eggs in each of my books releasing in 2022!

Coming next in March 2022 -
Orphan Duke: The Lonely Heroes, Book 7

ABOUT THE AUTHOR

Sam E. Kraemer grew up in the rural Midwest before moving to the East Coast with a dashing young man who swept them off their feet, and the couple has now settled in the desert of Nevada. Sam writes M/M contemporary romance, subgenres: sweet low angst, age-gap, cowboys, mysteries, and military/mercenary. Sam is a firm believer in "Love is Love" regardless of how it presents itself and a staunch ally of the LGBTQIA+ community.

Sam has a loving, supportive family and feels blessed by the universe every day for all that has been given. Sam's old enough to know how to have fun, but too old to care what others think about their definition of a good time. In their heart and soul, Sam believes they've hit the cosmic jackpot!

Cheers!

If you enjoyed this book, I'd appreciate it if you'd leave a rating and/or a review at Amazon.com, BookBub, and/or Goodreads. If you have constructive criticism to help me evolve as a writer, please pass it along to me.

You can find me at: https://linktr.ee/SamE.Kraemer

I'd love to hear from you!

Printed in Great Britain
by Amazon